D0952558

Praise for Kate Ormand's
The Wanderers

"The preternatural circus of shifters, budding young romance, and action-packed struggle against evil will appeal to readers of paranormal fiction."

—*School Library Journal*

"A swoony romance with a massive body count. . . . This more closely resembles a brutal, angst-drenched dystopia à la Veronica Roth's Divergent than anything else."

—*Kirkus Reviews*

"The world of shape-shifting characters has just gotten wider with the addition of this novel . . . Fans of supernatural series like Shiver will enjoy this book, with its similar themes and strong love story."

—*VOYA Magazine*

"Filled with excitement and whimsy, *The Wanderers* is an adventure story about shape-shifters, first love, and the endless search for a true home."

—Suzanne Young, *New York Times*–bestselling author of *The Program*

"*The Wanderers* is a dark, rich, and original story. I love the concept of humans with inherent shape-shifting abilities, and the circus setting is incredibly vivid—I could smell the musty, musky ring, feel the bright lights burning my skin. Kate has created an intricate and danger-filled world that's both cruel and beautiful."

—Melinda Salisbury, author of *The Sin Eater's Daughter*

"An utterly captivating big-top world filled with shape-shifters and dark secrets. I devoured this book! It was unlike anything I've ever read."

—Amy Christine Parker, author of *Gated* and *Astray*

"A fresh tale about shape-shifters that is sure to delight and astound."

—Danielle L. Jensen,
USA Today–bestselling author of *Stolen Songbird*

The Pack

The Pack

The Sequel to *The Wanderers*

Kate Ormand

Sky Pony Press
New York

Visit our website at www.skyponypress.com.

10 9 8 7 6 5 4 3 2 1

Library of Congress Cataloging-in-Publication Data

Names: Ormand, Kate, author.
Title: The Pack / Kate Ormand.
Description: New York, NY : Skyhorse Publishing, [2017] | Summary: Horse-shifter Flo and other orphaned shifters who once performed in a circus travel in a wild pack seeking a haven while eluding the Hunters that would trap or kill them.
Identifiers: LCCN 2017020354 (print) | LCCN 2017036905 (ebook) | ISBN 9781510712195 | ISBN 9781510712188 (hardcover) | ISBN 9781510712195 (Ebook)
Subjects: | CYAC: Science fiction. | Shapeshifting--Fiction. | Orphans--Fiction.
Classification: LCC PZ7.O63375 (ebook) | LCC PZ7.O63375 Pac 2017 (print) | DDC [Fic]--dc23
LC record available at https://lccn.loc.gov/2017020354

Cover design by Sammy Yuen
Interior design by Joshua Barnaby

Printed in the United States of America

"When the time comes for parting
And I give each a kiss
The thought will strike me
You much I shall miss."

In memory of Joyce Appleton (d. 2016)
and Harold Appleton (d. 1990), who loved to write

CONTENTS

Two lions met a woman in the woods.

Ro could tell right away that the woman was like them—a shifter, and a lion—in the way she held herself. Lions are proud creatures, and something about this woman, about the tall way she stood and the fierce glint in her eyes, told Ro she was pleased with herself. The woman smiled kindly, but there was an edge to her manner, her stance—something *off* that Ro couldn't ignore.

"Hello," the woman said. Her voice was softer than Ro expected it to be. It didn't match her image somehow. "I didn't realize anyone would be out here."

Ro and Chase hadn't expected to run into anyone either when they left their pack in search of a change of scenery, a chance to think out in the quiet forest. No one was ever in the forest.

"Who are you?" the lion pair asked the question at the same time, their words overlapping. They spared a glance at each other, but just a glance. The woman in the woods was watching them closely.

She had seemed to come from nowhere. One minute, Ro and Chase were talking about the warehouse, about

1

where they'd go when it was demolished, and then the woman was standing in the clearing in front of them. They hadn't heard her, hadn't sensed her, until she was right there.

"My name is Ava," she said. "And yours?"

The pair didn't reply right away. Ro wasn't sure she wanted to tell Ava her name. Chase made no attempt to either. Not yet, at least. They'd both learned to be wary of strangers, had both learned about trust the hard way.

"Where did you come from?" Ro asked.

Ava ran a hand through her hair, and Ro took a step back on instinct. Ava held her hands out in front of her then. "Whoa," she said, like she was calming a jumpy horse.

Ro scowled. Ava suddenly looked more troubled than she had a moment ago. Her eyebrows pulled together. Her white-blond hair stuck up where she'd just brushed it back. Her shoulders slumped forward a little, but she still held her hands out in front of her. She looked tired—*exhausted*—all of a sudden. Ro took another step back, and Chase followed suit.

"Whoa," Ava said again, softly.

They did not trust strangers—not shifters, not humans. The only people they trusted in this world were the other members of their own pack. Not the old pack, only the new one. And that trust had been earned.

"Who are you?" Ro asked again. Chase stayed silent beside her. He stood tall, alert. Ro moved an inch closer to him. "Why are you out here alone?"

Ro thought about the reason she was out in the woods with Chase—*Tia*.

Tia was the reason Ro had left the warehouse tonight. She had needed to get out for a while and clear her mind.

2

Chase wouldn't let her leave alone, claiming that it wasn't safe. He was right—it was never safe for them. And Ro had never felt she was safe—not with the old pack and not with the new. It was all part of the deal for shifters—always running, always hiding. Chase had insisted on joining Ro, and he knew why she needed out. He knew Ro's relationship with Tia had ended just before they'd left the old pack, the tension there becoming too much for all of them.

It had been a stupid argument—so stupid, Ro couldn't even remember what it was about. But she and Tia had kept it up. The old pack was behind them now, yet the aftermath of their breakup lingered.

Out in the woods, Ro had decided to go back and apologize. One of them had to make the first move and make things right between them. She missed Tia.

Ro and Chase had been on their way back to the warehouse when they crossed paths with the woman in the woods.

"I'm lost out here," Ava said quietly. Ro's attention returned to the woods around her, the woman in front of her, the darkness closing in on them. The night always snuck up at this time of year. "I'm looking for a new pack to join. Are you part of one, or is it just the two of you?"

The lions exchanged a look. Ro's thoughts moved to the others back at the warehouse, sitting around a fire, a warm glow dancing across their smiling faces. She would never lead this stranger into their camp.

Chase brushed dusty blond curls away from his eyes. He hadn't spoken much, and Ro wondered if she should have engaged in conversation with Ava in the first place. Maybe they should just turn their backs on her and walk away. But what was to stop her from following? They had to get rid of her, be sure she was gone, before they returned to camp.

Ava was out of place here. On closer inspection, she looked too groomed, too well, to have been out here long. To be living alone. To be in search of a pack. Chase was wearing a plaid shirt that was missing buttons; his light jeans had a hole in the knee. Dry mud clung to his boots. Ro's jeans were covered in grass stains and small tears. She and Chase lived well for wild shifters, but they still looked like they lived out in the wild—Ava didn't.

Something didn't add up with the woman in the woods. It seemed unlikely she was alone.

Suspicion grew inside Ro, but how could she handle it? How could they get away without triggering something?

Who is she?

The woman in the woods.

Ava.

"You're a lion," Ro said, just to say something. She was stalling, while she thought about what their next move should be.

"So are you," Ava replied. "Both of you—am I right?"

Ro and Chase looked at each other again. Then, surprising Ro, Chase nodded, confirming to Ava that they were lions, giving more away than Ro had wanted to. *Ava already knew,* she reminded herself. *Just as you knew about her.*

Ava lifted her eyebrows. She didn't seem either impressed or relieved to confirm that she'd found others like herself—something one would expect to experience after claiming to be lost and searching for a home. Ro opened her mouth to question this, to put an end to this, but a whooshing sound cut her off before her lips could form the first word.

Ava took a few steps back, widening the distance between them, as pain shot up Ro's leg. Ro stumbled, losing her footing. Chase reached out to grab her.

Whoosh.

Chase dropped her.

Ro hit the ground, landing hard on her shoulder. The pain spread down from her shoulder, up from her thigh, meeting in the middle to consume her. Chase almost fell on top of her, his side crashing into hers, adding to her agony.

What was happening? What was happening?

Ro turned her head to look at Chase. It felt heavy, hard to move. Her eyes were desperate to find focus, but her vision swam. Chase reached out, took Ro's hand. He squeezed; she squeezed back.

Everything went quiet.

Everything went still.

The stranger—*Ava*—stood above them. She was the last thing Ro saw before everything went black.

———

When Ro gained consciousness, she found herself in a dusty square room.

Her hands were bound with silver. The sting was sharp and immediate. She bit her lip and tried to block out the silver's bite as she shuffled to an upright position. Her movement stirred the dust on the floor. It burst into the air, swirling around her, tickling her nose. She sneezed and the jolt sent a wave of pain through her.

Ro examined her wrists. The silver band sat in a groove of skin that had already melted away while she was unconscious. The string bracelet she'd always worn had snapped and was on the floor beside her. The woman in the woods—she had done something to them. Ava hadn't been alone, just like Ro considered. They should've ran. They should've taken a chance, turned their backs on the stranger, and ran to the warehouse without looking behind them. But they didn't. And whoever was with Ava had shot both of them with some kind of tranquilizer. It must have been strong if Ro hadn't even felt the silver when it was forced onto her skin.

Chase wasn't awake yet. Ro shuffled toward him, her wrists stinging with every movement. The room was so small that she didn't have to scoot far to reach him. She left a short trail of scuffmarks and spots of blood as she went.

There were no windows, no doors leading off to other rooms. The only door, the one that led outside, was shut, but allowed some daylight to shine through the gaps, allowed in a draft that chilled the concrete floor to the point that it was almost painful to sit on.

There was junk in every corner, stacked high. As she readjusted herself, she hit a bucket, which fell and got caught in netting and knocked against something else. That object rolled toward her, stopping when it hit her hand. Her skin sizzled. Ro cried out and pulled her hand back, jerking away from more silver. Her wrists were almost numb with the sensation, but for the sizzling sting close to her bone. New contact hurt more.

Why would the lion woman have silver? It would hurt Ava to touch it, too.

Ro's mind drifted to the possibility of hunters, but she blocked that thought out like she was blocking the feel of the silver out. Or trying to. She couldn't panic—not yet.

Not yet.

But it must be hunters.

She took a deep breath, coughing on dust. Not yet. Not yet.

Chase moaned, pulling Ro from her thoughts. She quickly covered the rest of the distance between them. "Chase," she said softly. Chase groaned again, a small sound. He tried to lift his hand to his head. His eyes were squeezed shut, but flew open when he noticed his wrists were bound and burning.

"It's okay," Ro said, reaching for Chase before she realized she couldn't. He bolted upright, eyes wide. "It's all right," she soothed.

But it was not all right. It wasn't.

"Where are we?" Chase wheezed, his gaze darting around the room. Ro watched him process his surroundings, his brow creased.

Ro shook her head, even though he wasn't looking at her. "I don't know," she said.

"That woman," Chase said. He focused on Ro now, blinking in the low light. "The stranger. Ava. She did something to us?"

Ro nodded now. "Yes," she said. "But I'm still trying to figure out what."

—

Night fell quickly, suddenly, and white moonlight flooded through the small gaps in the door.

Ro and Chase could be anywhere, trapped in the tiny concrete building.

It'd rained earlier, so the room smelled damp, stale—the moldy wooden door, the wet earth scent coming in through the gaps. If Ro closed her eyes, she could imagine she was out there, on the other side of the door.

Chase's wrists were red, raw. He had been trying all day to pull his hands out of the silver so he could shift. But the silver was too tight, had sunk too deep.

Ro's shoulder ached where she had bashed it against the door countless times. But the bolt held firm, and the door wouldn't budge. Their situation seemed more hopeless by the second. Guilt gnawed at Ro when she looked at Chase, working at his bonds again, shredding his skin, watching it heal, and shredding it again as he tried to wriggle his hands free. She'd dragged him into this, just because she wanted to get out of the warehouse for a little bit, to put some distance between herself and Tia.

Look how much distance lies between us now.

Ro had wanted to clear her head, and her head was clear now. She wanted to go back. She so desperately wanted to go back.

She wondered what the others would be doing now. When would they notice that she and Chase were missing? What would they do? What would they think? She was afraid that Tia would blame herself if Ro never returned, if she never learned the truth.

Ro hit her forehead with the heel of her hand, accidently smacking her own eye with the other hand. *Why didn't I just say sorry? Why have I wasted all this time?*

What if I never see her again?

Ro shook her head, like she could fling the bad thoughts away somehow. Instead, Ro tried to focus on good memories, positive thoughts, and the belief that she would get out of this—both she and Chase.

Ro crashed into the door again. It held—again.

"They'll find us, Ro," Chase told her.

Ro only shook her head. Her breath came in sharp pants and she couldn't speak right away. Her throat felt closed up, her eyes stung, and tears warmed her frozen cheeks.

She crashed against the door again. Again. Again—

"They know we wouldn't just leave," Chase continued. "They'll know something's happened. And they'll find us."

He sounded like he believed it. Ro stopped and looked at him, sniffing back more tears. "Do you really think so?"

Chase gave her a small smile. "Absolutely. But let's make it easier for them by trying to get out on our own, shall we? Let me help you this time."

Ro nodded and cleared her throat. "Yes. Okay." She rolled out her bruised shoulder before running at the door again, over and over. Chase did the same.

But the two of them gave up before the door did.

Time merged into nothingness as the room faded light to dark.

Morning to night.

Clouds and rain, sun and wind.

Ro could see the fight going out of Chase. *We are already beaten.*

Ro's throat was too dry to make any sound. She lay on her side, facing the wall, thinking of nothing and no one.

The room was silent. The only noises that broke through the quiet were the soft calls of animals in the woods, the hush of the trees, the whispering of leaves on the ground. But then finally, *finally,* there was a sound.

A car engine somewhere in the distance.

Someone . . . someone was here.

Ro turned her head and looked at Chase, who immediately sat upright.

They heard a popping sound then, shattering the stillness in loud bursts. Shouting followed. Ro hurried to her feet and ran at the door again with newfound determination. *Thump. Thump. Someone find us. Thump. Someone hear this.*

"Ro," Chase said, taking hold of her arm. She shoved him off and crashed into the door again. "Rowena!"

She stopped, turned to face him. He was watching her, eyes wide. "It doesn't sound good."

Ro's heart leapt into her throat. "You mean . . . ?"

"Whoever it is is being shot at." He paused. "I'm not saying it's them, but . . ."

"Are you going to help me?" Ro snapped, gesturing to the door. They had to try; they had to do *something.*

10

Chase hesitated for a moment then said, "Make some space."

Ro stepped to one side and the two of them crashed into the door together, making as much noise as possible. Whoever came, good or bad, at least it was someone. At least it was something.

—

The door was unlocked.

Flung open so it swung on its hinges and smacked into the interior wall, sending a cloud of dust up into the air. It filled the rectangle of light, swirling, swirling. A figure stood before them. It was not the woman from the woods.

Instead, a hunter stood in the doorway with a wild look in his eyes.

Ro's breath caught in her throat. She stood still and the room closed in; she was unaware of anything but the hunter in front of her.

"Ethan, wait!" a woman yelled. She came up behind him, panting, blocking more of the doorway. The room felt smaller still. She wasn't Ava, either, but another hunter.

Ro swallowed hard, biting back her fear. She'd wanted something to happen, and here it was.

"I thought you said we had no use for the two of them?" the woman said to the hunter she had called Ethan. Her dark hair was pulled back tight, making her face all sharp angles and cold eyes. She was wearing the black uniform of hunters. "The labs have enough lions right now."

"Did you not witness what just happened back there, Ange?" Ethan barked. He had a silver gun in his hand, and he waved it in the direction they must have traveled from. Ange took a step to one side, avoiding the barrel of the gun.

Did Ava know the two hunters? *Impossible.*

Right?

"Yes," Ange said softly. "I did see."

"We lost the elephant, we let the others get away. And worst: we lost the damn horse. I *knew* we should have killed her immediately. If Dale wasn't such a—"

"You already made it clear what you think of Dale, Ethan."

"It's Ava's fault," he growled. "Dale didn't used to be like this."

Ange shook her head, a slight movement Ethan wasn't meant to catch. But he did. He cracked his knuckles. They were bruised and bloody. There was a nasty-looking slice on the palm of his hand and a dark bruise on his temple.

The words rang through Ro's mind. *It's Ava's fault. Ava's fault. Ava.*

Ava did know them, then. She was serving them in some way. It didn't make sense—why would a shifter help hunters?

"Help me with them," Ethan said, stepping inside the building. Ro's attention snapped back to Ethan as he entered the room. She and Chase were backed up against the wall, the silver around their wrists burning, burning. He pointed his gun toward Chase. Ange followed him in, the four of them—two hunters, two shifters—squashed up in the too-small room.

Ange ensured Chase's cuffs were secure first, her interference pushing them down into his raw skin. Chase yelled. Ange moved away from him, back to Ethan's side.

Ethan tutted at her. "Get it together, Ange," he said. Ethan steadied his arm, his grip tight on the gun.

Ange reluctantly moved toward Chase again.

With both hunters' attention on Chase, Ro took a breath and, before she could think too much on it, threw herself at Ethan. They both fell, landing hard on the ground. The shoulder she'd been using to ram the door cracked audibly, sending a shock of pain down to her fingertips and up across her back. A shot fired from Ethan's gun at the same time, earsplitting in the small space.

Oh. Oh. Ro scrambled to her feet, but her balance didn't cooperate and she crashed back down. *Where did the bullet hit? Chase. Chase?*

A continuous dull ringing filled Ro's ears. Ethan recovered quickly, though. "Shit!" he growled. "Grab him! Make sure he doesn't try anything." On his knees, he pressed his gun to Ro's head with one hand and raised his other hand to his own. "Shit."

"You okay?" Ange asked Ethan. She had a hold of Chase. He was still standing, though Ro could see he was in as much pain as she was.

"Do I *look* okay?" Ethan snarled. "I already had a hellish headache after Dale's beloved shifters booted me in the face and took off. God, I hope we find them."

Ethan got to his feet, pulling Ro up with him. Her limbs were too heavy and the room spun a little around her. Her feet scrambled on the floor until it felt solid enough beneath her. Ethan tightened his hold on her arm, securing her wrist in his hand. The silver pressed deeper into Ro's skin, and it was enough to snap her out of the dreamy, achy pull of her muddled senses. She screamed.

—

Ro woke next to Chase again, in the back of a car this time.

Her head ached and her wrists throbbed with the sting of silver. The pain was worse now. Fresh.

Chase had woken before Ro had this time. He stared out of the tinted window. Ro pushed herself up a little so she could see out, too, but there wasn't much to see. They were speeding down a stretch of flat road, streaks of muted color on either side of them. Trees lined the thin road and traffic seemed nonexistent.

"How long have you been awake?" Ro whispered to Chase. Her voice trembled and she wondered if Chase would pick up on it.

"Not long," Chase said, his voice controlled. She could see the worry in his eyes, though. Tear tracks lined his cheeks. He nodded toward the front seat, where the two hunters sat. Ethan was driving, Ange in the passenger seat beside him. "They haven't said anything."

Ro looked away from Chase, from the hunters, back out the window. She tried to process what happened, but it all seemed so unreal. She didn't know where the warehouse was now, how far they'd traveled, or in which direction.

Ange turned in her seat. "They're both awake," she told Ethan.

"Cover their faces. We're almost there," he commanded.

Ange climbed halfway over the seat and secured a burlap sack over Ro's head, but not before Ro caught sight of a large white building sticking up in the middle of nowhere like a single tooth.

Ro started to feel nauseous. The sack over her head made it impossible to breathe properly. She exhaled and it was hot against her cheeks. She inhaled and the air was stuffy and close. She tried to focus on breathing, on not panicking, but she was gasping beneath the material.

They soon stopped, but the bag wasn't removed. Ro's breaths were short, shallow—she couldn't take it much longer. The lion pair were pulled from the car and escorted the rest of the way on foot. The grip on Ro's arm was strong, keeping her upright and moving as she tripped, scuffed her heels, twisted her ankle awkwardly. She realized the grip belonged to Ethan, his voice startling her as he said, "E-two-seven-six. With A-three-two-one and two SuperNats."

A speaker crackled. "Species?" a voice replied.

Ethan hesitated for a moment. Ro remembered Ange saying the lab had enough lions.

"Lions," Ethan finally said with less confidence.

"I *told* you they wouldn't want them," Ange whispered.

"We had to bring *something* back," Ethan replied. "We have to have something to show or there's no place for us in the field. We're already slipping since—"

"Bring them in," the voice said, cutting Ethan off mid-sentence. Ro heard a beep and some kind of rattling—a gate opening?—then the four of them started walking again.

Once inside the compound, Ro was guided through a building—the breeze was gone, the floor felt smooth, the space felt smaller. Turning left, turning right, she didn't know if Chase was even beside her anymore or if Ange had taken him somewhere else.

Ro was walked to a room—a door clicked shut behind her. The bag was removed from her head. Her eyes took a moment to adjust to the brightness of the white room. The silver was taken off her wrists, the relief instant as the skin was finally allowed to heal. Ro exhaled, breathed in deeply, and then repeated the action. Her arms were then strapped to a chair, palms up, while she was still managing the sudden light, the chance to breathe, the relief of the silver removed from her skin. She had no energy left to struggle against her new bonds—at least they weren't silver.

In front of her, Ethan stood to one side while a woman in a long white coat approached her, holding a needle. She stuck it into Ro's arm and drew blood.

"You're lucky," the doctor told Ethan. "I accidentally killed one of the lionesses a few weeks back."

This information should have surprised Ro, but she knew what went on at the labs. Most shifters did. There were stories, and there were facts, and the two sometimes blended into one tale of experiments and testing and pain. A life in the labs was often a short one.

The room they were inside was small. The three of them crowded it. Ro was strapped to a white chair. The walls and floors were white tile, and the counters lining two sides of the room were white, too. There was a light above them, omitting a harsh white glow, glancing off the shiny tiles,

16

the silver instruments on the counter, the doctor's lab coat. Everything looked so clean, so sterile, so intimidating.

Ro choked on a scream as the doctor secured a silver band around her wrist. She bucked in the chair. "What is that for?" she gasped through gritted teeth. Her words came out hoarse and pained as it burned against her skin. She had only *just* gotten the first silver off. She didn't know if she could stand it again.

"And the male?" Ethan asked the woman. They continued their conversation as though Ro hadn't made a sound. As though they weren't hurting her.

The woman rolled her eyes. "No," she said. "We definitely don't need him."

"Damn," Ethan said. "So my team only gets one?"

The woman smiled, like it was a game. "Just one. Go log it then get back out there. I was looking forward to working with the horse. Quinn's team is chasing the assignment, and they're beating your numbers this year. If you don't find her soon, you could lose the job."

Ethan nodded stiffly. "We'll find her," he said, and then left the room. Left Ro.

Find who? Ro wondered, but then realized it didn't really matter. All that mattered was the burning, burning, burning, and what was going to happen to her, and what was going to happen to Chase.

The woman turned back to Ro. "Right," she said, picking up a clipboard. "Let's get you logged in."

"No," Ro said, struggling against the bonds. "*No!*"

"Relax," the doctor said coolly. "Fighting it won't do anyone any good."

Ro called on her shape, imagining the dark place, the cold, the heat, her light, smooth coat. But nothing happened. The woman tutted and shook her head. "I know what you're trying to do. I put a silver cuff on your arm, so it's not going to happen."

Ro struggled anyway, kept on trying, imagining her claws, her teeth, the way she'd roar and pounce on the doctor, fight her way out. Find Chase.

Chase.

Something told her he could no longer be found. "*We definitely don't need him,*" the doctor had said. And there was only one thing to do with a shifter that was not needed for the lab.

"You don't understand," Ro said. "I'm not wild—I have never hurt anyone! A woman in the woods—a lion—she tricked Chase and me. But we're good—we're *good*!" She stopped, searching the woman's face for any kind of reaction. There was nothing. "Please! My name is Rowena. I'm a lion, yes, but I'm also human, with friends who I care about, and a girlfriend who I didn't get to say good-bye to. You must know what you're doing is wrong, that it's—"

The doctor pierced her arm with a needle. "What is that?" Ro demanded.

The doctor didn't answer but abruptly turned her back on Ro and picked up a phone attached to the wall. The spiral cord was tangled up and the doctor had to lean forward. She pressed a button. "You can take her now," she said into the receiver.

"What about Chase?" Ro continued. "*Please*, just let him go if you don't need him here!"

"Enough!" the doctor snapped. The door opened a moment later and two hunters came to take Ro out of the room.

Her legs felt unsteady when she stood. Whatever the doctor had injected her with was taking effect—she could almost feel it moving through her veins.

With the doctor leading the way, they guided her to an elevator. When the doors opened again, they stepped out. The doctor swiped a key card on a heavy door and led the hunters down a long white corridor, passing room after room, each one with a sign on the door—a number, a species.

"In here, please," she said to the two hunters holding Ro, gesturing to an open door without a sign. The hunters heaved Ro inside.

There was a light on the ceiling, and a bed, a sink, and a toilet against the wall. A speaker in the corner. A hatch on the door. Ro noticed it as the door closed, trapping her inside. She rushed toward it, peering out into the hallway. The hunter reached out and closed the hatch, shutting her off, shutting her in.

She banged her fists on the door, slow and clumsy. Moments later, a voice came out of the speaker. She stopped and turned to look at it. It was in the corner, an ugly little box on the wall. "Welcome to Roll Point," the voice said. "Step away from the door."

1

THEY ALWAYS COME BACK

"Are you ready, Flo?"

I hitch my backpack up on aching shoulders and turn to face Jett. The light, misty rain clings to his eyelashes. I squint against its diagonal spray as it blows into my face. It's late in the day and growing colder, the sharp wind biting my cheeks. The sign swings outside the old inn across the cobblestone road from where I stand, creaking like it demands my attention.

And it's got it.

I give in and look back at the Flaming Horse Inn. The image of a horse surrounded by flames on a weatherworn sign is visible even from here. I didn't think we'd find ourselves back here, in this small mountain town so soon. If at all. We weren't here that long ago, though it feels like a lifetime. I guess it was another life, another journey. I had been a different person compared to who I am now. I hadn't seen what I've seen. Done what I've done.

"Yeah," I say absently, my gaze fixed on the swaying sign. My eyes start to sting and I blink some moisture back into them, snapping out of my trance and away from the path of memories the sign invites me to take.

A couple walks out of the inn, hand in hand. They move closer to each other as the bitterness of the temperature hits them. I remember when Jett and I walked out of those doors and huddled together against the chill. He had wrapped his scarf around my neck when we got back to the car. We almost kissed. But everything had been too much that day, too distracting.

"It's my turn to carry that," Jett says, easing the backpack off my shoulders. I straighten my arms to help get it off and refocus my attention on Jett now, working on forgetting the sign, the inn, the memories. But they tug at me, pulling me back.

"Is everyone else ready?" I ask as the weight shifts off my back. I roll my shoulders.

Jett loosens the straps on the pack and threads his arms through them. We're sharing Tia's backpack. It didn't have a lot in it—spare clothes, a refillable water bottle, a threaded string bracelet, a pair of small sandals, and a blanket. I kept most of it. Ro's name, surrounded by a heart shape, is plucked into the material at the bottom of the bag. Faint, but there. I wonder if Rowena knew it was.

Jett looks over his shoulder and nods. "Almost. Just waiting for Lola to give the word."

I follow his gaze. Ursula, Ruby, and Star are sitting on a low stone wall, resting until it's time to move again. Owen and Itch stand in front of them. Ursula swings her legs absently as she talks to Star. I hear her laughter, Ruby's too, and the sound makes me smile. It's been a long journey here. Spirits have dipped, moods have been low, and hope has disappeared entirely at times. But it all comes back; something always lifts us. Just the sound of laughter can do it sometimes.

After everything that happened with the cabin, none of the ex-circus members, including me, really knew what they wanted to do. None of us have been handed this kind of opportunity before—to leave and fend for ourselves. To live without rules and restrictions. We're part of a wild pack now, but none of us quite knows what that means, what it entails. We always had a role at the circus—we were given a chore, or an act to practice, and were told what to do and when to do it. We've never had to manage ourselves. With the threats of Ethan, Dale, the other two hunters, and the elders gone, we're finally facing the question: what next?

All I knew was that I wanted us to stay together. To join Lola's pack properly, not temporarily, and find our way as a team. I know we are stronger together—as animals and as humans. I know we will be okay if we stay together.

Lola came to us with her plans before any of us really had time to think about what to do from there. The only idea I'd had was to help captured shifters and to eventually find out what happened to my parents, but I know that wouldn't work. Not with our numbers and lack of knowledge. The battle at the cabin had been us versus four hunters, and we'd lost so many. We'd never get into a lab.

Since finding Ro and Chase seemed less likely—after Ava claimed she'd handed the lion pair over to the hunters—and our new pack had taken a hard hit with the loss of Tia, Dee, and Ebony, Lola told us about an opportunity that may give us all a chance. And it all rests on a rat.

Parrot sisters, Lola and Kanna, and white tigers, Jax and Hugo, are farther ahead of us, farther ahead than Ursula and the others sitting on the low wall. I wonder if the sound of laughter reaches them there. They're looking up at the mountain. I look up, too. The four of them will lead us up there soon. That's where we're supposed to find Rat.

I take another breath and wait for them to call us forward. It's only been a few days since the cabin—everything still hurts, though is healing well, and the memories are still fresh. After emptying out the cabin, keeping what we needed, burning what we didn't, we made our way here following Lola's lead. We erased every trace of the hunters, of their experiments, from the cabin. Nothing was left but the building itself and the remains of a campfire once we were done.

I stand waiting with my hands stuffed into my pockets. The coat zips up to my chin, fleece inside and waterproof outside, and reads: THE BAY CONSTRUCTION COMPANY on the chest with a purple swirl above it.

Star wanted to go back to the warehouse and stay there. She didn't like running. She wanted the circus, her friends, the other seals, the warehouse, the woods. She wanted to be safe, somewhere she *felt* safe. But the warehouse wasn't safe and it was being demolished soon. Honestly, no one but Star had wanted to stay in the area and everyone supported Lola's plan. So here we are.

I still don't feel like we're far enough away, though. We have too many connections to this place. It demands to be recognized, to be remembered. And I want to forget.

Over at the low wall, Ursula stretches her arms up, catching Star in a hug when she brings them back down. Ursula pulls her close, and Star rests her head on Ursula's shoulder. She looks tired.

Lance and Lucas pass the group on the wall, heading this way. Ursula smiles at them as they pass. They return it. Their smiles are fragile things, though. It's hard to see everyone hurting so much. I don't know how to make it better. I don't even know how I feel myself. Not yet, maybe not ever. Things will never be the same for us, and how well we adapt to this new life is yet to be seen.

Jett puts his arm around my waist. "It's strange being back here, isn't it?" he says. Lance and Lucas join us, hear Jett's comment, but don't say anything. We all seem to have fallen back into our groups. The wild shifters—Lola, Kanna, Hugo, and Jax—make one. The ex-circus members split into two—those who escaped together and those who were captured together. The brothers, Jett, and me—just like before, just like always.

"I'm trying not to," Jett continues. "But I keep thinking of then and now . . . and everything in between."

Lance and Lucas turn away, facing the mountain rather than the village. I close my eyes for a moment then say, "So do I." My thoughts fight over one another to be heard, and I can't hold them back as they all rush forward at once. I'm glad Jett has his arms around me, holding me up, as a wave of sadness and guilt consumes me. Like Jett, I try not to focus on the past too much, but there was *then* and there is *now* and all that's in between is too much to push away. Too much happened to ignore and simply move past. Like all things, it'll take time.

My heart aches for Logan, and I put my hand to my chest like I can heal it with touch. I miss him. I miss there being three brothers. Lucas and Lance don't seem right without Logan, and I'm certain they never will be. Something will always be missing. The loss is heavy, and I know we're all starting to really feel it now—now that there is time to.

"Hey," Jett whispers by my ear. "Are you with me?"

Lance and Lucas stand beside us, waiting quietly until we start moving again. They're so quiet now. They used to laugh all the time. The sound echoes in my memory. Another thing stored away. Another thing changed. The circus fire changed them, changed all of us.

"Yes," I say, turning in the circle of Jett's arms to face him. I draw a deep breath. "I'm here. I'm okay. It's just this place."

Jett nods. He knows. He understands. Always. "I know. I feel it, too," he says. "I think we'll be moving in a minute."

"To find Rat."

"Yeah," Jett says. "What a name."

This forces a smile from me. "He's a rat, too, you know?" I say, in an attempt to ward off all the negative energy filling me up. I include the brothers. "Did you guys know that? Rat's a rat."

"Oh," Lucas says, like he only just caught what I said. Only just realized I was speaking to him. "Yeah, we knew. Funny, huh?"

I hide my disappointment. It's something they'd usually laugh at. Make a big joke out of—a rat called Rat. It *is* funny. It'd be like my name being Horse or Jett's name being Bear. But no one laughs anymore.

I still try to ignore the changes among us, keep clawing for the way we used to be. If I can at least be like that on the outside, while still battling on the inside, maybe everyone else can, too. We can work at this together, be there for one another, pick each other up and all the pieces with it.

"Imagine if you were called Elephant," I say to Lucas.

Lucas's lips quirk up at the corners—almost a real smile. "Then the three of us would have the same name and everyone would have even less of a clue who was who," he says. He pauses then. Lance looks at his feet, his head dipped so I can't see his face. Lucas appears to almost physically choke on his words, putting a hand to his throat when he realizes he said "three." *The three of us.* The three of them.

I noticed it, too. But I didn't react, hoping Lucas wouldn't pick up on it, hoping it wouldn't crush the moment. But he did, and it had. Of course he did, and now I feel like I can't even help when I'm trying to. Maybe the pieces are too small, too scattered, for us to pick them all back up. Maybe some have to stay where they are, beyond repair.

Jett rubs my arm. I look at him quickly—he always sorts us out, always fixes things when they go wrong between us. And this is wrong, *all wrong*. Eyes wide, I search his face, but he shakes his head. He doesn't know what to do this time, either. Do I tell Lucas I'm sorry?

Probably not. That'll just draw more attention to it. I should just carry on as normal, whatever normal is, and not make a big deal out of it. So, I take a breath and say, "I still can't believe we're looking for the bear pack."

That's all I can think to do—push us off the subject. Away from the past and into the present. Right now, we're looking for the bear pack. Right now, we're going up the mountain to see if they're there. Right now, that is our goal.

Rat is part of the pack run by the bears from the attack article we discovered in a free local newspaper when we were last in this village. Lola, Kanna, Hugo, and Jax had all been part of the bear pack, but when hunters got close to their group, they'd fled along with some of the other shifters we lost at the cabin.

"The bears aren't there anymore," Jett says. "The hunters got them."

I nod. "True. But Lola says the rest are just as bad."

"Kanna said the same," Lucas adds, his hands in his pockets. The tips of his ears turn pink when we all look at him. "It does feel weird to be looking for them after reading about them all that time ago."

Lola said if we find the pack, we find Rat. Hopefully. He's trapped there, but Lola doesn't know for sure how much of the old pack is left. I don't want to lose this thread, this conversation between the four of us. I want to hold onto it, keep it close. "What do you think we'll find?" I ask.

The boys shrug. "I guess we'll find out soon," Lucas says, nodding toward Lola. She's calling us over. The brothers go ahead.

I linger for a moment before I leave the village behind, thinking about what awaits us on the mountain. I don't know what to expect, either. Answers, hopefully.

Rat was looking to move on to a bigger pack, one he discovered while out patrolling the area around one of their camps. He planned to leave, to join them. He told Lola and some of the others in secret. But his secret got out, and the leaders of his pack—the bears—found out. As punishment, they trapped him in a cage in his animal form. Lola had tried to save him before they left camp, but failed. So, we're going back for him now, and then we're going with him.

The pack Rat was looking to join is bigger than us, bigger than his pack, bigger than the circus. They're apparently well guarded, well hidden, and all with minimal incident involving hunters and humans. If that's true, then that's where I want to be, where I want all of us to be. At least for now. It would give me space to think about what I want next.

The wind blows stronger, bringing with it the scent of pine from the mountains and sending my hair flapping around my face and into my eyes. Jett helps me brush it back, smiling at me. I smile back and lean into him. We turn together and join the others around Lola.

I clutch my necklace in my fist. Jett had bought it here at a little store. I search the street for it now—The Horse on the Mountain, with its blue sign and chipped gold lettering. Lights are on inside, shining softly through the diamond-glass windows. Something sparkles on display, catching my eye.

We start toward the mountain, Lola and Kanna leading the way. It'll be dark soon. The sun casts a salmon-colored hue across the sky. Streaks of pink and orange brush the horizon. Up the steep path, the air is fresh. Awakening. It kind of makes me want to shift, to run up the mountain and feel the rush of cold air pushing against me as I climb higher, higher.

I haven't shifted since everything happened at the cabin. We have food and water from the hunters' stash (one of the only things we didn't destroy), and we're all healing well. There's no reason to shift other than wanting to.

"How much farther?" Star asks, coming to walk between Jett and me. She reaches for my hand and I take it.

"Not much," I say. Lola told us the camp wasn't too far off the ground, giving the pack easy access to the village.

Star frowns. "How can we be sure they're even here?"

"Lola said they'd never abandon the mountain. Not entirely. If they were scared off by hunters, they'd come back. If they're still out here, they're somewhere in these mountains. And we don't know for sure if the hunters found their camp in the first place. They started picking off members, but Lola and the others didn't stay long enough to find out. . . . Wait," I say, pausing. "Have you forgotten all of this? Lola said it all back at the—"

Star shakes her head, cutting me off. "No. I stopped listening because I still think we should have gone back to the warehouse." It's something she keeps saying, even though she knows it's coming down. Even though she knows it's too close to the cabin, too close to Violet Bay, to Iris and Greg, and maybe the elders, too. Too close to everything that's proven a danger to us in the past. "I don't like being here."

"Star—" I begin.

"I *know*," she snaps, her voice harsher than I've ever heard it.

Star wasn't part of the fight at the cabin, but I wonder how much of this she has absorbed. She still ran from the circus. She lost people, too. She was turned away from Iris's, but then found her way to this group, only to run into more danger. She was there when the warehouse was attacked—she was scared on the stairwell—and she saw the aftermath of the fight when she joined us at the cabin. She saw our wounds, saw the bodies.

"We could have found another place like the warehouse," Star says. "I don't like living outside."

I swallow hard. "We've always lived like this."

"Not always," she says sadly. "Not like this. We had tents, a big group, the elders. I felt safe before."

I don't point out that we were never safe, that we were likely in more danger throughout our entire lives than we are now. It still feels surreal that the hunters knew what we were all along, that they knew the second we joined the elders, the circus, the lie.

"And you don't now?" I ask.

Star shakes her head no. I glance at Jett. "Nothing will happen, Star," he says, taking her other hand. "The hunters are gone."

"They might come back," she says simply. "They always come back."

2
A VERY UNEXCITING BEAR

Star hurries us forward and walks the rest of the way with Ursula and Ruby.

It's not a long journey up, but going *up* makes it feel that way. My calves ache and my chest feels tight by the time we stop. I suck air into my lungs, so fresh and sharp that it hurts a little.

"I hope Lola knows what she's doing," Ursula says, suddenly beside me. She sounds breathless, too. We're a little way from the ground and the air is even colder up here. My teeth chatter while I'm standing still, and I rub my hands together to keep them warm.

Ursula cups her own hands and breathes into them.

"She does," I say with confidence. I trust Lola—she's smart and she's patient, she thinks things through, and she's brought us this far. "I think we're getting close."

Both Ursula and I fall silent as we watch Lola, waiting for the next instructions. I learned quickly that Lola is a natural leader and thankfully she's easy to follow. She's speaking to Jax now, both of them pointing ahead. A few moments pass before she turns to the rest of us

31

and raises her voice. "We'll make camp here," is all she says.

Most mumble their agreement and drop their packs, preparing the area for us to eat and sleep. Ursula, however, asks, "For how long?" She seems a little uneasy. I look at the area around us. It's all flat mud, tall trees, and uneven rocks. It seems as good a place as any to stop.

"Just tonight," Lola says. Then adds, "Hopefully."

"What do you mean by 'hopefully'?" Ursula asks. "Is it safe here?"

Lola and Kanna exchange a look. "We aren't sure how safe the mountain is," Lola admits. "That's why we'll move again once it's light. It should be fine if we don't stay in one place too long. We'll take turns on watch."

Ursula folds her arms. She doesn't respond right away. She doesn't seem herself, and I decide I should speak to her once we get a moment.

"We need a fire," Kanna says to fill the silence. Shivering, she picks up two pieces of wood to make a start.

"Do you think that's a good idea?" Ruby asks.

Ursula nods in agreement. "Yeah, won't that . . . attract things?"

Lola bites her bottom lip. "They're right," she says with a sigh. My shoulders slump—a fire would be really great right now. Kanna clucks her tongue. "Coats and blankets only," Lola adds.

Kanna steps away from the group. Lola watches her out of the corner of her eye. I do, too. But she doesn't go far, stopping beside Lance and Lucas, who are unrolling their sleeping bags.

I remember first meeting Kanna. She wasn't nice to us; she wanted us out of the warehouse and away from her group. I realize now that she was trying to protect her friends, and Lola—her sister. At the time, Ursula had told me not to take it personally. That Kanna wasn't mean, but angry. And I kind of get it now. I'm angry, too—at where we've been, where we are. It's not fair that we must live so cautiously, moving all the time, losing friends as we go.

Hugo joins them while Jax talks to Lola. The rest of us go back to unpacking for the night. Jett's found a good spot, and I place my bag down beside his. Ursula joins Owen, Star, Ruby, and Itch on the other side of the clearing. They're separate from the rest of us and I don't understand why—there's plenty room over here. I decide now's a good time to have that talk with Ursula, so I leave my things with Jett.

"Hey," I say when I reach her. "What're you doing all the way out here?"

Ursula's crouched over her pack. She shrugs. "It's a good spot," she replies.

The others don't look up from their individual tasks.

"Can I talk to you for second?" I ask quietly.

"What about?" she says with a frown.

"Everything."

She stands and we take a few steps away. "What is it?" she asks the moment we stop. There's an edge to her voice, something I'm not used to from her. This, paired with Star snapping at me earlier, strikes me as strange. I know we're all feeling a rush of emotions right now, but I don't know what to do with it.

"Is everything okay?" I say.

"Define 'everything.'"

I tilt my head. "Ursula?"

She sighs, her shoulders slumping forward. "I know," she says. "I know. I'm sorry." She shakes her head. "Everything isn't okay, okay?"

"Okay," I echo. "How can I help? What can I do?"

"You can't do anything this time, Flo," she replies, eyebrows furrowed. "We're wild now, remember."

"I remember," I tell her. "But we'll find the new group soon. Rat will—"

"I don't know if I want to do that," she cuts in. "So just let me figure it out on my own."

"But you're not on your own!" I say. "Please, Ursula."

Ursula takes a step back from me. I reach out to her but she angles her body away from me. "I'm sorry. I'm worried. And Lola . . . I'm just not so sure anymore."

I rub my forehead. "What does that mean, though?"

"I don't know if I want to find the pack like everyone else does. I don't know if it's a good idea. But everyone was so excited that I felt like I had to go along with it because it seemed like the best idea at the time and the safest thing to do, but now I don't know."

"Ursula, it *is* the safest. We've never been a small group like this. We've never been on our own."

"And look where that got us," she replies angrily. "I'm sorry, Flo."

"You don't need to keep apologizing."

"But I do. And I mean it. I just need time to figure it out, okay?"

"Okay," I say again. "Come to me—if you need any-thing. To talk, or anything."

She nods and turns away, heading back to Owen and the others. I want to make it better for her, but I don't know how, and she doesn't know how, and I don't think she really wants my help.

I close my eyes for a moment, taking a deep breath of the fresh mountain air. I let it sting my lungs with its chill. Then I go back to Jett. I'm sure Ursula will come around when we're settled with the new pack. It just seems scary now—not knowing. But when we meet them, we'll know if it's right. And there's nothing keeping us there if it's not. We're free now. Wild shifters, all of us.

As I pass Lola, Hugo, and Jax, I hear Lola hiss, "Great." I watch out of the corner of my eye, wondering what's happening now. "I needed her here with us!"

"I didn't know that!" Hugo whispers back.

The problem with whispering in a quiet, open space is that it still travels. "What's up?" I ask the three of them.

"Kanna and Lucas went on patrol," Lola says with a sigh.

"And that's bad?"

"No, but I needed her here, that's all."

"Why?" I put my hands in my pockets. Beneath the construction company coat, I'm still wearing the striped dress I got from Iris with my leggings and boots.

Lola glances at the rest of the group. I follow her gaze, see Jett and Lance sitting with their backs against a large rock, eyes closed, blanket over their legs.

I see Ursula's group in a circle, leaning forward to talk to one another, trapping warmth between them. As a monkey, Itch could shift and draw from the heat of his fur coat. But I know none of them will call on their animals when Ruby can't. They'll huddle together, wrap up in whatever blankets and coats are available, and keep warm that way.

Kanna and Lucas are still patrolling. No one is paying any attention to us.

"Because," Lola says, lowering her voice. "Their main base camp isn't far from here, but now Kanna is gone and I don't know when she'll get back."

I frown. "You were planning to go tonight?"

She bites her lip, but then nods once.

"When were you going to tell us?" I try to keep my voice quiet, but my hands are shaking. We're a *team*—we should have all known about this.

"When we got back," Lola admits.

"You can't do that!" I say, a little louder now. I look behind me. Jett and Lance are sitting forward, watching us.

"Great, Flo—why don't you just tell everyone?"

"I will!"

"Why don't you speak a little louder so everything on this mountain hears us and comes looking?"

I fall silent, then. Take a breath, a moment. "You should have told us," I say quietly. "Secrets aren't good for us."

Lola's eyes soften. She puts her hand on my shoulder. "I know. I'm sorry. We're still planning, and we'll tell everyone when we're done—I promise."

"Maybe we can help?" I offer. Lola's hand is still on my shoulder.

She shakes her head and pulls her hand back. "Next time."

I scowl—why will no one let me do anything to help them? I feel useless standing around waiting for something to happen. I want to make it happen. I want to be a part of this. "Tell me," I say. "If you're going tonight."

"I will," Lola promises, but despite all the praise I've given her in front of everyone else, my trust is slipping a little. And I don't want it to.

"If you do leave tonight—how soon will you have him?" I ask.

Lola looks at Jax before turning back to me. "Hopefully before tomorrow morning. Then we can move farther into the mountain. If everyone's okay with that."

I contemplate for a moment. "I think they are. But you might be losing Ursula."

"What do you mean?" Lola asks.

"I get the impression some of them don't trust this plan anymore. Maybe if you involve us more . . ."

"I'm trying, Flo. It's a difficult situation—we have to move fast and at the right time. Sometimes there isn't time to debate over what needs to be done." Lola looks over her shoulder at Ursula's group. "Do you trust me?" she asks. "Do Jett and the brothers?"

"Yes," I say with no hesitation. "As long as you don't keep anything from us."

She nods.

"We want to find the pack Rat told you about," I continue. "When were you thinking of leaving?"

"We were going to go now," Lola says. "Well, we were—before Kanna took off."

"She didn't know?"

Lola shakes her head. "Not yet. I told you—sometimes we make quick decisions."

Jax and Hugo stand slightly behind Lola. I notice they keep looking at each other. They seem worried. Is it because Kanna is gone?

Lola follows my gaze. "We still need to go," she tells them. "With or without Kanna. We can't wait on this."

Jax shakes his head right away. "We should wait for her," he says. "We should rest first—eat, drink, get our energy up."

"I told you—there's no time," Lola replies.

Jax frowns. "If he's there now, he'll still be there tomorrow."

"You don't know that!" Lola argues.

"Neither do you!" says Jax.

"Lola's right, Jax," Hugo says. Jax glares at his cousin. "We want to be gone from here by tomorrow. I agree that we should go now, while it's getting dark."

Lola takes a step forward. "Anything could happen between now and then. To us, to him. I'm not waiting. Hugo's right—the darkness will give us better cover."

Jax folds his arm. "Lola, we're off to face our old pack while we're at our weakest."

Lola tuts. "You're making it sound so much more dangerous than it is. If we can help it, we won't even see anyone."

Hugo rubs his temples and groans.

"I can come in place of Kanna," I offer.

The group's attention snaps back to me. "Why?" Jax asks.

"I want to do something. Standing or sitting around doesn't work for me right now," I tell him.

There's too much to think about, too much on my mind. Boredom pulls me in, memories surface, and I can't escape it. I want to help.

Lola offers a weak smile. "I don't know, Flo. I only wanted ex-pack members to go. I need them to trust us."

"You said you probably wouldn't run into anyone," I remind her.

"I said I hoped not to. I can't say for certain." Jax opens his mouth to add a comment but Lola hurries on, speaking over him. "And you're unfamiliar to them. They'll want to know who you are."

I shrug. "That's no big deal, right? I don't mind telling them."

"No," Hugo says. "Don't. They don't have a horse."

Lola and Jax nod in agreement. "I don't want them to know that that's what you are," Lola says.

"Why?"

"Just . . . trust me," Lola says. "They're unpredictable. I might be being overcautious, I don't know."

"I don't think you're being cautious enough," Jax says, but Lola ignores him.

"Okay," Lola sighs. "Just don't say you're a horse. It's better to be safe."

"And are you safe?" I ask. "Do they have other parrots and white tigers?"

"No," Lola says. "But they have an eagle and three tigers, so they won't be missing us too much."

"Unless something has happened to them since we left," Jax comments.

Lola frowns. "Jax, do you have to—"

"Okay," I say quickly before a new argument begins. Hugo grins at me. "What shall I say I am if someone asks?"

"A bear," Lola says with a smile. "A very unexciting bear. They'll have no interest in that. There were about five of them last time we were there, even without the two the hunters tracked. That's more than enough bears for one pack."

"Okay," I say with a nod. "I'm a bear. So, you're letting me come?"

Lola shrugs. "If the others are fine with that." Jax and Hugo give the go-ahead. "Okay, then. That's settled. Wear something of Jett's, too. Just to back you up in case one of them sniffs you."

I wrinkle my nose. "There's a sniff test?"

"No test, Flo," Jax says. "There's no order, no control."

"We just need to be prepared," Lola says.

"Right," I say. "Okay. I'll be right back."

3
INTO THE SKY

"Then I'm coming, too," Jett says.

I fold my arms over my chest. "I knew you'd say that."

"I care about you, and I don't want to be left behind wondering what's happening."

I wouldn't want that, either. I feel bad for asking him to—to stay here while I go with Lola, Jax, and Hugo. But I really want to help get Rat back, to see another shifter camp and how they live outside the circus. There's still so much I don't know.

"But I'm the bear!" I say. "If you come, it'll be obvious I'm stealing your scent."

Jett sighs. He takes his shirt off, gritting his teeth against the cold. I hand him my coat in exchange, but he holds the shirt out of reach.

"Jett! Lola won't let anyone else go anyway, and I really want to!"

Jett hesitates, but then tosses me the shirt. "Not happy," he grumbles.

After handing over the construction-site coat, I clutch Jett's shirt in one hand and pull him toward me with the

41

other. I press my lips to his then whisper against them. "I know. But it'll be fine. And they need you here—you're one of the strongest shapes."

"We're going, Flo," Lola calls. She's standing with Hugo and Jax, waiting for me.

I kiss Jett again before joining them. "Fill everyone in on what's happening," I tell him. "Lucas and Kanna, too, when they get back. Make sure everyone stays together."

Jett nods. "I will." He glances over my shoulder at Lola, Hugo, and Jax. "Be careful," he says to the group, but his eyes return to me.

"We will be," Lola says. "Don't worry." She turns, leading Hugo, Jax, and me deeper into the mountains she once called home. I look back at Jett as we leave, give him a reassuring wave and smile. He returns it halfheartedly. Then we're out of camp and I can't see him anymore.

—

Night falls quickly, taking me by surprise.

We haven't traveled far from the others, but Lola, Jax, and Hugo argue over the direction, and we change course several times until they've agreed. The moon is full and high, lighting our way.

Steep, rising slopes. Rocks jutting out. Paths become too treacherous to walk and we have to go back and find another way. Lola gets increasingly irritated that she can't remember the mountain like she used to.

"How come you haven't tried to get Rat back before

now?" I ask, panting a little from the effort of climbing over a series of rocks that covered the path.

"It hasn't been that long since we left!" Lola says quickly, defensively, as though to make sure I know she'd have returned for her friend before now if she could have.

"We were running at first," Jax explains. "I knew the pack would hunt us as soon as we took off. At least until we got far enough away for them to drop our trail and return."

"Yeah," Lola says. "And our departure wasn't as quiet as we'd hoped."

"We tried to take him when we left," Jax continues. "But failed, as you know. After that, we were looking for somewhere safe to settle for a while and let things calm down."

"Except they didn't," Lola says. "Your elders turned us away, and when we did find somewhere to stop, we got mixed up with hunters and your group, and Chase and Rowena went missing. This is the first chance we've had, really. And the best chance we have of getting him back."

I wonder how close a friend Rat is to the others. How close was the pack?

Lola must have known Rat well enough for him to confide in her about the pack he'd found. But it appears he wasn't keeping it quiet enough if the leaders found out—so who else did he tell? How many?

I don't know how much I trust Rat.

But I want to know where the pack is, so for now we'll have to go along with what he tells us. If we find the pack and settle there, who knows how often we'd see him anyway.

"They won't expect it now," Lola says. "I'm going to shift and go ahead to see what's there before we go any farther—okay?"

Jax nods. "Be careful. Is your wing feeling all right?"

Lola removes her coat and holds out her arm, examining the wound there. The skin is pink and puckered, healing well. "I think it'll be fine," she says. She drops her jacket on the floor, then jumps, shifting midair in a blur of red, blue, and green. The air quivers around her form. The rest of her clothes fall into a pile on top of her coat and she takes off into the sky.

As Jax, Hugo, and I wait for Lola to return, I'm reminded again of the night in the woods when Lola flew ahead to scope out the cabin before coming back to tell us she'd been spotted. Other images flash in my mind now: Dee's leg in the bear trap, watching Tia drop to the ground, seeing Lance crush Dale's skull. And the bear again—Ebony. Always the bear.

I remember Lola's caw when Ethan stabbed Ebony in the woods. When I thought it was Jett. It's a sound I'll never forget. It echoes through my dreams, repeats in my mind. I see the knife coming down again, again, again. The bear's back arching, the hunter running into the trees. I chase him. I chase him into the darkness.

I rub my eyes and pull myself back to the present. I came here to get away from those thoughts. I'm not in one of my nightmares now. I lean against a tree, tipping my head back so it rests on the cold bark.

"Tell me what to expect," I say to distract myself. I speak quietly. The mountain is so still, so silent. I keep my voice low as not to disturb it. It feels like being somewhere else—somewhere between worlds, like when we shift and enter the Blackout. It's almost comforting. My limbs tingle with the thought of the shift—of the cold, of the heat, of my coat and the way it makes me feel. I quickly shut down the thought. I am a bear tonight, and that's only if anyone asks.

"It depends how full the base is," Jax says softly. "We don't really know what happened to them after we left. We could run into some trouble, we could run into a lot. Or none at all. It all depends who's there and how many. Lola will come back with the information, and then we can decide how to play it."

I bite the inside of my cheek, wondering exactly what we'll find there.

"Are you worried?" Hugo asks. Then says, "Don't be," before I have chance to answer. I shake my head anyway. I'm not nervous, exactly, just eager to get this done. The sooner we locate Rat, the sooner we can move on.

I want to find the camp, to feel safer than I do now. To finally let the past be in the past. To know I'm staying put somewhere. The circus stayed in each location anywhere between two weeks and two months, and each place was usually familiar to us. I've never felt more lost than I do now. But, at the same time, I've never felt so free.

4
DARK DELIGHT

"How many?" Jax asks the moment Lola returns to us.

She shifts right before she hits the ground, landing securely on her feet. I stumble back from her landing spot as her form changes. She moves so quickly and expertly—Lola can shift faster than anyone I've met. She seems so aware of herself, of her surroundings.

"Give her a chance to transform first," Hugo chides while Lola's bird beak flattens out into her mouth and chin.

Lola shakes out her hair, running her hand through the strands. Her fingers tangle in a knot and she winces and pulls away a blue feather. "Ouch," she says, dropping it. Its color is magnificent. "That took longer than usual."

Quietly, I step closer to Lola, no longer needing to give her the space to shift, and gently take her arm. Turning it over, I inspect the bullet wound again. "It's probably because of this," I tell her. It looks more swollen than before, while the skin readjusts around it.

Lola smoothly extracts her arm from my grip and pulls it back, looking closely at the patchy skin there. It's hard to see in the dimming light, but the skin is clearly shinier and raised up where she was hit in the wing with the silver bullet. It's healed but not entirely—serious wounds take time to completely disappear. "It doesn't really hurt anymore, though," she says, frowning.

Jax bobs from foot to foot, clearly eager to get going and making sure we know it. Hugo notices Jax's impatience and rolls his eyes.

"Are you okay?" Hugo asks Lola.

"Yes," Lola replies, lowering her arm and quickly pulling her clothes back on.

"So, before Jax explodes, how many are in camp?" Hugo says.

"If we're doing this, I want to go get it done," Jax replies quickly. "That's all."

"Even if Lola is hurting?" Hugo says, tilting his head to one side.

Jax looks from Hugo to Lola. "Are you hurting?" Jax asks, his voice softer.

Lola shakes her head. "No," she says. "I just feel funny still, but I'm fine."

Jax closes the distance between the two of them, wrapping Lola up in his arms. He kisses her forehead. "Sorry," he whispers against her hair, but it's loud enough for me to hear. Hugo hears, too, given the grin on his face.

"Sometimes he just needs a little push in the right direction," Hugo says beside me.

"Are they together?" I ask him, not taking my eyes off the pair. Jax holds Lola against him and runs his hand through her long hair. I'd suspected there was something more between them but there had been nothing to confirm it.

Hugo shrugs. "Who knows? You'll get used to them."

I laugh quietly as Lola and Jax break apart. Lola and Hugo exchange a look, a smile tugging at Lola's lips.

"Well," Lola says, clearing her throat. She tucks her dark hair behind her ears. Jax stays beside her. "We're in luck," she continues. "Kind of. I only saw Gretchen and Tomas on guard duty. The rest of the camp was empty."

Jax's eyes widen. "Really?" he says. "We should go in now. Before they get back."

"What are their shapes?" I ask. "Gretchen and Tomas."

"Beaver and mouse," Hugo says.

I smile. "This is going to be easy."

"Not necessarily," Hugo says. "Gretchen's got a mean bite with those sharp front teeth of hers." He holds out his arm, showing me an old scar on the inside. "See."

I gasp. "What did you do to get that?" There are pink puncture wounds on the soft part of his arm, just above the elbow. The skin looks stretched too tight around them—Gretchen must have bitten hard to leave a mark like that, for it not to heal and disappear like most injuries do. Only the bad ones stick around as reminders.

Hugo furrows his eyebrows. "I tried to save Rat. While she was on guard duty."

I swallow. "Oh. . . . Kind of like what we're doing now then."

Hugo nods. "Exactly like. Only she's got Tomas for backup this time."

Jax snorts. "Tomas is a traitor. Everyone knows that." He turns to me. "He was always in trouble for sneaking off and trying to join new packs, then coming back when he couldn't find one or they wouldn't accept him."

I frown. "Did he find Rat's pack?"

Lola shakes her head. "No one other than Rat found them from our group. Rat said that they're so well organized that they wouldn't let someone like Tomas even get a whiff of them."

"And you trust Rat—one hundred percent?"

"Why would I be here if I didn't?" Lola says. "Don't you?"

I shake my head. "I don't know him. But I trust you."

Lola crosses her arms. "Then why ask?"

"Because I have to," I tell her. My heart beats fast in reaction to the confrontation, to what we're about to step into and what we might find. I want to start moving now; I don't like standing still when I feel this full of nerves and energy. "For peace of mind."

Lola lets her arms drop back to her sides. "Anything else you want to ask for peace of mind?" she says.

"Let's start walking," I say. "I'll ask on the way."

So we do. Lola leads the way, Jax beside her. I hang back and talk to Hugo, the scar on his arm flashing in my mind as we make our way toward the person who made it.

"Why does your ex-pack keep Tomas around if they know they can't trust him?" I ask Hugo, carefully stepping over a fallen branch. I try to understand how they live, how things work there. I've never known anything but the circus, and this between running and hiding and trying to find somewhere new to belong. If you ran away from the circus, you weren't ever allowed back, so why could Tomas go back again and again to the pack he continually betrayed?

Hugo shrugs. "They taunted him," he says. "Kept him as a pet of sorts. It's worse punishment than letting him go seek out a new way of life. He's always got silver embedded in his skin so that he can't shift. And someone always keeps an eye on him so he can't sneak away. Gretchen's watching the camp, but she's babysitting Tomas, too, if things are like they used to be." Hugo sighs. "It's cruel, what they do to him."

"It's just to show what they can do," Lola adds from ahead of us. "How far they can take things."

Hugo runs his finger over his scar. "That's not even the worst of it."

"What's the—?"

Jax holds up a hand in front, cutting off our conversation of scars and silver and imprisoned shifters. Their ex-pack seems worse than the hunters, and suddenly I wonder why I came along to face shifters like that. *Because you want to help. Because you want to do something and move forward. Because you want to know.*

I crouch down when Lola and Jax do. Hugo does the same beside me. We creep forward and I wonder how close we actually are. Is the camp just beyond those trees? Are we already inside it?

I look around me. Everything looks the same—tall trees, hard ground covered in pine needles, rocks and caves, the whip of mountain wind through my hair. Then ahead of us I see the faint pulsing glow of fire.

I wait for Jax or Lola to give the signal to move forward, thinking about what the camp will be like, what it could possibly be like. The pack members seem so brutal, and I wonder if their way of living reflects that. Every time I try to picture the camp, though, I think of the circus—the only real shifter camp I've known. Nothing else seems to be able to break through that mental image. I've got nothing else to work with but the image of a rat in a cage and a boy with silver in his skin. So, it can't be like the circus, can it? We had our flaws, some pretty big ones, but this pack isn't like us, not at all.

"Where did you see Rat?" Jax whispers. We're all pressed close together, low to the ground. Jax straightens a little, scanning the area ahead.

Lola's expression is a mixture of anger and worry. Her eyebrows are pressed down as she scowls at what I assume is the camp, biting down on her bottom lip. "Still in the cage, over that way." She points to our right. "We just need to grab it and go. We'll get him back to our own camp, and then we'll all move on straight away."

"You didn't tell the others that part," I say. "They won't be ready to move on."

"I'm kind of making this up as I go, Flo," she tells me. "There's only so much I can plan for, so just bear with me, okay?"

I frown and look away from her, trying to focus on what's through the trees. But I can't see anything.

"Let's move in," Jax says. "Slow and quiet."

Panic surges in my veins and my hair sticks to the back of my neck. It's not warm on the mountain, but I'm hot beneath Jett's shirt and coat.

We stop again, right on the outskirts of camp. I can see it now. I hardly dare to breathe as we edge forward. The space is clearly lived in, but not at all like the circus. Rocks and logs serve as seating. A campfire burns low in the center. Hammocks sway gently between tree trunks. It looks abandoned, but I know its occupants could return any moment. And I don't want to be here when they do.

Small bunks made from wood are dotted around in no apparent order, most under the shelter of branches or tucked into grooves in the mountain. My breath catches in my throat when I think I see a pile of bones beneath one of the hammocks. I shudder and look away.

There are ropes in the trees and some kind of podium on the ground, which is where Gretchen and Tomas are sitting to keep guard. The space is not looked after. It's not homey, it's not cared for.

My eyes drift up to Gretchen and Tomas, where they sit on the edge of the raised platform, their legs dangling from the side. Gretchen sways hers absently without a care, but Tomas sits more stiffly, like he can't relax.

Gretchen—the beaver—has dark short hair that is straight and shaped around her face. Her lips are tinted purple, and I wonder what she used to do that. Berries, maybe.

Tomas—the mouse—has an angry red mark on his face. It winks in the moonlight, and I realize silver has been embedded in his cheek. His hair is completely shaved, so I can see his scalp shining white against the night. There are dark shadows beneath his eyes, making his whole face appear sunken.

"Okay," Lola whispers. "Follow me—don't say anything. I can handle Gretchen."

I take a breath, but my chest feels tight, and I follow Lola out into the open. Both Gretchen and Tomas get to their feet as soon as we step out from the cover of shadow. Tomas is a little slower to react than Gretchen is, but he follows her lead and is the first to speak. "Who's there?" The words squeak out of him, showing us his lack of confidence and his fear.

Gretchen elbows Tomas in his side, shutting him up. "Stop!" she demands of us. She speaks clearly and assertively. I start to worry about her—surely the pack wouldn't leave the camp in the hands of someone not able to defend it. Tomas doesn't concern me, but Gretchen is taller and meaner than I imagined she would be when I first learned her shape. I think again of the bite mark on Hugo's arm and take a step closer to him.

"It's us," Lola replies, keeping her voice calm and steady. "Lola, Hugo, and Jax." She leaves me out, and I'm glad—I don't want Gretchen's attention drawn to me. The newcomer. The stranger. The horse pretending to be a bear.

"Lola?" Gretchen gasps, momentarily letting her guard down. But it doesn't last, as her next words are laced with suspicion. "You came back?"

"I'm not sure," Lola says. "We're thinking about it."

Jax separates himself from us, edging his way toward what looks like a pile of stock. It's all haphazardly stacked up—boxes, barrels, bags, blankets. I hear faint squeaking coming from that direction, too: the cage. Can Rat sense us? Can he sense his friends?

"Jax," Gretchen snaps. He stops moving toward the cage. His stance is suddenly casual, but I can see the worry in his eyes. His gaze darts from Gretchen to Lola. "And Hugo," Gretchen continues. Hugo visibly stiffens beside me, and Gretchen's mouth spreads into a wicked grin as she says Hugo's name. "How's the arm?"

Jax quietly releases a sigh and continues moving slowly toward the cage now that Gretchen's attention has moved away from him.

Hugo clears his throat. Our shoulders almost touch, and Lola stands close to his other side. "Just fine," he replies.

Gretchen tips her head back and laughs—high-pitched with dark delight. "Don't you think I know why you're here?" she says, wiping at the corner of her eye. Tomas stays silent, a step behind Gretchen, still and straight-faced. "You can stop edging toward the cage now, Jax. I know you want Rat."

"Then let us take him," Lola says quickly. "We'll just get him and go. No one else is here."

Gretchen tilts her head. "Aren't they?"

5

THE LAUGHING SISTERS

A stretch of silence passes between us and a shiver runs through me as Gretchen's words hang in the air.

Aren't they?

So, someone else is here. They must be. I look at Lola—could she have missed others in camp if they were sheltered beneath trees or inside one of the small caves? I look around us, searching for movement.

Gretchen jumps down from the podium. Her feet land on the ground with a thud. A branch snaps beneath her boot. Tomas stays put. "There's no way I'm letting you take him," Gretchen says, sauntering toward us with a smile fixed in place.

"You can't stop us," Lola says sternly, taking a step forward. She doesn't shy away from Gretchen like the rest of us. I want to leave, get away from this girl with the purple-tinted lips and malice in her eyes.

Gretchen's smile widens, her face threatening to crack with bewildering amusement. *She's enjoying this.* Which means we should probably be concerned. I look up at Hugo, but he keeps his expression neutral. Just like Lola, and just like Jax. I wonder what my face is telling Gretchen about how I feel, and I focus on straightening my expression to match the others.

"It's not me you need to worry about," Gretchen says. The joy in her voice makes my blood run cold, but I work on not *showing* it. I keep my shoulders back, my head high, my gaze fixed forward, my eyes on her. But my breath catches in my throat, and it all falls away when laughter fills the air—a startling and childish sound.

"Hyenas," Lola hisses through gritted teeth, stepping back to rejoin Hugo and me.

Humming to herself, Gretchen turns her back and climbs up to the podium again. She turns to face us, then sits, crossing her legs like she's settling in for a show. The children used to sit in the circus tent like that, in front of the first row, as close to the ring as they could get. Faces painted, balloons in hand, eyes wide with wonder.

Jax makes a sudden dash for Rat's cage. His hand wraps around the handle just as the hyenas come into sight. Hugo moves closer to me, his arm brushing mine. "*This* is the worst of it," he mutters under his breath. I swallow hard and watch the hyena girls approach.

I stay completely still as the three of them circle us in their human forms, laughing and snapping their teeth. I can't hold it when one comes near, flinching each time teeth nip at the side of my face or long fingernails scrape through the ends of my hair.

What does Hugo mean, "this is the worst of it"? What will the three of them do to us?

Our group stays rooted to our spots as the hyena girls push closer, push in. My heart beats painfully—pounding, pounding, pounding—as they stamp their feet to the same rhythm and tilt their heads to the sky. They laugh and snap and taunt us until I feel like I can't take it anymore. Only Lola speaks. Only Lola tries to stop them. But her efforts are wasted.

I feel numb but for the beating inside my chest. What do we do? Where do we go? The world spins a little around me as I await Lola's next instructions, my limbs tense and ready to run.

My legs want to move, but I keep myself put. Hugo, Lola, and Jax know these girls. They'll know what to do. My running could mean my death. At the very least, it could start something and put the others in danger too. So, I hold on and watch Lola, copy what she does. She seems oddly calm, watching the hyenas out of the corner of her eye, standing straight and still. I mimic her posture and focus on holding it.

Jax is still over by the stockpile, holding Rat's cage in his hand. Could he run? Could he go get help? He moves the cage so it's out of sight, but I think Gretchen and the hyena girls all know he's got it.

Hugo's fingers find mine and he grasps my hand reassuringly. His touch says, *We're together. Don't worry.*

"Good to see you, Lola," one of the hyena girls says in a singsong voice. It's the first time any of them have made a sound more than snapping, growling, and laughing. Her voice is terrible—raspy and rhythmic like a creepy lullaby. It raises the hair on my arms.

All three of the hyenas stop moving to stand before Lola, and I get to study them properly instead of in flashes as they circled us. All three have stained lips like Gretchen but, in a moment of terror, I can't decide if it's berry juice or blood—I wonder if the bones beneath the hammock belong to one, or all, of the hyenas.

The three of them momentarily focus their attention on Lola, leaving the rest of us unobserved. Jax takes the opportunity to move closer to us.

"Who are they?" I whisper, my voice shaky. I study their long, dusty-blond hair. It looks like it has never been cut, reaching down to their hips, straight but tangled. Each girl wears it differently—with braids and twists and flowers. They wear brown tunics with a tie at the front holding the material together and slouchy boots. Their legs are bare and muddy.

Hugo doesn't look away from them to answer, which is probably why they hear him when he says, "They're known in the wild as the Laughing Sisters."

The title catches their attention. "*Don't* use that name for us, Hughie." The same girl who spoke before now moves away from Lola and over to Hugo and me. We're not far—a couple steps—but she takes her time reaching us, like it's all part of a game I don't know the rules to.

"We don't like it, do we girls?" she says over her shoulder. The other two whimper and shake their heads. Then the one who spoke, who I assume is the leader, looks at me and tilts her head to the side, coming to a stop right in front of me. "Lola!" she gasps, though her eyes don't leave me. "You've brought fresh meat with you!"

"Look," another says, pointing to Hugo and my joined hands. "Hughie's claimed her all for himself."

"Tut tut," the third girl says. Her sharp gaze darts from our hands to my face. "So selfish, Hughie. Share?"

"She's not meat," Lola says, her calmness cracking. I think I've stopped breathing. "She's a friend."

"A friend who's a . . .?" They sniff the air around me. "What are you, friend?"

I swallow hard. I'd *really* like to go now. I look at Lola and try to communicate this to her, but she doesn't look my way—her full focus on the hyenas. "I'm a bear," I say, trying to keep my voice steady. I'm not sure I do, but I don't have time to think on it as laughter bursts out of them once again.

Their laughter rises. "A bear. How dull."

"We're going now," Lola says suddenly, and relief floods me.

The hyenas stop their teasing. "So soon?"

Lola nods, her jaw clenched.

"Chase you?" the sisters suggest. Panic rises within me again, shadowing any relief I might have felt. I understand now that they mean to hunt us, and I wonder: what will they do if they catch us? I glance at the bones again.

"No, Viv," Lola says. "We're not here to play games."

I look back at the podium, noticing that Tomas and Gretchen are gone. *What happens now? What part of the game is this?* I wish I understood them, knew what they wanted from us, what will come after all this teasing and madness.

Viv—the leader—smiles, wide and menacing. "Then why are you here?" Lola opens her mouth to reply, but Viv cuts her off. "How about we let Eve guess?"

Eve claps her hands rapidly, excited. "I like a game," she says. "Let me think . . . Oh! I know! They're here to save Rat the rat. Rat the useless, double-crossing, sneaky, squeaky rat. Am I right?"

Viv smiles. "That was too easy." She strokes her sister's hair. "Much too easy. Zoe?"

"Too easy," Zoe agrees. "The game shouldn't end so soon."

Viv shakes her head. "No, it shouldn't."

"We're going now," Lola says again. She starts to back away this time.

Hugo tugs on my arm. Somehow my frozen limbs respond to my desire to move and I let Hugo guide me backward. I can't see Jax out of the corner of my eye, even though I know he's there—I can hear Rat squeaking—but I'm too nervous to turn and look at him, too aware of how fast one of the sisters could strike if I looked away for even a second.

Viv throws her head back and laughs. Zoe and Eve nip at her neck. She decides what happens here. "Go on, Lola. Run, run, run. We'll give the four—oh," she pauses, looking over at Jax and Rat. "I mean, *five*, of you a head start. Try not to drop that cage, Jaxon."

"Viv, I—" Jax begins, but Hugo grabs Lola with his free hand, his other still firmly in mine. He spins us around and we run. Jax is quick to follow with Rat's cage.

Laughter chases us into the trees. And so do the hyenas.

6

AS SILENT AS THE NIGHT

"Split up," Hugo suggests, releasing Lola's hand. "Divide their attention."

"That's a terrible idea!" I shout over the noise in my ears. As I run, the cool air stings my cheeks and my ears quickly start to ache with the cold and the force of the wind. "Aren't we going back to the others?"

My voice is loud with panic and Lola shushes me.

I lower my voice, but it's difficult while we're running—hard to hear, hard to speak. "We should warn them!"

"No!" Lola hisses. "They'll follow us back there."

"We can take them together," Jax says. "Lead them back. They'll think again when they're up against all of us."

"Only half of our group is strong enough to take them," Hugo argues. "And we don't know if Lucas and Kanna are back."

He's right. Ursula, Owen, Ruby, Itch, and Star have no experience fighting. Kanna and Lucas could still be out of camp, which leaves the four of us alongside Jett and

Lance against the three hyena sisters. It could work. We'd stand a really good chance of beating them, but there's too much that could go wrong, too many people who could get hurt or worse.

"No," Lola repeats at the same time as I say, "It's too big a risk."

Lola adds, "If one of them gets away, they could lead the rest of the pack back to us. We wouldn't be able to move quickly enough—they'd track us down." She pauses for breath. "We couldn't take on the full group."

"They might not be as large a group anymore," Jax points out.

"And are you willing to take that chance?" Lola retorts. "It's bad enough that they know we're here." She growls in frustration. "This isn't how I wanted things to go."

"I warned—" Jax begins.

Lola barks, "*Don't!*"

There's a crashing sound behind us, followed by maniacal laughter. "They've shifted," Hugo barks. "Go!"

"Find somewhere to hide. Head back to camp when it's safe," Lola says hurriedly. She and Jax split off, leaving Hugo dragging me through the darkness. I pull my hand away, knowing I can run faster with both arms free.

"What will they do if they catch us?" I pant. I ask the question even though I think I already know the answer.

Hugo doesn't reply, and I realize I'm not sure I actually want him to. His silence, and my imagination after seeing the three sisters, combines to paint a picture in my mind of blood and teeth and bones under a hammock.

They're not going to catch us. They're not going to—

Another high-pitched noise comes from close behind us.

Hugo slows and points to a small cave, an open mouth in the dark landscape. "In there?" he whisper-shouts. I nod and start to run toward it, but then hesitate. I'm not sure I want to be on the ground. The hyenas could have us cornered if they worked out where we were hiding. We'd be trapped between the bloodthirsty sisters and a dead end. *No.* We can't go inside. It's too dangerous.

I skid to a stop. "No," I say, thinking quickly as the noises get louder, closer. I look around, not even sure which way we've been running—up or down, toward our camp or away from it?

I look up. *The trees.*

"Up there," I say, pointing at a tall pine tree with sturdy-looking branches. They start low enough on the trunk for me to reach with a boost. "Help me," I say, and Hugo hurries to cup his hands beneath me, making a step.

Taller, Hugo manages to reach the branch himself—just. We're lucky to both get up here in good time. The mountain has gone quiet around us, and I'm silent with it for a moment. Then I start to climb.

The tree is thick and tall with tough branches, though they get thinner and weaker the higher I climb. The bark is rough against my hands, scratching the skin, plucking at the fabric of my clothes. There's only so far I can go before I have to stop. I shuffle close to the trunk, hidden by the needlelike leaves.

Straddling the branch I stopped on, I test if it can hold my weight. Then I hug the tree trunk, leaning my forehead against the cool bark. My breathing comes fast and I close my eyes in an attempt to slow it, to calm myself. The cool air and scent from the tree help settle my nerves.

Hugo stops on the branch just below mine. He sighs and holds the tree trunk like I do, his legs dangling down beneath him.

"Are they—?" I begin.

"Shh!" Hugo whispers.

A moment passes in a heartbeat, and the sound of scuffling starts up from below, followed by soft giggles. They must sense we're close by as they creep between the trees.

I see Viv first, back in her human form. Her pale skin is visible in the moonlight, smears of dirt and little scratches covering her arms, legs, and torso. Her messy hair is free from its braid and falls down her back in waves. "We know you're out here," she sings. "Come out, come out, little bear."

Me.

"We don't bite."

Zoe and Eve come into view then. They hold their hands to their mouths, biting back laughter in response to Viv's comment.

"She's very good at this game," Zoe says, right beneath the tree. I hold my breath even though it hurts. *Please don't find us.*

"She's very quick for a cuddly bear," Eve adds. "Very, very quick."

Viv holds up a hand, shushing her sisters. I look down at Hugo, wide-eyed. I want to know what he's thinking but he doesn't look up. My palms sweat and my grip on the tree doesn't feel as steady as it did. My legs shake, and I imagine the branch snapping and sending me down to the ground, landing right in the middle of them.

Taking a shaky breath, I press myself closer to the tree trunk, careful not to move too much in case I make a sound. Do they know we're here? Are they messing with us even now? I close my eyes—I can hardly stand it any longer.

Viv gasps suddenly, and with my eyes closed, I'm sure she's spotted us. She says, "Mommy's home," after a stretch of silence and my eyes fly open in time to see her shift and cry out. Eve and Zoe follow her lead, and the three of them turn and run back toward their camp. I let out a long breath and peel my hand from the tree trunk to wipe away the sweat on my forehead.

Hugo breathes a sigh of relief. "That was really close."

I can't speak yet, so I wait until Hugo starts to climb down. Then I focus on climbing out of the tree after him.

It's a slow descent with my muscles still locked up in fear. Hugo catches me at the bottom and I hug him. I'm relieved that the hyenas are gone, that my feet are back on the ground, that we can move again and go back to camp, to our friends, to where I feel safest.

Hugo gets his bearings and I stand back, leaning against the tree we just climbed out of. I turn my head so my cheek is resting against the trunk. The cold roughness feels good against my warm skin.

"This way," Hugo says. We walk back slowly until he's certain the direction we're going in is the right one.

Everything looks the same to me, from tree to tree, one rock to the next.

"Who's Mommy?" I ask as we walk in single file, Hugo in front.

"I don't know." Hugo shakes his head, bewildered. "The new leader of the pack, maybe? The bears are gone, and I don't know who took over after that."

"I guess it doesn't matter," I say. "We've got Rat now and we can leave. We never have to see them again."

We both fall as silent as the night. I tilt my head up to the sky, counting stars and waiting for morning to come.

1
FREE FROM THE CIRCUS

The camp is just how we left it.

The people are just how we left them.

Lola and Jax have beat Hugo and me back and are already sitting in the clearing with Rat's cage. Their faces are scratched, but otherwise they look like they're okay. The others are packed up and ready to go, waiting for the two of us to return.

Relief washes over me as I take it all in. We're fine. Everyone's fine.

Jett is first to reach me. He brushes my hair away from my forehead, where it sticks to my skin with sweat. "Rough night?" he asks.

"The worst," I say. Hugo breaks away and joins the others.

Jett gathers me into a hug. "I was so worried about you," he says against my hair. "I haven't taken my eyes off the trees, waiting for you to get back."

"I'm here," I say, hugging him tighter. The other way around and I'd have been going out of my mind. Especially if Lola and Jax returned and told them what'd happened.

Who's to say we'd have ever returned this morning? "I was worried about you, too," I tell him.

We break apart and I wave to Lola. Kanna is sitting beside her sister. Jax approaches Jett and me. "We haven't been back long," he says. "Coming to let him out? We were waiting for you."

Jett nods. "We knew you'd come back," he says with a kiss to my temple. I take his hand and we join the others gathering around Rat's cage. We sit in a haphazard circle, ready to release him.

From my place between Ursula and Jett, I turn to speak to her as everyone gets settled. "I'm sorry about before," I tell her.

She smiles tightly. "All forgotten," she says.

"How are you feeling now?"

She shrugs in response and I frown, but decide not to push her. Conversation has never been hard with Ursula, not like this. I'm not sure what to do.

Lola calls attention, with Rat's cage resting on her lap now. "So," she starts. "We got him. We did run into *some* trouble—"

"We almost got eaten by a pack of hyenas," Jax confirms.

"Yes. Thanks, Jax—they know," Lola says. Hugo nudges Jax to shush him and a small smile tugs at my lips. Our victory feels good. Still, the sooner we speak to Rat and move on the better—I don't feel safe staying put too long in case the hyenas were to follow our scent back here.

"Anyway," Lola continues. "We're all packed up and should move on as soon as we have Rat back. I don't want to leave him in this cage a second longer, and he can tell us which direction to go in." She smiles brightly, like she wants to say, *Finally! Something is going right for us!*

My own smile widens—this is it. What we've been waiting for.

Then Ursula stands up beside me and my smile falls away. I get this instant feeling, a deep ache in my chest, and I just know that something is wrong. The way she's been acting, it must have been building to this, whatever she's about to say. I look up at her, tears already filling my eyes. *What is it? What's wrong?*

"Before we start," she begins. I sit up and reach for her hand, hoping she will take it. *Let me in. Please.* She does, but she doesn't look at me.

"Ruby, Star, Itch, Owen, and I have been talking about . . . things," she continues. My grip on her hand tightens. "From around the time we joined you all after the fight at the cabin, we've been discussing what's next for us. I know we weren't a part of the fight itself, but we saw what it did to you and what you did to them."

"Ursula?" I breathe. I look over at Star and Ruby, at Owen and Itch, one by one. They won't meet my eyes. They aren't looking at anyone but Ursula.

"Since then there's been this divide between us. The five of us have felt it. You all went through that together, while we were back at the warehouse."

I shake my head. "That's not true. Whatever role we had that night, we're still all part of the same pack." I swipe at a tear with my free hand. "What's going on?"

"We're leaving, Flo," Ursula says, almost in a whisper. She raises her voice so everyone else can hear her. "We're leaving. You've got us this far, and we're so grateful for that, really. But the five of us—we're not fighters! We're not in this like the rest of you are. And we don't want to join a big pack where everyone's new and we don't know who to trust or what's going to happen from one day to the next."

"Ursula—"

"No, Flo," she says, cutting me off. "I'm sorry, but whatever it is, no. There's nothing anyone can say to change our minds. We've thought hard about this, considered all our options, and we've made this decision together. I wouldn't be sharing it otherwise."

Her palm still sits in mine, and I hold tight as I stand. Ursula turns to me and I still don't let go. I can't. This might be the last time I stand beside her like this. She puts a hand on my shoulder. "But where will you go?" I ask.

Ursula closes her eyes. She takes her hand from my shoulder to wipe away tears. I fight against my own. "After what happened at the circus, and seeing what happened to Logan, Pru, Tia, Dee, and Ebony, I realized that this—" she gestures to the whole group with her free hand "—isn't as safe as I thought it was. And I don't want to see my brother's life end that way. I don't want to see anyone else suffer. I don't want to lose any more friends. You've adapted well to this life, you all have, but I haven't— *we* haven't—and we don't want to do it anymore."

I search Ursula's face, hoping to catch a hint of doubt there. Hoping, despite what she said, that I can convince them to stay. That promising we can defeat anything that's thrown at us might change her mind.

But I don't know if we can defeat everything that comes our way. I don't know what this next stage holds for us. She's serious—she's leaving. All five of them are leaving, and I'm bursting to say *No!* and to fight against their decisions, but I know I shouldn't, couldn't, because it's *their* decision, and there's no room for promises I don't know I can keep. Ursula is almost eighteen, and I know she can lead them—she got them away from the circus and took them to Iris's when it burned down. They found the warehouse and Ursula hid and protected Star and the others when the hunters attacked it.

As much as I'll miss them, their lives aren't mine to risk, aren't mine to decide what to do with. Free from the circus, this isn't a decision any of us have faced before now. I want to find the new pack—that's my choice. I want to be part of that. If they don't, then all I can do is support that. Maybe they will be safest in a small, quiet group. They're smart—they've proved it. They'll be okay—I have to believe that they will.

Everyone's standing now, moving in to say good-bye. "You're going right away?" I say to Ursula.

She nods. "Yes, I think that's best. We want to get a good start and make the most of the day before stopping at nightfall."

"Why didn't you say something sooner?" Lucas asks, and I only now notice that he, Lance, and Jett are standing behind me. They're all I'll have left of the circus.

Ursula gives a small shrug. "We weren't sure until now. I mean, we almost were, but I didn't want to rush off until we were certain. It's not a decision we've made lightly. You've helped us get this far, but I can't lose Owen the way we've lost others."

"I know," I say. "I get it, I do. It won't stop me from missing you, though."

She smiles and rests her forehead on mine. "I'll miss you, too, Flo."

We hug until someone tugs on my sleeve, and I break away from Ursula to see Star standing beside us, tears spilling down her cheeks. I pull her to me, holding her close. Jett steps forward to join the hug, and Star wraps an arm around him, too.

Ursula, Owen, Ruby, and Itch continue to move around the group, hugging and saying good-bye to each of us. I pass Star to the brothers and they make her laugh so much that she stops crying. I'll have to watch them leave soon. Let them all go. And I know I can't go with them, because that's not the path I've chosen. I don't like the way things are right now, either—the fire at the circus, the fight at the cabin, the hyena chase—but I believe the pack we're seeking is right for me—a place I might be able to call home.

I'm done running.

THE TESTING

The speaker crackled.

"Stand back from the door."

Ro did as the voice commanded, backing up until she could feel the cool surface pressing against her skin through her thin jumpsuit. She shivered.

The silver on her wrist had been left there for days now. She was beginning to think they would never take it off.

She hadn't been out of her cell yet, so she hadn't been able to see the other shifters and how they looked. Did they all have silver on their wrists? Did they all do as they were instructed? Was it easier that way?

She wanted to talk to someone.

Her meals had been brought to the little hatch in the door, twice a day. The food was bland, the water not enough. Her stomach grumbled through the night.

The door opened.

Two hunters stepped inside and beckoned her forward. One walked in front, the other behind, as they escorted her down the corridor. She passed door after door, wondering who or what was on the other side of each.

They walked down to the floor below, winding through corridors with more doors. The last door opened, and she peered in to find the doctor's office. The place she'd been brought to first by Ethan.

She swallowed. Tears warmed her eyes, but she worked on holding them back. It was easier to concentrate on that than on whatever was about to happen.

This must be the testing.

"Take a seat," the doctor instructed.

When Rowena didn't move right away, one of the hunters nudged her toward the chair equipped with the arm restraints.

She sat.

The hunters strapped her down and took the silver cuff off her arm. She sighed with relief. The change was instantaneous; the burning stopped and her skin began to knit itself together. It itched a little, but she couldn't do anything about it.

Ro tipped her head back. Her eyes closed against the bright lights over her.

Something pricked her arm.

She jolted upright, bucking in her chair. "*Hold her,*" the doctor commanded.

The hunters pressed down on her shoulders and wrists. She shouted for them to let go. She fought, but not enough, as the doctor continued her work.

Soon, whatever the doctor dosed her with took effect. She felt woozy. The room swayed. The doctor appeared out of focus. Ro stopped fighting.

She swam in and out of consciousness as the machines beeped beside her.

8
THE RAT RUNS

We move on immediately after we say good-bye to our friends.

As much as Lola doesn't want to leave Rat inside the cage any longer, she's waiting to open it now. No one really feels like celebrating our small victory, because we've lost something. Again. The momentary excitement that things were going right for us after we rescued Rat was crushed when Ursula announced she'd be leaving us. So, I'm glad to move on from here now. I don't want to risk anything else going wrong—like the hyenas returning with the rest of their pack.

We head off in search of a new site to settle where we can release Rat, while Ursula, Owen, Star, Ruby, and Itch head back down to the village. And after that—I don't know. I can't stop thinking about it—which direction they'll travel in, where they'll end up, what they'll meet on the way.

Star walks backward, waving as she goes. Little Star. I wave until I can't see them anymore. Then I kind of feel like I can't breathe. Because they're gone now. That's it. I have to force myself to stay in place and not go running after them.

I turn around, face my own path, and suck air into my lungs.

The rest of us travel farther up, deeper into the mountain. The path we're following becomes steeper before cutting off altogether. And still we go higher. My ears start to feel a little funny, the wind and cold numbing them.

When we stop, it's outside the mouth of a cave, high up in the mountain.

I rub my arms and tuck my chin down into the construction company coat I took back from Jett before we set off. He's carrying our backpack, even though I think it's my turn. I've lost track, and he doesn't seem to mind. The fleece lining is soft against my skin and I breathe through my nose, deep calming breaths. Thin clouds of air form in front of my face, disappearing as quickly as they appear. There one moment, gone the next. It makes me think of Ursula and the others. Already, I can't stop wondering where they are, how far they've traveled. They could be in or just outside of the village below us and it wouldn't make any difference because the distance between us is huge now.

Jett rests his palm against my lower back. "Thinking about Star?" he says.

I exhale. "All of them."

"Me, too," he replies. "They're smart, Flo. They've been through as much as we have—they know what they're doing."

I shake my head, unsure. "They weren't in the woods. They don't know how to fight."

"But they know how to hide," Jett counters. "They know how to stay out of sight."

"They didn't stay with Iris, visit Greg at the doctor's office. They weren't captured and held in the cabin. They didn't see the cells, spend time with hunters. They weren't there at the end. I'm worried, Jett—I can't help it."

"I'm worried, too," he admits. "But they still experienced everything through what we shared with them. They still ran from the circus, and they did well on their own. Remember that."

I turn to look at him. "What if it's not enough?" I whisper.

Jett puts his hands on my shoulders, his touch gentle. He leans forward so his eyes are level with mine. "You'll drive yourself crazy with the 'what ifs,' Flo."

I fold my arms. "I care, that's all."

He offers a small smile. "I know you do. It's one of the best things about you, the way you care for others, the way your nose crinkles a little right here—" he taps the bridge of my nose "—when you're worried about someone. But we have to look forward, not backward. I remember how guilty you felt after the circus. I don't want to see you put yourself through that again. We all let them go. We had to respect their decision."

I nod. "I know." He hugs me then, warm and familiar. I close my eyes and push the sadness out and away.

Jett kisses the top of my head. "They'll be okay. We will, too."

I nod again. Even though I don't know if they will be. I don't know if *we* will be. But we'll go on anyway, because that's what we do.

I pull back from Jett. "You always know what to say," I tell him.

He smiles.

"It's infuriating," I add with a little shove and he laughs, clinging to me and pulling me to him. "Know-it-all," I mumble, and he laughs more.

"Cave's clear," Kanna says as she comes out of the entrance with Lucas.

I turn away and walk to the edge of the pathway opposite. Trees mostly shield the view of the little village below. I can see the taller buildings, like the church steeples, but not the store or the inn or the people.

Behind me, Lola, Jax, and Hugo spread their blankets out on the floor of the cave. I watch over my shoulder as Kanna, Lucas, and Lance join them. There's not much space left, so I help Jett shrug off our pack and take my own blanket, unraveling it beside the others for Jett and me to sit on. Then there's nothing left to do but open the cage.

"Everyone ready?" Lola asks.

"*Yes!*" Kanna says impatiently. "He's been stuck in there way too long."

Jax nods, his eyes resting on the cage. "Open it," he says.

Lola flicks the latch and the small barred door falls open, hitting the blanket with a soft thud. We wait in silence. I'm too nervous to move at all. I'm not sure I even breathe as the little rat emerges. He sticks his nose out and looks at us. Rat edges farther out of the cage—gray fur and a long pink tail.

Then the rat runs.

Kanna squeals and lifts her legs. Hugo lunges and misses, Rat narrowly escaping his cupped hands. Rat runs right toward me. Jett and I move together at the last moment, forming a solid barrier in Rat's escape route with our legs. I quickly snatch him off the ground and crawl forward with one hand to put him back in the cage. He wriggles in my grasp as I gently guide my hand through the small barred door. Lola slams the door shut again as soon as my hand clears it.

"What's going on?" I say, sitting back.

Lola sighs, her hands still on the cage. "This is bad." She puts her hand on her forehead. "He's been in the cage for . . . weeks. Maybe a little over a month. I think he's forgotten."

Kanna nods. "All that time he was stuck in the cage, unable to shift back to human. And now it looks like he can't remember how to."

I swallow, disappointment settling in. Our whole plan is falling down around us. The next step relied on Rat telling us where to go. "He's stuck like that?" I say. No one can be this unlucky. Can't this one thing—this *one thing*—just go right for us?

"For now, at least," Lola confirms.

Hope sparks inside me. "We can get him back?"

She bites her lip. "Maybe. We can talk to him, remind him who he is."

"And that'll work?" Jett says.

Lola puts her hand on the cage again. Rat sniffs her palm through the bars. "It could. I mean . . . I think so. Eventually."

Kanna stands, pulling Lucas up with her. "We're going to find firewood," she announces. Lola starts to shake her head, and Kanna quickly adds, "It's too cold not to."

"But if someone sees . . ."

Kanna shrugs. "If someone comes, they'll wish they hadn't."

Lola tilts her head. "Kanna," she sighs. "We're not invincible. We just lost five of our group. Another five in the woods around the cabin."

Kanna puts a hand on her hip. "It's either face what may or may not come, or freeze to death. Your choice."

Lola looks to the rest of us. "Are we okay to assign watch duty, then?" she asks. I nod along with the others. Lola sighs again. "*Fine.* But don't go far. And I'll need you to talk to Rat, too, Kanna. Hugo, Jax, you, and me—we knew him and we need to tell him who he is, what he likes, what he looked like. We'll take turns."

"All right," Kanna says to Lola, her hand locked with Lucas's. "You go first."

9

JOIN THEIR GAME

Days pass, one bleeding into the next—orange, light, pink, dark.

The days are long and the nights are longer. We sit in the glow of the campfire, blackness stretching toward us. The sky is inky blue, clear enough to see the stars.

We keep the fire going.

We keep the watch going.

Rat still hasn't done anything. There was a moment, late yesterday, when it seemed like his shape was a little fuzzy—like he was shifting. But then it stopped. I wondered if I'd imagined it, but Jax said he saw it, too. Rat is still inside the cage, but someone stays with him all the time—talking to him or simply keeping an eye on him in case there's any change at all.

"I think he's remembering," Lola says now, breaking a long stretch of silence. We tend to fall quiet when it grows dark. We listen to the chorus of insects, the howl of wolves in the distance, the shushing sound of the wind whispering through the trees. The crackle of the logs on our fire. It's calm on the mountain.

"How do you know?" Jax asks. He's lying on his back, closest to the fire, his backpack cushioning his head. Our food is getting low, our water lower, and everyone's energy is dipping. Lack of supplies is just another problem we're going to have to face—and soon. We didn't plan for this—for Rat not to remember. I thought we'd be with the new pack by now. I think we all did.

Most of us sit slumped around the fire now, backs resting on our packs or against overturned tree trunks or rocks. Those who aren't here are on watch. Lola sits with Rat cupped in her palms. He hasn't tried to run today.

Jax moves to sit by Lola. Kanna is sleeping on Lola's other side and doesn't stir. Hugo is listening, but he stays just inside the cave with his back to the wall. The firelight only just reaches him there. Lance and Lucas are on watch, and Jett is out there keeping them company—even though his own watch with me is up next.

"He's looking at me like he's listening," Lola says.

I shuffle closer and watch Rat. He does look like he's paying attention . . . kind of. He watches Lola, his nose twitching, though I could just be imagining it in my desperation for him to change and remember his human side. We all could—we've been watching him for days, waiting for a sign.

Lola and Jax start talking to Rat, trying to coax him out of his shape. "Do you remember me?" Lola says, like I've heard her say to him so many times. "I'm Lola—your friend. I'm a parrot, but at the moment I'm human. Do you remember what that's like? To be human?"

I tune out and jab the fire, adding a few more pieces of wood. I move closer to it, thinking about later when I'm on watch with Jett and nowhere near the camp's warmth. It's boring out there, too. Being on lookout allows my mind to wander—to the elders and where they are now, to the hunters who've surely discovered what happened at the cabin, to my friends and if they're safe.

Night drew in quickly, early. And the mountain woke up when it did. The flames dance in the night and I huddle closer still.

Jett returns to camp and sits beside me. Our thighs touch and I lean my head on his shoulder. "Hi," I whisper.

He puts his arm around me and kisses my hair. I breathe in his scent, but it has changed. While we were part of the circus, he smelled like lemon and mint, or sometimes the buttery scent of popcorn or the smoke from the campfire would stick to his clothes. Now that's all gone. He smells like his surroundings again, but this time that means pine and freshly turned earth. Like he belongs out here with the mountain air in his lungs and a landscape of scent on his skin.

Jett's fingertips trace circles on my back and I close my eyes. "What are you thinking about?" he asks. It's a question he asks often, but also one he almost always knows the answer to already. I suppose he can tell when there's something on my mind and usually also what's caused it.

"Everything," I say. "Mostly about the new pack, though, and what we might find when we get there. Also about the old pack, and what's left of it. And about the hyenas. I keep remembering they're still out there. I told you that it was the Laughing Sisters, didn't I?"

"Jax did," Jett says.

"Oh," I say. "Have you heard of them?"

"Yes," he says. "In stories. The sisters are only roughly ten years older than we are, but dark tales reach far."

"I hadn't known they existed before now," I confess. "Will you tell me their story?"

Jett smiles softly. "It'll only give you nightmares."

I smile back. "We've done this before."

"Your first show night," he says.

I nod. "You told me the story of 'Lydia the Wolf' that night. Then my first show was next and everything was fine until the hunters showed up." I press my hand to my stomach.

"Don't think about that bit," Jett says. His arm moves around my waist and he rests his palm on top of mine. My burn is completely healed, a scar left in its place, but there's a sensation there—a deep memory of how it felt and what it caused.

"Distract me," I say. "The story."

"It's more a rhyme," he tells me. "The triplets and I used to scare each other with it as children, but Nora made us stop if she ever heard us."

"I don't remember that," I say. "Or I never heard you."

"Nora made us stop," Jett repeats. "She said it was childish and that we'd scare the others and each other."

"You were a child," I say.

Jett gives a short laugh. "Exactly. But it did make Oscar cry once, gave him bad dreams. He lost sleep, his chores slipped, his schooling suffered, and he told Nora. So after that she banned the song from camp."

"We're not in Nora's camp now," I say. "Tell me. I promise not to cry."

Jett smiles again. "Don't say I didn't warn you," he says. "It goes like this . . .

Three sisters, born on the same day,
Hyena cubs destined to find their own way.
The world was cruel, their mother died,
The three sisters barely survived.
Their anger was deep, as was their sadness,
And the three sisters slowly slipped into madness.
From that time, for years to come,
The three hyenas became known as one.
The Laughing Sisters—stay away,
Or join their game and become their prey."

I tilt my head up and close my eyes, soaking in the steady baritone of Jett's voice and remembering the three hyena girls.

I think about their tatty tunics, tied at the waist. Their bare legs—scratched and muddy. The way they snapped their teeth with a playful edge, a hint of something sinister beneath their singsong voices. The laughter that followed us through the trees when we ran.

A shiver runs through me as I imagine Jett and the triplets singing this rhyme, none of them really knowing what kind of creatures they were whispering about.

"It's creepy," I admit, imagining a younger Jett with the brothers, scaring one another with the sisters' rhyme. I stretch my arms. "We should go swap with Lucas and Lance. They've been on watch for hours."

Jett kisses my cheek, my jaw. He stays close and says,

"Stay by the fire a little longer. I'll go tell them." His breath stirs my hair and I shut my eyes again. He moves away and I shuffle closer to the fire, missing his warmth. I hand Jett his blanket, and he wraps it around himself before heading off to our lookout point to trade places with the brothers.

I watch the flames, enjoy the last few moments of light and heat before I join Jett. I'm thinking about the Laughing Sisters when Lola suddenly shrieks, "Ahh!"

She startles me, and I almost miss the moment Rat transforms back to human. I push up onto my knees and watch his tiny pink paws grow and shape into hands, his gray fur change to tanned skin. The white tuft in his fur adjusts to messy brown hair with a white streak in the front.

Kanna startles awake as Lola gets to her feet, Jax beside her, a big smile on their faces. Rat stumbles, and Lola and Jax hurry to grab an arm each, steadying him. I stand, too, but stay where I am, across the fire from them.

"Rat?" Lola says. "Are you . . . *you*?"

Rat looks at her. The silence between them seems to stretch on forever. Lola and Jax step back as Rat finds his balance.

Rat rushes forward then, gathering Lola into a hug.

He kisses her cheek enthusiastically and she laughs. "Thank you, thank you!" he says, releasing her and moving to hug Jax.

Once Rat has greeted Kanna and Hugo as well—his four ex-pack members—Hugo hands him some clothes. Rat pulls the worn black pants on first, then a polo shirt with the Bay Construction Company logo on the chest, a coat like mine, and brown work boots. When he's done, he turns around and his gaze lands on me first.

"Flo?" Rat says. I nod nervously and he hurries over, taking my hands in his. His grip is firm and his hands are warm against my cold ones. "I heard them say your name while I was . . . in the cage. They told me about you. A horse! I've never met a horse. Thank you for helping rescue me, Flo." He looks down at our joined hands. "The hyenas didn't hurt you, did they? They didn't bite you?"

"No, why?" I say quietly. "Will I turn into one?"

Rat throws his head back and laughs. "I'm pretty sure that's only werewolves. And they don't exist," he tells me.

My cheeks warm and I look over Rat's shoulder to see the others watching us.

"Where's Jett?" Rat asks.

I pull my hand from Rat's and gesture behind me with my thumb. "That way," I say. "He's on watch."

"And the twins?" Rat says. His words come out fast, excited. He's finding his voice again, taking in his new-found freedom.

"Brothers," I correct him.

A crease forms between Rat's brows as he lowers them in confusion. "They aren't twins?"

I lower my voice. "They were triplets," I say. "They recently lost their brother, so we call them 'the brothers.' Or 'Lucas and Lance.'"

Rat lets go of my other hand and places his on his chest. "Gotcha," he says.

He hurries off to meet them before I can say anything in response.

"He can't keep still," Kanna says.

Lola backs up, her smile bright. "Now let's hope he remembers where to go."

"We should have asked him right away," Jax says, sitting back down by the fire.

"Give him a minute," Lola replies teasingly. "We'll ask him when he's finished meeting everyone."

Hugo sits down beside Jax and nudges him. I linger by the fire, not sure whether to sit down again or go join Jett on watch.

I decide to wait until Rat comes back with the brothers, rather than interrupting. "He's friendly," I say.

Hugo smiles. "He is. I feel good about this."

"Me too," I say. We're almost there.

Rat returns with Jett, Lucas, and Lance. The four of them join us around the fire. "We shouldn't leave the lookout for too long," Jett says, leaning against a rock rather than sitting down. I go stand beside him since it's my turn out there as well as his.

Lola agrees. "We won't," she says. She shares some food with Rat, who eats it quickly. "There's not much more," Lola tells him. "We're running out of supplies. We were . . . we were hoping you'd know where to find the pack you talked about. Remember? Before they put you in a cage, you were going to leave."

Rat nods, still chewing. Jax passes him his water bottle. Rat drinks all of it.

"Rat?" Lola prompts. The rest of us are silent, watching and waiting.

He wipes his mouth. "I remember," he says. "I was

out patrolling the mountain with two of the bears. They didn't want to be with me, so they split off to work a different part. I was annoyed at how they treated me so I went a bit farther than I'd been before and a pack of wolves stopped me and turned me around."

"Wolves!" I exclaim, thinking of Lydia's story. "But if they sent you away, then how did you find out about their pack?"

Rat wipes his palms on his pants. "They saw what the bears did to me and they followed me a little ways back. They must have made their mind up about me because one night when I was alone, making my way back down the mountain to rejoin the bears and the pack, they told me about their pack, about how large it was and that they take in strong new members and thought I'd fit in well there. I asked if I could bring some of my friends—" He glances at Lola and smiles "—and the wolf said yes as long as they proved themselves to meet the standards of the pack as I already had."

"How had you?" Lucas asks.

"Navigating the mountain alone. For days. Returning to a pack that treated me like shit. Remaining loyal. They were impressed."

"But you were disloyal to your pack when you said you'd join the wolves," Lucas points out.

Rat frowns. "Why wouldn't I join the wolves? I was loyal to that awful pack until I had to be. Presented with an alternative, of course I'm going to take it. They wouldn't expect me not to, surely."

Lucas raises his eyebrows but doesn't say anything else.

"Wait," Jett says. "So how would your friends prove themselves to the pack?"

Rat scratches his head. "I don't know. They didn't tell me everything. Just . . . enough. They've got to protect themselves, too."

"How do you know you can find them again?" Lola says. "After all this time."

"Easy enough," he says. "I know where I was, and I used to think about going back there all the time. That pack is somewhere in these mountains, and the wolves can take us there. They'll see us coming."

"How soon can we go?" I ask eagerly.

"We can head that way as soon as it's light," he says. "If that's all right with all of you?"

Lola swats him on the arm excitedly. "Yes!" she says. "We'll leave in the morning. Is it far?"

"Maybe a day," he says. "To the point where I found the wolves. Then I don't know after that. They came to our camp while I was in the cage. Tried to push us farther down the mountain. The pack pushed back, of course. Too stubborn to budge."

I go cold, thinking of the hyenas. Of Gretchen's berry-stained lips and Tomas's silver cheek. "So your old pack knows they're out there? What if they go looking as well?"

"They won't," Rat says confidently. "They don't like civilized living. They make their own rules. They'll stay put, I assure you."

"Who's left?" Hugo asks.

"Plenty," Rat says. "Hunters only took out about

eleven of us. Cassandra's in charge now. The freaky hyenas call her—"

"Mommy," I finish.

Rat smirks. "She's a red fox. I think it confuses them."

"How did the pack even tame the Laughing Sisters?" Jett asks.

Rat laughs now. "They're not tame! But they respect Cassandra, so she controls them."

I shudder, wondering what Cassandra must be like to have control over the Laughing Sisters.

Lola clears her throat. "So we aren't far?" she asks. "We'll find them tomorrow?"

"We'll find them tomorrow," Rat confirms.

10
DO NOT ENTER

We set off in the gray, early morning light.

The clouds are swollen with rain. I keep my water bottle in hand, hoping to fill it up when the storm starts. The others do the same.

We start off slow and don't pick up speed. Rat's in the lead and seems a little confused. "I know where I'm going," he tells us. "I just need to find my bearings."

"You've lived on this mountain for a long time," Lola says, concern lacing her words. "Do you really know where you're going?"

"Yes!" Rat insists. "I was a rat for a long time, too. Things are coming back but take time. I'll get us there."

"Is there a river or stream we could stop by?" I ask. "To fill our bottles and bathe."

Rat rubs at the stubble beneath his chin. "There is, but it's quite a way off track."

"So how much time would it add to our journey?"

"If it's off track at all, it adds too much time, don't you think?" Rat says. "The Laughing Sisters, Gretchen, and Tomas know we're on the mountain. They'll tell the rest of the pack. They could still come looking for us."

Rat looks to Lola and I do, too. She nods—he's right. My shoulders slump.

"Besides, it looks like it's going to rain," Rat adds. "Keep your bottle handy."

I wave it in front of me halfheartedly as we set off.

Rat and Lola lead the way with Jax, Hugo, and Kanna close behind. I trail along just behind them while Jett hangs back, talking to the brothers about a noise they heard while on watch.

"What was the noise?" I ask over my shoulder. "Us or something else?"

Lance shrugs. "It came from the other direction, so not from camp."

"Like a rustling sound," Lucas adds.

"An animal," I decide. "We're not familiar with the sounds the mountains make during the day or night. It must have just been an animal, don't you think?"

"Probably," Lucas agrees. "But not all animals are what they seem, are they?"

Jett frowns. "There's a lot we don't know about the mountains, Flo's right."

"It could have been anything," Lance adds. "Or anyone."

I swallow. "Well, we've left that behind now so I suppose it doesn't matter anymore."

"Unless it's following us," Lucas says. We remain silent and he sighs. "That was called a joke. It's probably nothing, like you said."

"Yeah," I say with a forced smile. "Probably." But it's rarely nothing when we're concerned.

As the sun rises higher in the sky, its rays peeking out from behind the heavy clouds, Rat tells us about the new pack we're expecting to find. They are deep in the mountains, set up in a place that is defendable and secret. "No one would just stumble across their base," Rat tells us. "Or at least it would be extremely unlikely."

I trip on the uneven path, falling into Kanna. "Careful!" she hisses, grabbing hold of Hugo's arm to steady herself.

"Sorry," I mumble as Rat continues relaying information.

"They patrol far and wide. They have many defense posts close to camp, and their shifters branch out to search the surrounding area. That way nothing that could be a threat gets anywhere near their main camp."

We go through a narrow pass. Steep rock on either side, reaching up. We pass a weatherworn once-red sign that reads CAUTION: DO NOT ENTER.

There's a jagged slice of gray sky above us. "Humans have died here," Rat says. "Shifters, too, I reckon."

"How do they die?" Jett asks.

"The rocks break away, see." He points to where a few chips of rock skitter down the side. "It's a long walk through."

I notice netting on the side of the mountain, patching it up, holding it in place so the rocks don't break, slide, and fall. That and the sign just shows how close to human civilization we still are, even if it doesn't feel like it.

Another caution sign ahead warns us to turn back, tells us this is not a safe passage. Rat taps it as he walks past. I glance at Jett, his worried expression mirroring how

I'm feeling. We're not immune from danger just because we're not completely human. The signs still apply to us. As though sensing the sudden unease of the group, Rat says, confidently this time, "This is the way to the pack."

11
FOUR STRANGERS

The path gets narrower before coming out the other side.

When it opens up again and I see trees and open space, I sigh, relieved. The group as a whole was silent for almost all of the journey through the narrow pass. Rat was the only one talking about what he expected we'd find. So far, it's what I've wanted to hear, and I just hope these shifters live up to the picture Rat's painting of them.

"We're here!" Rat declares, stopping suddenly. The mountains rise up in the distance, trees covering every surface for miles on either side. We're high up. *Really* high up. And there's no sign of human civilization this far out. It's like we passed through a veil between their world and ours. *This* is our world, our territory. I can feel it.

"Stop!" an unseen person shouts. But we have stopped, all of us. Rat seems pleased with himself. The owner of the voice emerges from behind a boulder above us. Three more come out from behind trees. The four strangers surround us. "Raise your hands and stay still."

I hesitate, but Rat raises his hands immediately and says, "It's okay! Do as they say."

I remind myself that I want to be in this pack and that we've come a long way and risked a lot to find them. I raise my hands above my head.

Three of the strangers circle us, checking our pockets and backpacks while the one who spoke stands watch over us. She's a little older than us, with fiery red hair. She's barefoot, wearing jeans with tears in the knees. Her jacket is tied around her waist, leaving her upper half covered in just an ivory tank top. I'm cold just looking at her bare arms. She must be the wolf girl. I heard—in one of Jett's stories—that their body temperature is high. Freckles cover the wolf girl's tanned face and arms, reminding me of Ebony.

"Shapes," she says. "Call them out." She points to Rat. "You first."

"I'm a rat," he says. "We have met before. I—"

"You," she says, moving on to Lola before Rat can finish.

"A parrot," Lola says. She links her arm with Kanna's. "We're both parrots."

The girl's eyes drift over Kanna and rest on Jax. "White tiger," she guesses. She nods at Hugo. "You, too. Am I right?"

"Yes," Jax and Hugo say together.

The girl shakes her head and smiles, though it's not a particularly friendly expression. "So easy to spot. It's the eyes." She turns to Jett now. "Next."

"Bear," Jett says simply. The girl doesn't comment, seemingly uninterested. I take a step closer to Jett before the wolf girl stops me with her sharp eyes.

"Wait your turn," she says to me. Jett looks back, a knot of worry between his eyebrows. "The twins," the girls continues. "What are you?"

"Elephants," Lucas says flatly.

She nods. Then her gaze rests on me again, making my skin prickle. She looks at me as another member of her group starts patting her hands roughly down my coat and reaching into my pocket. "*Now* it's your turn."

I clear my throat. "Horse," I say loudly so she can hear me. I hesitate for a beat before asking, "And you?"

Jett stiffens and the girl narrows her eyes for a moment, considering my question. I asked to see if she'd tell me, to see if she'd trust me with that information after she demanded it from us, to see if she really is Rat's wolf girl.

"I suppose it's only fair," she says. "I'm a wolf."

"We all are," the girl behind me says. "Kind of you to ask."

I can't work out if she's being serious. I swallow. "I've never met a wolf," I tell them. "Only heard about them in stories."

"All good, I hope," the girl behind me says.

The wolf girl on the rock grimaces. "Let me guess," she snarls. "'Lydia the Wolf'?"

I nod.

"Remind me to tell you another if we allow you to stay."

"How do they earn their places?" Rat asks. "I've already earned mine."

The wolf girl frowns at him. "That's not how it works," she tells him. "You'll see soon enough."

The other three wolves rejoin the girl at the front, waiting below the rock she's standing on. I finally get a good look at them and notice they're all tanned and freckly. The two girls share the same shade of scorching red hair, and the boys a darker red-brown. I wonder if they're all related.

"But you do remember me, right?"

"We wouldn't be having this conversation if we didn't," she says.

Rat beams with pride. "Okay, good. Just checking."

I watch the lead wolf jump down from the boulder and talk to the others, fascinated by how they work. I realize they're a pack, not just part of *the* pack, but a pack of wolves themselves. I wonder what their shapes are like—how big they are, the color of their fur, the sharpness of their eyes, and the strength of their jaws.

"Darius," the lead wolf says. "You lead the way with the rat and the parrots. Sam can follow with the white tigers." Sam isn't wearing a shirt, and I notice both his and Darius's feet are bare, too. The male wolves take their places at the front and lead off. "Brea, stay with the elephants. And I'll escort the bear and the horse."

We follow Darius and I keep my gaze set ahead, on him, even though I can feel the wolf girl's eyes on me. "We've been watching you for days, you know?" she says. I twist my ankle on the edge of a rock. She steadies me by the elbow, her touch warm—maybe the stories *are* true. "You had no idea we were there."

That must have been the noise Jett and the brothers heard. "Actually, we did," I say proudly. "We heard you last night."

She smiles tightly. "That wasn't us," she says. "Someone else has been watching you, too."

I skid to a stop. "What?"

Jett and the wolf girl stop, too, and look back. "Who?" Jett asks, looking from her to me.

"We don't know," she says. "We tried to find them but they retreated. Now come *on*." She starts walking again and I jog to catch up.

"The hyenas?" I think aloud. I wonder if they've been following us all this time, if we're still playing their game. Though, they didn't strike me as being patient enough to simply hide and watch us; surely, they'd have engaged with the group in some way. Their laughter echoes in my mind.

The wolf girl is shaking her head, her red curls bouncing on her shoulders. "No. The Laughing Sisters don't work that way."

"Then who?" I ask, even though she already told me they don't know. I'm freaked out that someone was following us, and if it wasn't the hyenas, I have no idea who it would be—the elders? Gretchen and Tomas and others from the pack? Who would follow us, and for what reason?

"I don't know," the wolf girl repeats. "They're not following you anymore, anyway. So, forget about it. If they come this way, we'll find them."

As we near the camp, more shifters emerge from their lookout stations around the perimeter. A message is passed on that a meeting has been called and we're to wait somewhere with the wolves until everyone's ready.

I didn't know what to expect—I still don't—but it seems as organized as Rat and Lola said it would be. It seems right, safe.

The wolves lead us into the heart of the camp while we await the meeting. I don't speak as I take it all in. Their base is huge, and I know I'm only seeing part of it. Everything is camouflaged in forest-green, earth-brown, and sandy tones. Hammocks hang between trees, blending in with their surroundings. Rope ladders lead up to platforms, hidden high in the branches. Thin rope bridges connect between them, stretching from tree to tree.

Thick logs surround several campfires, with seating carved out. Wooden screens section off what I assume is the bathroom area—the barrel and watering-can shower system is just like ours was back at the circus. I think that's the first place I'll visit once we get accepted into the pack.

Handmade wooden tables hold an assortment of ingredients—bags of rice, potato sacks, vegetables—pots, pans, and a mismatched stack of wooden plates, bowls, and cups. My stomach cramps with hunger. I lick my dry lips and finish off my water bottle. It didn't rain—the clouds passed—so I'm drinking the last of it. Looking at the ingredients on the table, I think about a meal around a warm campfire with a cold cup of water. I think about the water in the cans washing the dirt and grime off my skin. Of smelling of soap instead of sweat and earth.

Two water containments stand on either side of the food prep table. DRINKING WATER is carved into one, and WASH BOWL is carved into the other. This system also reminds me of the circus, only better. And I almost feel like I'm home.

"This place is incredible," I whisper to Jett.

He nods his agreement, still busy taking in everything around us. It's like nothing I've ever seen before. They've become a part of this mountain, made it their own, made it a *home*—somewhere they want to stay. Somewhere free of unease, absent of worry, with nothing to fear from one day to the next.

The wolves all sit on or lean against a large rock in front of us. They seem excited for what's to come, but each time any of us ask, they refuse to give anything away. "You'll have to wait and see," the lead wolf keeps telling us.

So, we wait as the camp organizes itself around us.

12
NO KILLING

They're ready for us.

The pack assembled quickly, gathering in a large clearing on the other side of camp. During the short wait, we each were given a cup of soup and a piece of bread. I feel better for it and it helped warm me up.

The wolves lead the way, finally giving up some information on where we're going, but still keeping quiet about exactly what we're doing. "We use the clearing like an arena," Brea tells me. "But we don't use it often."

"When was the last time?" I ask, trying to picture it. "What for?"

Brea rubs the tips of her fingers across her chin. "The last time . . ." She pauses, thinking. "Oh!" She laughs. "The last time was a tournament some of the tigers tried to set up. Tigers are such show-offs—do you know any?"

I think of Pru and nod.

Jax clears his throat in response to Brea's comment, walking just behind the two of us. Brea tsks. "I don't mean *you*!" She looks at me and grins then shakes her head. "Anyway, they set up a competition. Performances and routines—that kind of thing. Not many people were into it, so only a few entered and they had trouble finding a judge who was willing to suffer through everyone's performances."

The lead wolf is walking just ahead of us. She turns back. "Brea, if you're finished?" she says. Brea blushes and nods. The leader nods back and raises her voice. "No more chatting now," she instructs. "Walk them out into the Pit professionally, okay? The chiefs will be watching them . . . and us."

The Pit? That doesn't sound good. And the *chiefs?* That kind of sounds like the elders. I get a sudden bad feeling, but I shove it back down, reminding myself that I want this. I do.

Brea glances at me out of the corner of her eyes, a smile teasing her lips. *What's funny?*

"The Pit?" I mouth.

She nods excitedly. "That's the *professional* name," she whispers. That's when I realize she was smirking at the lead wolf's orders, not at whatever's about to happen in the Pit. I think. We carry on in silence.

When we get there, I find that it's not really a pit. I was imagining an inescapable hole in the ground. There's a large, bare circular patch of land, flat and clear, which I assume is like the ring at the circus. The mountains stretch up on either side, like the circus tent. Cut-out paths, ledges, and cave openings are filled with shifters looking down at us, reminding me of the benches and the audience with their snacks and face paint, cheering, caught up in the experience. It's just like that now, without the snacks and face paint. There must be a couple hundred shifters here. I wonder if it's the whole camp, or just part of it. Seeing such a large number of shifters in one place is both overwhelming and comforting.

The wolves stop in the center of the Pit. There are more shifters on the edge of the circle, and a small raised platform at the head of it all makes the podium Gretchen and Tomas sat on back at the hyena's camp look rushed and uneven. This one is sturdier but around the same height as theirs, raising those on it about three feet higher than the rest of us.

On the podium are five shifters, who I assume to be the "chiefs." One sits on a central wooden chair with a tall back carved with intricate patterns. Two sit on each side on chairs not quite as grand, but just as detailed.

The five shifters stand. The one in the middle says, "Thank you, Cady," to the lead wolf. That's the first time I hear her name used. "You can stay for the trial or return to your station. The choice is yours."

Cady glances at me. Her eyes sparkle before she turns back to the chiefs on the platform. "Thank you, Mal," she says. "We'll stay."

Mal nods, and the wolves take a place at the side of the circle. The feeling of being back in the circus ring is overwhelming, with an audience ten times the size. I start to feel nervous about what's to come, but the thought is cut off when Mal addresses us. "Newcomers," he starts. "Welcome. I am Mal, leader of this pack and head of the chiefs." He has a kind face, much older than the elders. His salt-and-pepper hair is shaved short, as is his facial hair. He's all stubble and tanned skin and wrinkles around the eyes and forehead.

Mal wears a brown poncho, all the chiefs do, and the sides blow in the wind as he gestures to the woman to his right, asking her to speak. "I'm May," she says. "Mal's twin sister. He is older by a minute, which is why he's in that chair and I'm not." She elbows him in the side and he smiles, the lines on his face deepening. Her hair is dark with strands of gray. "The two of us are gorillas."

The chiefs sit down.

"As you can see," Mal says. "Our pack is scattered through the area surrounding us here, high in the mountains, away from human trails, hidden in enormous caves and under the shelter of trees, guarded day and night. We are safe, protected, secret. But we only achieve this through our members, which is why we are selective about who we allow to join."

I take a deep breath. I knew this was coming—I knew there was some way we had to earn our places—but still I feel unprepared. Lola looks worried. "We've come a long way to find you," she tells the chiefs.

Mal smiles sadly. "I understand that you have," he says. "But if, say, the Laughing Sisters showed up here to ask for a place among us, we would not grant them access because they cannot be trusted, cannot be tamed. We know this already. But we don't know anything about your group."

He watches us for a moment. The silence drags out between us.

"If," Mal then says, drawing out the word. "If there are enough of you that perform well, then you may all stay. It depends how valuable we deem the majority."

"Perform?" Jett says. He leans in to me and lowers his voice. "Like at the circus?"

I shrug, but I don't think so. I don't suppose we'll like it, whatever it is. The crowd stays quiet throughout all this, as though they're collectively holding their breath.

"Perform, yes," Mal says. "Before we accept a new member, there is a trial. This is yours. You now know who we are and what we are. You will get the chance to step forward and introduce your group before the match—"

"*Match*?" Lola shrieks. She rounds on Rat. "You never told us any of this!"

"I didn't know!" Rat retorts.

Mal looks exhausted as he tries to explain this to us. He turns to May and she takes over with a no-nonsense expression. "*Yes*," she begins. "Each aspiring new member is pitted against an existing member in their animal forms as a test of skill and commitment."

Lola's eyes widen. "What? Like, a fight to the death?"

A chorus of snickers and chatter emit from the crowd— the first time they've reacted to anything. Mal holds up his hands to silence them.

"Goodness, no!" May says. "That would be extremely dramatic. No, one contender must clearly beat the other to win. But no killing is permitted."

"*Has* anyone ever died during one of your tests?" Lola asks, glancing at Kanna, who looks furious.

"No," Mal says, taking over again. "We would never allow it to get that far. It's our way of knowing if a group will be an asset or a burden. After that, if you're accepted, it'll be on a trial basis, with another series of tests to find your strengths and what you can each offer to the group."

Lola spins around, putting her back to Mal. Kanna and I do the same, and the rest of the group steps forward so we're closer together. "So what shall we do?" she says.

"It's this or back out there on our own," Lance comments. "Lucas?"

"I'm with you," Lucas says, clasping his brother's shoulder.

"So the elephants are in," Rat observes. "I am, too. With or without the rest of you." Then he adds, "Sorry," like it's an afterthought.

I frown. He wouldn't even be here if it weren't for us. But . . . we wouldn't be here if it weren't for him, too.

Rat separates himself from us, stepping forward to be closest to the platform.

"*Rat*," Lola scolds.

"I'm sorry!" Rat exclaims, looking over his shoulder. "But I've waited a long time to come here. I'm not leaving for anyone."

"And you just failed the loyalty test," Kanna mocks. She turns to Lola. "I'm in if you are."

"Us, too," Jax says. "If the rest of you are. We've got nothing to lose."

I glance at Jett and he nods. We're doing this. "And us," I say.

We break up the huddle and turn back to Mal. "Okay," Lola announces. "We'll take your test."

13
WILD AT HEART

"Interesting," Mal says. "A mixture of wild and working."

The audience stays silent. They had listened to Lola explain our shapes and where each of us came from, including what we went through to get here.

"Working shifters are a rare thing indeed," May adds. "A circus, you say? Very interesting."

"Yet it seems the working are wild at heart," Mal says. "Taking down four hunters is no easy feat."

"We lost five shifters doing so," Lola reminds them.

"More if you count the circus," I add. I place my hand on my scarred stomach, and try to push the memory of fire from my mind.

Mal announces, then, that the second part of today's test will begin. "If we're still satisfied by what we learn from your group today, you will be escorted to separate living quarters to continue your trial."

"And after that?" Lola prompts.

"After that, if all goes well, you'll move into the main camp with everyone else."

Lola dips her head. We only know so much about this camp—that they're big and well protected. Rat couldn't tell us much more, and it seems like Mal and May won't either. Not until we've proven ourselves. If we join, will we be assigned specific jobs? Will we hunt? Patrol? Will we be able to stay together? If we want to leave—can we?

Right now, we need the protection of this pack. To be turned away would mean we'd have to rethink everything. We could run into the Laughing Sisters on the way back down the mountain. We'd have parted with Ursula and the others for nothing. I nudge Lola's side and nod. We should go ahead and deal with the rest later. Her eyes spark and I know she's thinking the same thing.

Lola looks back up at the podium. "That sounds fair," she says.

Mal claps his hands together. "Then let us begin." Cady and the wolves escort us to the side of the Pit. "We'll start off small," Mal announces. He leans in at May's side and whispers something to her. She watches Rat and nods along.

"The rat will go up against Boo," May announces.

Boo walks out in front of the platform. She has short black hair, shaped around her face, and she isn't wearing any clothing in her human form. No one pays any mind to her nakedness—used to it, as we were always encouraged to be.

Rat smiles. Boo is small and, at first glance, she seems an easy target. I can't work out what her shape is, but it must be something small for her to be paired with Rat. Maybe a mouse or a bird.

Rat closes his eyes, preparing to shift. For a moment, I wonder if he'll have trouble with it—being stuck as a rat for so long is bound to have an impact on him—but he transforms quickly. His clothes collapse onto the ground and he scampers out from beneath the pile of material.

"Showtime," I whisper.

Mal nods to Boo and she shifts into a bat. With a blink, she's transformed and I gasp in awe. "Well, that's not fair," Lola mutters. "She can fly!"

Rat stands up on his back legs, his tiny paws raised as Boo swoops down on him. "So not fair," Kanna agrees. "I hope we get it this easy. I'd take a Rat out in a second."

Lola tilts her head to the side.

"What?" Kanna says, her voice high. "I would! And so would you."

Boo knocks Rat onto his back. He awkwardly rolls over, recovering from the hit. He resumes his position before Boo strikes again. She dives. This time, Rat latches onto one of Boo's wings, using his tiny claws to cling on. Boo tries to fly upward, but Rat's grip is firm. She lifts him off the ground before the two of them crash down together.

Boo wraps Rat in her wings, encasing him, but he manages to wriggle out and step onto one before she can take flight again. He sits on one wing as Boo flaps the other in an attempt to free herself.

The crowd cheers. I'd forgotten about all the other shifters watching the fight. I glance up at the chiefs to find they're not celebrating, just watching and analyzing. Their facial expressions give nothing away. It reminds me of the hunters on show night at the circus.

I look back at Rat and Boo, still struggling on the ground, and wonder what the chiefs are seeing in their battle. Is Rat representing us well in his fight? It seems fairly balanced so far.

"Is he winning?" Jett asks. "I can't tell."

"I think they're a good match for each other," Lucas says. "No clear winner yet."

Boo's back in the air now. Rat's running along the clearing, following her flight path. But before anything else can happen, a scream rings out from up in the mountains. Rat and Boo carry on, but the attention of the crowd is now split.

Another scream follows.

Another.

The fight stops.

Everyone is looking up the sides of the mountains now, searching for the source of the screaming, trying to figure out what's going on up there.

The carved-out paths and ledges up the sides of the mountains turn to chaos in a heartbeat, and still I don't know what's happening. Everyone's scrambling either up or down, knocking into one another in their hurry. Owls and eagles, parrots and bats, take to the sky, escaping the dangerous pathways.

On instinct, our group moves closer together. Jett takes my hand. The chief members stand. Mal shouts orders. Other shifters hurry in to protect them.

Mal has a hard time being heard. With so many shifters in one place, he has no chance reining them in while panic ensues. It's like the circus all over again. And with that thought in mind, I finally see the hunters.

14
SHATTERED BY A SCREAM

I blink once, twice.

Did I imagine it? The figures in black, pushing through the chaos, weapons in hands, targeting shifters. *Hunters*—here?

Jett lets go of my hand. His grip moves to my arm, tight and sure. The sudden shift in contact snaps me from my thoughts. His touch is urgent, firm. *We have to go.*

Yet the group stands frozen around me. "This can't be happening," I say, breathless as I watch the chase up on the mountainsides. This place is supposed to be untouchable. How did they find it? How did they get in?

I turn to Jett. His eyes are wide, panicked. "It is," he says, his voice quiet. "It is. Come on!"

He pulls me with him before letting go. It's enough to force me into action. "Let's go!" I yell to the others, and I take off down the path, Jett close behind me.

Everyone follows. I keep looking back to check. Even though the ground is uneven and the path is unfamiliar, I have to make sure no one is left behind, no one is caught.

Rat is lost in the crowd. I didn't catch sight of him at all after I saw the first hunter. I don't know if he'll escape or get caught. I can't think about it. As long the rest of us are together—that's what matters to me. But I still hope he's safe—that he gets out of this and can finally be free.

We stay close. More and more hunters fill the paths, the cave entrances, the mountains. They've reached the ground now, too. They're closing in.

"They're everywhere!" Lola calls as we run away from the Pit.

"What do we do?" Jax yells. He's holding onto Lola with one hand, his other wrapped around Hugo's wrist.

"Run!" Kanna shouts. "Keep running!"

"And stay together!" Jett calls over his shoulder.

A net lands to the side of Hugo. Jax tugs him out of its reach. My mind flashes briefly to the image of Jax beneath a net of silver in the woods by the cabin. Of Dale edging toward him, arm outstretched, gun in his hand, silver bullets ready to fire. I blink and the image is gone.

I dare a look up at the rocky ledge to find a hunter rushing down to retrieve the fallen net.

The eight of us pick up speed, going back the way we came, though we're unfamiliar with the layout of the camp and, in the lead, I'm just guessing the direction. *Away*—I just need to get *away*. We can figure out the rest after that.

"If we get split up," Lola yells. It's hard to hear her with the wind rushing past my ears as we hurtle down the mountain slopes. "Meet back in the village."

We weave through the tree trunks, which are growing thicker and closer together. My feet keep a good pace, stepping where they should, staying ahead of the others, but my mind is elsewhere. It's back at the circus, reliving the night of my accident and running from the camp with Jett, the triplets, and Pru. We ran from the Pit like we ran from the big top—the chaos behind us and around us.

I still can't fully process what I saw back there as being real. That they caught up to us again so soon. How *did* they find us? Where did they all come from, and all at once like that? The pack was everything it promised to be. We were almost a part of it, almost home. Then all of that was shattered by a scream.

When will this stop? Will we *ever* be free from hunters? Will we ever be safe?

I already know the answer to that. We never have been and we never will be, and it would be foolish to truly think otherwise. I allow myself to forget their threat sometimes, but they're always there, chipping away at the back of my mind.

Danger, danger, danger.

The sound behind us rages on—birdcalls in the sky, roaring and growling, shouting and screaming—but becomes more distant. I start to think we might actually get out of this—but then what? Finding the pack was everything. There was no plan B. We risked a lot to get Rat back.

I look behind me, but I can't see anything from here. As I turn back, I crash into a tree trunk, throwing my hands up in front of me to take the impact of the hit. My knuckles crack and the rough bark scratches the skin away. Lola, Kanna, and Lucas overtake me. I pull back my hands, holding them close to my chest and stumbling forward. Everyone has passed me now, but Jett and Lance stop just ahead.

"Flo!" Jett calls back. "Are you hurt?"

I shake my head and pick up my pace, catching up with the two of them. "No," I say. "Go, go—it's fine."

They both take off in the direction of the others again, but Jett hangs back a little to allow me to catch up. My hands throb, but the cuts will heal easily, taking the pain away with it.

Lola skids and stops up ahead. Lucas and Kanna crash into her. It takes another few steps for me to realize what's happening. Four, five, six thumps of my feet against the ground and my heart in my chest. Then I see them.

Two hunters are blocking the way.

15
A CHOICE

I hurtle to a stop behind Lola and the others.

There's a rushing sound in my ears, and I struggle to catch my breath. For a moment, no one moves. Then between one blink and the next, Jax shifts, his clothing tearing as a growl rips from his throat and the white tiger stands protectively in front of the group. Hugo shifts, too, backing up his cousin.

A could-be hunter—I'm not certain—steps out behind us. Her steps are careful, quiet. The way she moves, and the way the hunters don't react to her presence, makes me think she's with them, but she's not wearing the black uniform. I angle myself so I can see all three of them, not comfortable having my back to either side. Jett takes a discreet step toward me and I reach out for him, holding his sleeve between my thumb and finger. The slight contact grounds me and I take a shaky breath. I know we're going to have to act, to fight our way out of this. There are eight of us and three of them, and we've done this before.

The woman up front looks close in age to the elders, but the guy can't be more than eighteen or nineteen. His hair is black, and he sweeps a curl from his forehead. He has dark eyes, too, that from here look as though they match the color of his uniform. The woman beside him is dressed the same way. Her hair is light brown, streaked with gray, though most of it is tucked under a black baseball cap.

The woman behind us, the one who isn't wearing the typical hunter-black, is younger than the other woman but older than the guy—he's the youngest hunter I've ever seen. Her hair is dark like his, too. She's wearing a white coat and wool hat, dark jeans, and black boots. She looks too clean for the mountain, too noticeable.

Lola and Kanna stay behind Hugo and Jax's white tiger forms, blocked from the hunters. Lola is standing slightly in front of her sister. Lucas and Lance cover Kanna's sides. Jett and I are the only two split from the huddle. I want to be closer to them—the distance between us is only a couple steps to the side, but feels too wide. I don't want to make any sudden movements, afraid of what it could start if the hunters get the wrong idea.

Hugo inches toward us, though, filling some of that gap. I should have moved instead of leaving it up to him.

"Easy," the hunter says to Hugo as the white tiger settles in place. The hunter has his hands forward, empty of any weapons or silver. It's unclear if the other two are armed or not, though.

Hugo stops and the hunter lowers his arms, straightening his back. His gaze finds mine then, looking over Hugo, past Jett, right at me. It roots me to the spot, him looking at me like that. He's a hunter and I'm a shifter.

Enemies. But he's staring at me, not breaking contact, and my skin itches and my eyes start to water before I have to blink and turn away. Then he says my name.

"Flo?"

My bones turn to ice. I'm afraid if I move, they'll shatter. I inhale, but air doesn't feel like it's reaching my lungs. Did I hear him right? Did he say . . .?

I whip around to face him again, putting my back to the girl behind us in a moment of panic, of confusion—how does he know my *name*? He must have my file, but why? Did they come from the cabin? We burned everything, but I'm sure they could get copies easily enough. So they're here because of what we did. But why is the focus on me?

"How do you—?"

"There's no time," he says. He shakes his head and the curls he brushed from his forehead flop back down. "Hunters and shifters could come this way at any moment. We need to move."

I stare at him, so confused I can't do anything but just . . . stare.

What?

Are they sympathizers? But even sympathizers wouldn't seek shifters out to help them, would they? Look at Dale, with his relationship and deals with Ava, and the way he did little to step up and help us when we were locked in the cabin, burned by silver, alone and afraid. The one behind me adds, "Ava sent us."

I gasp and take a step toward the brothers, dragging Jett with me. I press in close to the rest of the group.

Ava—she's alive. She escaped with Nora and Hari. Are they with her? In on this plan of rounding us back up or whatever it is they're doing? How did she find us? Hugo growls low, baring his teeth.

"*Ivy*," the male hunter hisses. "What the hell did you say that for?"

So he didn't want us to know that piece of information. What else are they hiding? We should fight them now, while they're distracted, and run before any other hunters or shifters come this way.

"It's the truth!" Ivy replies, her voice high. Her gaze flicks from him to us. "She doesn't want to hurt you, Flo. She wants to help you. We've been tracking you since—"

"Stop!" I yell. I don't want to hear what she has to say—I don't want anything to do with the elders or the hunters. I just want to *go* with my friends, disappear again until we can figure out what to do. But if they tracked us this time, what's to stop them from tracking us again and again. Will they ever lose our trail? I lower my voice, cautious of drawing any more unwanted attention. "Don't come any closer, don't *say* anything else. We're not letting you take us to the elders or to the labs."

"Not the elders," Ivy says. "Just—"

"She *said* stop speaking," Lucas snarls. "Get away from us. We won't back down."

"We know that," the male hunter says. "We saw what you did to the others."

"Okay, Quinn," Ivy says. "Let's stop there." She looks to me. "Flo, this has nothing to do with Nora or Hari. It's only Ava who sent us."

"It makes no difference!"

Ivy pauses for a second, a look of irritation flashing across her face. "We aren't taking you to the elders or the labs," she continues. "We're sympathizers, all three of us, and Ava has some information she wants you to have. You should come with us."

I shake my head no before I can even process her words. Dale did nothing to help us, and even though Ava did step up at the end, she was still the reason hunters captured us in the first place. Getting mixed up with her again could be very bad for us. I'm determined to move forward, to get out of all this trouble. Going back to Ava would take us a thousand steps back, throwing us in the absolute wrong direction.

"You can tell us here," I say. "Then let us go."

Ivy shakes her head. "It's something Ava wishes to deliver herself."

"How could we ever trust you?" I say.

"Or Ava," Kanna adds with a scowl.

"She did help you escape," Lola says quietly.

"But she was the reason we were there in the first place," Lucas says to Lola and the sisters nod their agreement. "The reason that Logan . . ."

"We can't seriously be thinking about going with them, right?" Kanna quickly says. She hooks Lucas's hand with one finger and he pulls her closer to his side.

"We aren't here to hurt you," Ivy says.

"Just to trick us," Kanna sneers.

Quinn tilts his head. "What would be the point in that? If we wanted to bring you in, we could do it without the debate."

"Really?" Kanna replies. "I'd love to see you—"

"Kanna, stop," Lola says quietly.

"Like you said," Kanna adds quickly. "You saw what we did to the others."

"*Kanna,*" Lola snaps, grabbing her sister's arm. "I mean it."

"Willa," Quinn says. The woman beside him turns to look at him. Quinn steps behind her and removes a backpack from her shoulders—one with thin black straps that I didn't notice she was wearing.

"Not yet, Quinn," Willa says, trying to stop him. But he's already got the pack. He drops it to the floor and crouches down to unzip it. He moves fast, I notice.

We seem to stiffen all at once, sucking in a collective breath and waiting for what comes next, for who'll make the first move and start what we all know is coming.

"They aren't coming with us willingly," Quinn says, looking up at Willa. "So what choice do we have?" He lifts out two guns and drops the bag. Jax and Hugo growl. Quinn turns back to us. "Ava asked us to bring all of you to her, *if possible.*"

He hands a gun to Willa. "Here, take this. Just in case."

Jax launches himself at Quinn while his arm is still outstretched. He drops the gun before Willa can take it, and his own gets trapped beneath him as Jax brings him down. Kanna breaks away from the group, rushing forward to kick the gun out of the way. Lola shouts after her as Kanna tackles Willa to the ground. Lola and Lucas both hurry toward her.

A CHOICE

Quinn tries to free his gun, and the silver exterior sizzles against Jax's fur. He pulls back, giving Quinn the opportunity to release the gun and point it toward him.

Quinn pulls the trigger.

16
NEW TARGET

A silver dart slams into Jax's side.

I gasp. It's just a dart gun, like the one they used on me in the cabin when I escaped my cell. Except that dart didn't affect me other than returning my shape to human, but whatever Quinn used seems to be slowing down Jax a lot.

Jax shifts back to human and stumbles to the side, unsteady on his feet. He pulls the dart from his shoulder, dropping it to the ground. Leaving Kanna and Lucas holding Willa back, Lola runs to Jax's side, catching him before he falls. She lowers him to the ground as Quinn pulls the trigger on his dart gun again with a new target. Lola goes down this time, a dart in her thigh.

Kanna screams, releasing Willa. Quinn turns his aim on her. "Stop!" Ivy and I yell at the same time. I'd forgotten she was here, behind me.

"Not unless you cooperate," Quinn says, his dart gun still aimed at Kanna. He's panting, and his black curls are sticking to his forehead.

Kanna snarls. "I don't take orders from you. You shot my sister!"

Quinn scowls and adjusts his grip on his weapon, knuckles white. His arm shakes, but he doesn't drop his aim.

Before anyone else gets hurt, I blurt out, "I'll come with you!" I continue, quickly, "I'll come to Ava. But not the others. If she has information for me, then I'll come alone to get it and then I'll leave and return to my friends."

I don't believe it will be that simple, but looking at Jax and Lola slumped on the ground, Quinn with his gun pointed at Kanna, Lucas holding Willa back, and everyone else poised to fight, I realize I could end this now. No one else has to get hurt. We could fight, and we could win, but we could lose people again, too.

"Flo—no!" Jett says. The brothers are shaking their heads, too.

Still on his knees, Quinn looks to Ivy, considering. "No," Ivy says in response to his glance. "Ava said all of them."

"*If possible*," Quinn recites. "It's not possible."

"It is!" she argues. "They just don't understand."

"None of us are coming with you," Jett says. "Leave us or fight us—there's no other option here." I whip around to face him. He looks right at me. "There's not, Flo," he says quietly. "There's no way any of us would let you leave with them."

Mind seemingly made up, Willa suddenly yanks her arm out of Lucas's grip and lunges for the gun on the ground. Quinn squeezes his finger on the trigger of his own gun, shooting Kanna with a dart. She starts swaying, turns to Lucas, and holds out her hand. He goes to her, leaving Willa's path free. She's feeling on the ground for the gun while Quinn finds his next target.

Everyone bursts into action—everyone but Ivy, who still stands in the same spot and watches on, calling for us to stop, wait, think about this. No one listens to her.

Lance, Jett, and I run for Quinn at the same time. He only has time to take out one. He gets Lance in the thigh with a dart just as I reach him and hit the dart gun out of his hand. Jett shoves him to the side and he tumbles over, wet patches of mud on his knees.

Hugo, still in his tiger form, ran for Willa at the same time we went for Quinn. I see now that he got to her, but she hasn't given up. Lying on her back, she pulls a knife from her waistband and plunges it upward. Hugo moves to one side, but the blade still slices him, painting white fur red. He roars and brings his claws down on her chest. She doesn't even have time to scream.

I look away quickly. It's all too familiar. I feel like I'm back in the woods, in the cabin with Dale and Ethan and the other two hunters, chasing us through the trees. Quinn's eyes widen and he stays put on the ground.

"Stop! Stop!" Ivy calls out again. "This has gone too far!"

I look at my friends on the ground, unconscious. Lucas is holding Kanna in his arms, his brother lying beside him. Only four shifters and two hunters left standing—if I'm counting Ivy as a hunter. Then she does something to surprise me, to confirm it. She pulls her own dart gun from her coat and aims it at me.

"I'm sorry, Flo," she says. I stare back at her in a moment of disbelief—she was telling us to stop! She didn't want us to fight, and now she's joining the fight herself? Was she tricking us? Making us think she was on our side? Why is she doing all of this for Ava—why are any of them? What could be so important?

Jett pushes me over, narrowly missing getting shot with the dart himself. Hugo leaves Willa's body and charges at Ivy. Quinn's clear to get up again. Lucas springs to his feet at the same time.

I take my coat off quickly. "Keep me clear of them," I say to Jett.

Then I close my eyes and shift.

17

THE HORSE WITHIN

It feels good to find my shape again.

It seems like it's been so long since I've been a horse, and it's like I'm now rediscovering just how powerful it makes me feel. The Blackout welcomes me back, wrapping me in darkness, sucking me into its depths. I crave the cold, the beginning of the transformation. And then it comes, answering me.

My skin prickles, my bones crack like ice, and my shape starts to take me. I feel my body expand, change, as the heat comes to let loose the horse within me.

Jett quickly scoops up my broken necklace and puts it into my coat pocket before anyone else even notices he's moved. I regret not taking it off first, but there was no time. In the moment, I was only thinking about being a horse and defeating the hunters trying to deliver us to Ava.

Ava. She's forcing us to act. She's brought this situation on us. All of this—all the lives she's risking to track me down. All the shifters back in camp, who're being captured and killed. I stand here with my friends, half of them injured or unconscious. This doesn't tell me Ava is changing. This only tells me she's just as reckless and thoughtless as she's always been in her aim to get what she wants.

She wants my friends and me this time.

She can't have us.

Hugo charges at Ivy while Jett shifts beside me. Ivy loses her dart gun quickly, but Hugo is forced back into his human shape somehow. I see a nasty red burn down his side as he stumbles back from Ivy. She's clutching a silver baton in each hand, forcing Hugo back with them.

They came prepared to take us in. Caught us off-guard. Four against two, I remind myself, though it doesn't make me feel better. I did this last time, as our numbers dropped—the hunters killed us, we killed the hunters, it felt like it would never end, and definitely wouldn't end well. For either side.

I'm thinking the same thing now.

Quinn and Ivy move together and stand side by side, Quinn with his dart gun and Ivy with a silver baton in each hand. For a moment the two of them watch us, and we watch them. It's like the Pit—them against us. But this isn't like the Pit—this isn't a controlled situation, a performance. This is real. This *is* a fight to the death. And I'm not losing any more friends.

Before anyone else can make another move, Quinn shoots at Hugo, perhaps seeing him as the biggest threat. Lucas, on the ground with the others, protecting them from further harm, seems to have been forgotten. He gets up, laying Kanna down, and tackles Quinn from behind.

Lucas wrestles the dart gun from his hand. Quinn's aim is off, but he still shoots and gets Hugo, who lets out a whimpering sound as he loses his balance and falls.

Jett and I face Ivy. Quinn is still distracted with Lucas, whose nose is bloody. Quinn knocks him down. Jett and I move in, testing for a reaction from Ivy. But she's clearly been trained for this, and she stays put, letting us come closer. Ivy worries me the most—she's unpredictable. I can't work her out.

Quinn takes Lucas out with a blow to the head and he falls. I startle, stop. Quinn hit Lucas so hard I heard it, felt it. Jett stops, too.

Lucas groans and turns his head. His chest moves.

I look back at Quinn then, fury running through me. He shouldn't have done that. He shouldn't have done any of this. He should have stepped aside and let us go—Ava isn't worth this.

The sudden silence around us is deafening. *What do we do?*

Quinn decides that for us. He holds the dart gun in sight, obviously having picked it up again during or after his scuffle with Lucas. Jett and I stumble backward at the same time, but in one swift movement, Quinn aims it at Jett. He pulls the trigger and a dart flies out, landing in Jett's leg. How many darts does that thing hold? As though hearing my thought and needing to answer it, Quinn shoots twice more. Both silver darts hit Jett in the stomach, sizzling. He shifts back and falls.

Lucas starts to stir and Quinn tosses the dart gun to Ivy before rounding on him. She runs for me. I turn and kick out, knocking her over. The dart gun fires as she falls, hitting Quinn's shoe. He yelps, hops on the spot, then stumbles, landing beside a disorientated Lucas.

Ivy recovers, brushing leaves from her hair. "Quinn!" she gasps when she sees him.

"It only got my shoe—it's okay," he calls out.

She looks back to me. "I'm not even part of the team anymore!" she cries, spitting soil from her mouth.

I charge for her, my hooves kicking up dirt. I knock her to the side and though she loses her balance, she doesn't fall. I turn, run again, hitting her harder. She falls, rolls onto her stomach, and looks up at me. If I was quick, I could trample her. Quinn, too.

I start to run, thinking maybe I could just knock them unconscious until I can get my friends out of here, but Ivy holds her hands out in front of her. "Wait! Wait!" she yells. "She has Rain! Please!"

I hesitate, skidding to a stop. *Rain?* The toddler from camp. She was with Iris last time I saw her, so what is she—

I hear a crunch behind me.

I turn. Quinn's recovered one of the fallen dart guns and fires it. Four times. Each dart lands in my chest or shoulder—*thud, thud, thud, thud.* I screech and rear back, shifting somewhere in between. I fall onto my back with a *crack* that knocks the air from my lungs, and between one moment and the next, both hunters are standing over me.

Quinn's triumphant expression is the last thing I see before everything fades.

18
NEVER SAFE

My eyes flutter open.

A moan escapes my lips, and I tilt my head to the side. It feels heavy, like someone's standing on it, pressing down.

Then I remember: four darts hitting my chest and shoulders, releasing whatever substance they held to force me to lose consciousness.

I see the others sitting up, tied hands resting on their laps.

"Flo!" Jett says. "Flo?"

It's too loud.

"It's okay," Jett says. "We're okay. It just takes time to wear off."

I hear heavy boots on dry mud coming closer. The tip of the boot nudges my side. I whimper—everything feels too close, too loud, too real.

"Get off her!" Jett shouts. The sound of his voice rings in my ears. Everyone's talking over one another now. The hunter stands over me, shouting back, and it's just a string of muddled words pressing on my eardrums.

"Stop!" I shout, but I don't know if the word comes out. Tears escape my eyes and I speak again, "Stop."

The others quiet down. The only person who speaks is Quinn. "That's all of them," he says, dusting off his hands. "Flo's the last one and she's coming around. Let's move them."

"We're not going anywhere with you!" Jett snaps.

"You don't have a choice," Quinn replies.

I feel rope against my wrists as the fog in my mind starts to clear.

"We can't go yet," Lola says from somewhere close by. "Flo's hardly awake."

"It'll wear off in a second," Ivy says.

Quinn hauls me to my feet and I notice the rope around my hands is connected to the others. All eight of us are in a row, the rope linking from one to the next. I'm already wearing my coat. It's been zipped up for me and comes down to mid-thigh. My legs are freezing, the rest of my clothing ruined. My boots are on my feet. The others who shifted are left in scraps of clothing, too. Jett's wearing Quinn's hunter jacket and a scowl on his face.

I'm still nauseous from the shift, from being pulled from my shape and knocked unconscious. "How long was I out?" I ask.

"Not long," Ivy replies. "We moved undercover while we waited for you all to come around." I look around, but everything looks the same, though I see scuffmarks on the ground where Ivy and Quinn must have dragged us all. "The tranquilizers work fast, and move quickly through your body, flushing out fast, too. They're good for when we need to capture and question a target but not have them out of it for hours."

I turn away from Ivy, not interested in hearing hunter tactics. I pull at the rope around my wrists, which only serves in tightening its hold.

Quinn tuts and shoves me. "Give it up," he says. "Can you stand? We're going."

I shake my head, even though I think I could. But if I stand, we start moving. Instead, I close my eyes and call on my shape.

Nothing happens.

"I said, give it up," Quinn repeats. "You're not going to be able to shift until the serum is completely worn off. It usually takes a couple hours, and I don't have time to wait. Now—get up." He tugs on the rope.

I glare at him. "I can't."

"Let's try it," he says, hauling me to my feet. He holds my face in his hands and looks into my eyes. "You're fine."

I pull back. "You said you weren't here to hurt us!" I snarl, tugging on the bonds some more. I know it's no use, but I don't know what else to do, how else to fight back.

"You're hurting yourself," Quinn says.

"Then take this off me!"

Quinn shakes his head. "Soon. Let's go." He takes the lead with me, and Ivy walks at the back behind Lance. Everyone else walks in between, single file, and connected by the rope.

I look at my feet, watch them take each step, leading me somewhere I don't want to go. As my mind starts to clear, I replay what happened before Quinn and Ivy beat me. The darts took us down one by one, and Ivy

screamed something about Rain. That's why I stopped—
that's what distracted me.

Wait! She has Rain!

Who does? Ava? If Rain is in trouble, we should know
about it. She's one of us and we'd want to help her. I look
back at Ivy, eager to ask her what she meant, but she's too
far away. Something tells me I'll have plenty time to ask
her as I look down at my bound wrists.

The rope rubs against my skin as Quinn pulls us along.
Soon, I see a black van in the distance. It's parked on a
flat, winding road at the bottom of a steep hill. There are
no other vehicles around. "Did your friends leave?"

"No," he says. "Ivy brought the van. She didn't park
near them. She's not on the team since . . ." He clears his
throat. "Ava wants to be the one to explain things."

"Well you've started now," I prompt.

"I shouldn't have. Ava will tell you everything.
Finding *you* was our mission." He looks at me. I hold his
gaze. "We just had to wait until the right time."

I scowl. "And when did you figure out it was the right
time? When you saw we were finally safe and happy?"

Quinn sighs. "I'm not your enemy, Flo."

I huff a breath and remain silent. Of course he is.

"You're never safe, you know," Quinn continues.
"Don't be tricked into thinking you are just because a
group is big and organized. We're bigger. We'll always be
bigger. Look how quickly we took them down."

Tears warm my eyes, but I push them away. I can't let
him get to me. I can't let myself believe that, because then
what's the point in even trying?

"How did you find them?" I ask, to distract myself and to understand. I didn't think it was possible to attack them like that, and certainly not as easily and successfully as they had. "They've never been attacked before."

"We've been tracking your group since you left the cabin." I turn and look back at the others, noticing Jett, Lola, and Lucas are listening close behind. I think of the sound in the woods, of Cady telling us someone else was following us but that whoever it was wouldn't get into camp. But they did, and so many of them. Cady and the wolves stayed for the fight—they had abandoned their post. How many others did the same? How many were tricked into a false sense of security following years of no incident. The defenses were down and the hunters came in.

"It's one of the biggest missions I've ever had to pull off," he says with a sense of pride. "I needed you for Ava, but the others wanted you for the labs. Keeping them away from you was the hardest thing."

"There were so many of you," I whisper.

"Yes," Quinn says. "We were about a day behind you until you stopped on the mountain. The numbers started building once you led us here. We caught the hyenas who chased you and others in their group. Then we called for backup—lots of it—when we saw where you finally stopped."

"Yeah," I say bitterly. "You hit the jackpot."

"My mission was you," Quinn says matter-of-factly. "I'm the mission leader so I could lead my team after you, then send them one way while I captured you for a different purpose."

"A lot of shifters will suffer so you could get me while the others were distracted."

Quinn clears his throat. "I had wondered how I was going to do it when the time came, but the opportunity sort of presented itself."

I think of everything that happened back there. How many shifters must have been captured, their lives ruined or ended. Did the wolves get away? Did Mal and May? I can't help but feel a little relieved that the Laughing Sisters are off the mountain, but it's not enough to quell my anger. I elbow Quinn in his side as hard as I can.

He stumbles and clutches his side, but quickly recovers. "What the hell?" he snarls, shoving me back. Jett pushes him, too, his rope tugging everyone else forward.

"Stop it!" Kanna calls from near the back, stumbling with the rest of the group.

"Don't try anything again, Flo," Quinn warns, stopping at the van. "I mean it."

"What more are you going to do?" I snap back, holding up my bound wrists. "You being the group leader is bullshit."

He grabs my shoulder and shakes me. "I have told you nothing but the truth. You fought back. You killed Willa. And despite all of that—" He shakes his head. "Just take help when it's offered, Flo."

I snort and pull back from him, but there isn't far to go. "After I've spent my entire life hiding from hunters, after everything they've—*you've*—done to us in the past few weeks alone? I don't need your help, and I don't trust in it, either."

"Fine," Quinn says, eyebrows drawn. "But there's nothing you can do about it." He shrugs. "And I *am* the leader, just so we're clear. With my team, and right now."

"Won't your *team* be looking for you?"

Quinn starts walking again. "No. We don't hang around if someone goes missing. They find their own way back eventually. Usually."

"Great work ethos," I say. "Is that why you left Willa in the woods?"

Quinn sucks in his bottom lip. "Don't talk to me about Willa. You killed my friend and hurt my sister." He looks past me and cups his hand around his mouth. "Ivy!"

"You attacked us!" I argue. I don't feel as confident as I sound, though. We've known a lot of death lately—on both sides—but we did just take a life, hunter or not.

Ivy makes her way up the line.

"We tried to bring you in calmly," Quinn says. "But you wouldn't cooperate." He unlocks the van and swings the back doors open.

Ivy jogs the rest of the way and stands beside the open door. She reaches for my arm and takes hold before I have a chance to react. By the time I pull back, her grip is strong. "Sorry about this," she says.

"About wha—" She secures a silver cuff on my wrist. Pain shoots up my arm.

Silver.

Not again. Not again.

"HEY!" Jett yells.

"It's just while we're in the van in case the serum wears off," Ivy says.

"Transporting live cargo can be dangerous," Quinn adds with a grin.

"She'll be fine," Ivy adds. But how could she know? How could she ever know what it feels like to have your skin burned like this?

My vision blurs, my ears feel blocked, and I move my limbs too slowly. Ivy unties my wrist, leaving the silver cuff in place, and guides me to the van.

I lie on the floor of the van, clutching my arm, while Ivy and Quinn work their way down the line, starting with Jett. When Ivy brings him in, he almost falls on top of me, his side crashing into mine. I turn my head to look at him. He reaches out and finds my hand.

THE GIRL

There was a group in the waiting room.

It was the first time Ro had been there. The first time she'd seen other shifters.

They sat in rows in the corridor. Eight, including her. No one made a sound. No one looked at anyone else. All eyes were cast downward, except Ro's.

Four hunters stood by the doors—two in front of the one she'd been lead through and two in front of the one she assumed she'd go through next. She didn't know what was in there, but everyone seemed scared, quiet.

Ro's arms were bruised. Her wrists were raw, the silver cuff having been reapplied after each testing. She couldn't remember anything about the tests they'd done on her so far. Every time she woke up in her cell, in a heap in the middle of the floor, the silver having burned a new ring in her skin. It shocked her awake sometimes. Sometimes she could actually sleep through the hunger and fear, when the knowledge of what they'd done to Chase didn't keep her up and thoughts of Tia quieted down.

Ro noticed the other shifters wore the same clothes as her, had the same cuffs, the same bruises. She fought tears, looking at them. She didn't know how much more of this she could take, certainly not a lifetime's worth.

But how could she ever escape? She knew she would never get out—shifters who were taken to the labs didn't leave.

Beside her, a young girl sat statue-still. Her head was dipped and her hair hung over her face like a curtain.

Ro glanced up at the hunters. She didn't know if speaking was permitted, though she guessed not.

She turned back to the girl and whispered, "I'm Ro, what's your name?"

The girl flinched but didn't reply. Ro noticed the girl's eyes were rimmed with red like she'd been crying.

The door opened and another hunter stepped through. He held a clipboard and called out a number. The girl beside Ro stood. Her bare feet slapped the cold floor.

The girl lifted her head. Her steely gaze fixed on the door she was heading for.

Ro watched her go. Watched until the door closed behind the girl and seven shifters were left waiting to be called.

If she can be brave then so can I, Ro thought.

When the door opened again, and the hunter called Ro's number, she stood and forced the same hard gaze. But it cracked as soon as she stepped into the room.

19
RED AND WHITE

When I open my eyes, I'm still in the back of the van.

Jett isn't beside me anymore. No one is. We aren't moving. The van door is open. There's nothing but daylight and me back here. The silver cuff is gone. My wrist is mostly healed.

My head hurts. Panic hits me, fuzzy and uncertain. My senses are slow to kick in, my reactions trailing along behind. *Where's everyone else?*

"Finally," someone says, startling me.

I raise my hand to my forehead, squinting against the light. I notice dried blood on my arm.

I see colors: red and white. Then I hear voices.

"Well, shit, Ivy," one voice says—familiar but not. I massage my temples, willing this foggy feeling to pass. "She actually woke up."

"I didn't think it would have such a bad effect on her. Everyone else is fine."

"And you know what the touch of silver feels like to us?" the voice snips.

"No," Ivy replies.

142

I rub my eyes and sit up slowly. "Ivy?" I say.

"I'm here," Ivy says. "Ava, too."

I flinch and move back. My wrists are no longer tied, but my movements are weak and clumsy.

"It's all right, Flo," Ava says. Her voice, the memories connected to it, come rushing back. I open my mouth, but words don't come out. "I'll explain everything when you're feeling more yourself."

"Jett," I manage to say. "Jett. Where is he? Where are my friends?" My voice rises.

"They're fine," Ava says. "They're here. Settling in outside. You're safe, I assure you. Rest until you feel you can stand, then come out and see for yourself."

I lean against the back of the van. Ava's wearing a red coat. Her white-blond hair is clipped back, her chin tucked into a thick scarf around her neck. "Go and get Jett," I demand.

Ava turns to Ivy. "Go on," she says. I meant for Ava to go. I don't want to see her, don't want to speak to her, but Ivy does as she's asked. She hops off the back of the van and leaves me alone with Ava.

Ava is also perched on the edge of the van. She shuffles in a little farther and the vehicle moves slightly with the shift in weight. My vision tilts again and I cover my eyes with my hand.

Ava tuts. "Trust them to use silver. I didn't want any of you to be hurt," she assures. "Just give it a minute."

"I've experienced this before," I tell her, anger in my words.

She clears her throat and turns away.

"Why did it affect me so much this time?" I ask. "Why did I pass out when no one else did?"

"Lance did," she tells me. "But not for long. It's because of the tranquilizers they used. You were all in a weakened state. The introduction of silver and the pain it causes was the reason some of you were unconscious. I'm sorry, Flo."

I ignore her apology.

"Why did you bring us here? I told the hunters I didn't want to come to you." My voice sounds muffled to my ears.

"It's important," Ava says. "I'll explain everything when you come outside."

"But I said I didn't want to come!" I say, my voice clearer now. "I said no!"

"Flo, I—"

"No! Wait," I say. "I appreciate that you helped us escape the hunters' cabin. We got out and I saw what you did to Ethan so we could get away. But you have to understand that I still blame you for all of it. I blame you for every life lost before and after that. I blame you for my parents! So I can't do this . . . I can't forgive you."

"I'm not asking for your forgiveness," Ava says calmly. Her eyes shine with tears. I've seen her cry, plenty of times. It doesn't make me feel anything. "I still lost something in all of that."

I shake my head. I can't think about Dale.

"That's not why you're here. I have something you'll want and I want something in return. It's strictly business."

"What—?"

Ava holds up a hand. "Rest," she says. My head aches and I lean back again.

The van dips again and I look up. Jett crouches down in front of me. "You're awake," he says. He smiles.

My own face cracks into a smile, despite everything. I'm relieved to see him here. "What's happening?" I ask. "Where are we? Where are the others?"

"We've been setting up while you slept."

"Do you believe her?" I ask.

"I don't know," Jett says quietly. "I'm still trying to work things out. None of us really know what's going on yet." He turns his head, glancing at Ava, who's still hovering behind us. "Ava won't tell us anything until she's spoken to you."

Ava nods once. "That's right," she says, standing. She takes a few steps from the van but hovers close.

"So what have you been doing?" I ask. My sight seems to be returning to normal, and things have kind of stopped spinning.

"Do you want to see?" Jett asks. "Do you feel like you can stand? I'd love to get you out of this van."

I nod slowly. "I think so. I think it's wearing off."

Jett helps me to my feet and we slowly make our way to the open doors. He's wearing jeans and a checked shirt beneath his coat. The clothes look clean, and I wonder where he got them. Did Ava give them to him? Ava hurries over when she sees us. She holds her hands out to help me step down, but I don't take them and end up almost falling over. She catches me, though.

I shrug out of her grip when I find my balance and move away with Jett.

"We'll talk when you're ready," Ava calls after me. "You're going to want to hear what I have to say."

20

THE LION'S DEN

I already know I'm going to turn Ava down.

Whatever it is, it's not something I want to get involved in.

But for now, I need air. I need to walk off the stiffness in my legs. I need to see where we are and see for myself that everyone else is okay.

Jett stops as I put my hand against the van's exterior. It's cold against my palm. It's only a short walk—I can hear everyone—and Ava strides past, leaving us to it.

"We can find out what she wants and then leave," Jett says once she's out of earshot.

"Or we can just leave," I offer.

Jett tilts his head. "I don't know—it might be better to find out why she tracked us down like she did. The more we know, the better. If we run, she might follow. And if we don't know what she wants, we're at a disadvantage."

My shoulders slump.

"We'll try and put up with Ava until we find out what she wants," Jett says. "Then we're gone."

"I don't know if I can do that," I tell him. "It's like two sides crashing together: she helped us, she betrayed us. I can't sort it out in my mind. And I know she won't say anything I want to hear. The sooner we get out of here, the better."

"Okay," Jett says. "I get it. We'll figure it out—don't worry."

Worry is all I do. It feels like worry is all there's room for.

We start walking again. I let go of the van and Jett guides me around it. "Where are you set up?" I ask.

"Just through that path there," Jett says, pointing ahead.

There's a gap in the bushes, and a trodden-down, flat stretch of earth between it serves as a pathway. I smell the campfire first. It smells of home. Then we push through the bushes, along the short path, and I see the smoke and the camp and—

My breath catches in my throat. I stand still, just on the other side of the path, right on the edge of camp. "It's just . . ." I begin.

"I know," Jett says.

This could be the circus. The only thing missing is the big top. Everything else is set up just like it used to be—before.

There are fewer tents, fewer people, but it's all here. Or, at least, it looks that way.

Six tents are set up in a large arc with plenty of space between them. A campfire in the middle is lit and crackling, and the cooking area and washing bowl are set up to one side of it. There's a laundry area near the showers. And two trailers a little farther back, near the tree line. The trailers—does that mean Hari and Nora *are* here?

"The elders?" I say.

Jett shakes his head. "Just Ava. The other trailer is for Ivy and Quinn."

Lola and Kanna rush over to us. "You're awake!" Lola exclaims.

"Just," I say with a small smile. "Still trying to take all of this in."

Kanna crosses her arms against the cold. She turns to look back at the camp. "What's going on?" she says quietly.

"I still don't know," I say. "I'll find out soon."

"Do you have any idea what Ava might want?" Lola asks. "All she said to us is that she needed to see you first. I don't get that—why it has to be you, I mean."

I shrug. I don't either, but I get Ava and that things are never straightforward with her. Whatever it is, she probably could have told everyone, but she kept us here by withholding the information until I was awake.

"She said she has something I want," I tell them. "And she wants something in return for it."

Lola frowns. "Do you have any idea what it might be?" She looks from me to Jett.

"I don't," I say. "I can't imagine there's anything she has that I would want badly enough to stick around. So it'll all just be a waste of time. A waste of life." I look back at the camp, the inviting glow of the campfire, and think of Willa's body on the mountain and the shifters who must have died in the Pit today. Because of Ava. "I wouldn't get comfortable."

Lola nods. "Okay. You coming?" she says, turning back toward the camp. "Clothes are in your tent."

148

I look down at myself, remembering that I'm only wearing an oversized construction coat and boots. Goose bumps prickle over the bare skin on my legs. "Yes," I say, moving to follow.

"That one is yours," Kanna says, pointing to the little yellow tent. I know it's not actually my old tent—it can't be—but it looks just like it. "We're neighbors."

I wave to the others as I pass the campfire. They're playing cards together. I want to tell them not to settle in here, that it could be dangerous. Another part of me wants to let them sit and relax because being on the road is hard.

"I could use a shower," I say, noticing that I'm the only one who still looks dirty. Kanna and Lola both have wet hair and clean clothes.

Kanna smiles and points toward the tree line. "That way. There's probably a towel in your tent."

I unzip the tent and notice a pile of clothes and a towel. I grab it and head over to the tree line to shower before anything else.

———

Once I'm clean, I slip my boots off and climb inside the yellow tent.

I find socks, jeans, a sweater, and a scarf inside. Jett waits outside.

"Did all this stuff come from the circus?" I ask, wrestling the sweater over my head.

"Some of it," Jett confirms. "Ava told us that the elders took what they could when the circus was attacked.

Because they were part of the deal with the hunters, they didn't rush out and leave most of their stuff like the rest of us. Ava also said she's been set up here for a few weeks, waiting for us."

"Why would she do all this?" I say. "What could she possibly want that's worth all this effort?"

I notice a plain chain on top of the jeans, clearly meant to replace my broken necklace, which I pull out of my coat pocket. *How did she know I'd broken it when I shifted?* I tip the pendants onto my hand and secure them on the new chain.

I finish wriggling into the jeans and shuffle over to the edge of the tent, pulling my boots back on over the thick socks. It feels good to be clean and wearing fresh clothing. To be wrapped up warm again without rips in the fabric, dry mud, and wet feet.

I stand and take a breath. "Better," I say.

Jett nods. "I guess there's nothing left to do but . . ."

"Find out what Ava wants," I finish.

Jett nods. "She said she'd wait for you in her trailer. Ivy and Quinn are there, too. She said when you were well you were to go over there. When you're ready."

"Are you nervous?" I ask him.

He nods. "Are you?"

"Yes," I tell him. I zip the construction coat right up to my neck, the necklace tucked safely underneath. "She's planned all of this too well."

"It does seem a bit much," Jett admits. "But we're making the most of the break, the rest. Look at every-one." He glances over his shoulder and I follow his gaze. Kanna and Lola have joined the card game now.

"They seem happy. And that's good, at least just for the time being," Jett says. He looks back at me and smiles. "Go see what she wants . . . before we get too comfortable."

I swallow hard. "I will. Which trailer?"

Jett points to the one farthest back from the camp.

"Okay," I say, taking a deep breath. "I'm going."

He gently presses a kiss to my lips. "For luck," he whispers.

I head over to the trailer, the feel of his lips still on mine. Back into the lion's den like I never left. Maybe I never did. And maybe I never will.

21
OLD WOUNDS

I open the trailer door without knocking.

The conversation happening inside stops. For a moment, only silence and memories lie between Ava and me. She's sitting on a cushioned bench around a small table with Ivy and Quinn. The blinds on the window next to the seating area are fully open, letting the pale light from outside paint the small space in soft gray. Despite the dullness, Ava's trailer is neat and spacious, not cluttered and stuffy like Hari's was. Everything's got a place here, an order. Except me.

"Flo!" Ava says. "I hope you're feeling better. Come join us."

I take a hesitant step forward and the door slams shut behind me. "How did you know my necklace was broken?" I ask, feeling the cool chain against my neck. "Where did you get the chain?"

"It was mine," Ava says. "I don't have use for it, and I found the pendants loose in your pockets."

"You went through my pockets?"

"The bear claw fell out while you were in the van," she says. "Please, Flo—come join us."

152

I sit on the very edge of the bench, next to Ivy and across from Ava and Quinn.

"I hope you're comfortable there, Flo," Ava says, taking in the way I'm sitting.

I shake my head. "Not really," I say. How can I be comfortable around her? How can I relax inside her trailer, lean back against the seat, have a regular conversation? None of that exists where Ava is involved.

"A lot has happened in the time we've been apart," she says.

"Just tell me why you brought us here," I reply.

Already the walls appear closer. Already it feels like there's less air in here to breathe. I want to be back outside in the camp with my friends. But I want to know what Ava wants from us, so I can dismiss it and move on and then all of this is over.

"We'll start with the moment we parted ways. When I threw the keys to you."

I nod stiffly. "Thank you for that," I say. "But Logan got shot in the forest when the hunters chased us. He's dead."

"I know," she says, not meeting my eyes. "Dale got in touch with me right after you escaped. Ethan was furious. He had five shifters, then suddenly none. His team have—*had*—never taken a hit like that. He and Ange—the female hunter—took the lions Dale and I had captured to the labs to buy more time and cover for the trouble they were having with you and the others. It gave Dale time to slip away and tell me everything that'd happened."

"Chase and Ro," I breathe. "The lions you tried to trade for us. The ones you captured to get us out. We came back to find them—they were friends of our new pack."

Ava closes her eyes for a moment. "I asked Dale not to go back, but . . . he didn't listen, too worked up with everything that was going on at the cabin."

"The hunters took more of our group, then attacked the rest of us at the warehouse the rest of us at the warehouse we were hiding in. We didn't have much choice but to go back and face them."

Quinn leans back, shaking his head. His hair looks freshly washed, dark curls falling into his eyes.

I fold my arms and ignore him. "The hunters attacked us," I continue, addressing all three of them. "It's them or us."

Ava wipes at her eyes.

"And I suppose Willa was . . . what?" Quinn says.

"Willa attacked Hugo."

"Hugo attacked Willa!" Quinn argues, clutching the edge of the table. "She wasn't going to harm you. Neither were Ivy and I. You forced us to act more aggressively to ensure your capture."

"Willa pulled a knife out! She tried to use it on Hugo!"

"A white tiger was pinning her down! What would you do?" I fall silent and he says, "Exactly."

I swallow hard. "Hunters attacked the mountain camp," I say more calmly, though my hands shake beneath the table. "You cornered us. We were *not* just going to follow strangers—*hunter* strangers—who claimed they had our best interests in mind. Of course we'd fight back in that situation."

Ava holds her hands out. "That's enough. What's done is done. Now isn't the time to be blaming each other and arguing over right and wrong. It won't change anything."

I take a breath. Quinn does, too, leaning back in his seat.

"Quinn, are you all right to be in here?" Ava asks him. "Because I need to speak to Flo. I'd rather you were here, but this shouting is no good for anyone."

"I'm not leaving," he says firmly. "I'm fine."

Ava narrows her eyes, her irritation clear.

"Who are these two, anyway?" I ask. "Why are they helping you?"

Quinn's staring at me again. I keep my focus on Ava, trying to ignore him. Ivy stays quiet beside me. "After Nora, Hari, and I met up with Dale again, he informed us of the problems his team were facing with you and that they were going to try and draw you back in," Ava begins.

"We both knew it was dangerous, and Dale told us that if anything happened to him, it was likely his secret would come out—which it did." She glances at Quinn. "Dale was Quinn's uncle, and Quinn reached out to me after Dale's death. He told me the lab discovered where Dale's loyalties really lay, and then started investigating the rest of the group. They pulled our information—everything on the circus. And Hari, Nora, and I are now high targets."

I swallow and dare to look at Quinn. I find he's still watching me, his dark eyes unwavering even when I look back at him. I can't work out if he hates me or wants to help me. Why would he find Ava and warn her if he wasn't a sympathizer like his uncle? I still don't fully understand the role Quinn plays in all of this. I don't understand the role *I* play in all of this.

"What do the hunters want you for?" I ask Ava.

"To kill them," Quinn answers. Ava flinches at his honesty. "Ava, Nora, and Hari pose a threat to security. There's no telling what Dale shared with Ava during their relationship. The three of them are a risk to the organization."

"Then why haven't you taken her in?" I ask quietly.

"Because I have something of theirs," Ava says. "Simply put."

Quinn looks to Ivy. I turn in my seat to see she is silently crying.

"There's no need for that, Ivy," Ava says. "You remember Rain, don't you, Flo?"

"Yes," I say hesitantly, still watching Ivy. Her eyes spark at the mention of the toddler and I wonder what the connection is. When Ivy shouted something about Rain, I figured the little girl must be in trouble. "Is she in danger? She was at Iris's last time I saw her."

"She was," Ava says. "Rain is not in danger. I had Iris keep an eye on her when the circus ran into trouble. Rain is Ivy's daughter."

My eyes flick between Ava and Ivy, trying to grasp onto this new information. "Rain is . . . ?" I trail off. "You're a shifter?"

Ivy shakes her head, her eyes still filled with tears. "No," she says. "I'm not. Rain's father was." She casts her eyes down.

"It's why she lost her place at the EOS," Quinn says. "They found out about her relationship. They took Maxx—Ivy's partner—away. Ivy got Rain out before they came for her, bringing her to Ava. Dale said Rain would be safe with Ava at the circus."

Quinn reaches across the table to take Ivy's hand. He looks to Ava, his hand still clutched around his sister's, and nods for her to continue.

"I was keeping Rain for the circus until Ivy could leave with her, but obviously we had some trouble," Ava says. "And obviously, I wanted something in return."

"Obviously," I mutter.

Ava ignores the comment, giving no indication if she heard or not. "So I kept Rain with me until calling in a favor from Ivy and Quinn to deliver you to me. As part of the agreement we made, they delivered you, handed over their weapons, and are staying on site until we've tied everything up between us."

"I'm Rain's uncle," Quinn adds, but I'd worked that out for myself.

"Why did you have them hand over their weapons if you trust them?" I ask.

"So you might be able to trust them, too. There's nothing that is a threat to you here—no silver, no tranquilizers, nothing that could make you feel more uneasy. I hope it helps."

My mind buzzes. My vision feels suddenly as cloudy as it did with the tranquilizer serum running through my veins. Maybe it hasn't entirely worn off. Or maybe I just can't believe what I'm hearing. "So you're back to killing and kidnapping?" I ask Ava. "I don't know why I'm surprised. I didn't think for a second that you might have changed."

Ava frowns. "This is a dangerous world, Flo. Things are never as straightforward as they seem."

"And where is Rain now?" I ask, sliding closer to Ivy.

"Coming soon," Ava says. "Iris will bring her to us. Ivy can have her back and then leave as and when she pleases."

"And the rest of us?" I ask. "When can we leave? What do you want from us?"

"That's another matter," she says, lifting up a large file. She drops it onto the table, the thin wood rattling under its weight. "The rest of you are here because of this. This is Dale's file—the one he kept on the circus children. He had it for years."

I stare down at the brown case file, with its frayed edges and handwritten notes. "There's stuff about me in there?"

"About all of you," Ava confirms. "Where you were found, what happened to your parents—everything."

I reach for it and Ava slams her hand down on top of it, stopping me.

I startle, pulling my hand back. "I . . . I thought you were giving it to me."

"It's not good news, Flo," she says. "I want you to be prepared for that."

A wave of disappointment washes over me. I don't know what I was hoping to find in there. My parents, alive and well? Details telling me where I can find them?

"Tell me," I say, my voice cracking. "Tell me what's in there. My parents—are they alive?"

"Flo," Ava says evenly. "Breathe. This isn't the right time to get upset."

I stand suddenly, without realizing I had made the decision to move. One minute I'm sitting, breathless on the cushioned bench. The next I'm on my feet, slamming my hand down on the table between us. Quinn reaches for me across the table and I shoot him a warning look.

Ava puts her hand on Quinn's arm and his posture relaxes. "Flo," she says again, in a voice meant to calm me.

"No! Just tell me what happened to them that day," I demand.

"They were taken to the labs," Ava declares. I crash back down onto the bench, my knees giving way. Ivy puts a hand on my side, grounding me. I rest my hand on the table, gripping the side, my breathing coming too fast. "They're no longer alive—I'm sorry," Ava adds in a small voice.

I push myself up again, needing to leave this room, this trailer, these *people.*

This is what she brought me here for? To cut open old wounds? To hurt me all over again?

Ava stands, too, as I head for the door. "Wait! Flo, there's more."

"I don't want to hear it!" I yell, not turning around. I fling the door open. "I don't want to know more!"

The others are still sitting around the campfire. They look up when they hear me yelling. They rush to stand, run toward the trailer.

Ava hurries on anyway. "Your mother was pregnant when they took her."

I stop, turn.

"She delivered the child at the lab facility—a girl."

My world falls apart, taking a piece of my heart with it. *A child. A girl.*

"You have a sister, Flo," Ava continues. "She's still there."

The steps vanish from beneath me and I fall out of the trailer, landing on hard mud. *"What did you say to her?"* I hear. *"What did you do?"* A chorus of panicked voices.

Someone grabs me. Multiple hands lift me. I'm pulled against someone's chest. I smell the outdoors on his clothes, the smoky campfire.

"Flo." I hear the whisper, feel it—my name on Jett's lips.

My eyes close, numb to all of it.

22
THE CIRCUS CHILDREN

I sit alone on the outskirts of camp, clutching the file to my chest.

When I first recovered from the shock, a horrible nausea rushing back with me, Ava got me a cup of water. I'd sat leaning against Jett's chest. Quinn and Ivy had stayed inside the trailer, giving us some space. I could hear them talking quietly to each other, though I couldn't hear what they were saying.

Hugo, Jax, and Lance were the first to go back to the campfire, where they waited for news. Kanna and Lucas soon after.

Lola had stayed the longest, brushing the hair back out of my face. "She's so warm," she kept saying. "What did you say to her?" she asked a few times.

But Ava wouldn't tell.

Ava waited with us until I sat up and looked at her again. "I'm okay," I told Lola and Jett, though even I wasn't convinced by my croaky voice, the way I kept touching my palm to my forehead. "I just need a little more time with Ava. I'll tell you all what's going on soon, I promise."

Jett scooted backward and got to his knees. My thighs were cold from sitting on the floor, pressed against the hard mud. "Flo?" he said, searching my eyes.

I nodded to him. "I'm fine, really."

He didn't want to leave me, I could tell. He furrowed his eyebrows in confusion. None of them understood, not yet.

Jett and Lola left me with Ava, and she guided me back into the trailer. She had made some sweet tea for me once I'd finished the water. Then she handed me Dale's file and told me I could take it wherever I wanted, do with it whatever I wanted.

I took a blanket from her, tucked the file under my arm, and walked in the opposite direction of camp. I laid the blanket out under a tree and sat with my back against its trunk.

I'm still sitting against the tree.

The file is still closed on my lap.

Ava told everyone to leave me alone, give me some space, and so far they have. Even if they don't want to listen to Ava, they seem to understand something big is happening. A car arrived a short time ago and I watched from this distance as Iris handed Rain over to Ava.

I heard Ivy before I saw her. She shrieked and rushed to Ava, taking Rain out of her arms. She held Rain close and cried against her. Rain started to cry, too, and the two of them went into the other trailer.

Poor Rain has been through so much and she's so young—too little to understand most of it.

I think about my own sister growing up in the labs. She'll be thirteen now—I know that much without having to open the file—and the lab is all she's ever known. If I can believe Ava, she's still alive.

I put the file down in front of me, tucking one of my legs beneath me. Jett and the brothers will want to see it, too. But I have to open it first. I take a shallow breath, staring down at it. I can't get enough air into my lungs.

Ava had said there are pictures inside. She warned me that there's a lot of information that I might not understand, but she and Quinn will help explain it if I want them to. She told me about charts and numbers that might not make sense to me.

I had asked Ava what my sister's name was, and she said she doesn't have one. That fills me with so much sadness it's almost unbearable. My sister is a number, owned by the lab. I wonder if she knew our parents, and if they ever told her about me.

I open the file.

The profiles are in alphabetical order by first name of the circus children. Circus shifters stare back at me from the pages, most of them lost to us now from years ago or weeks ago, as I flip my way through to letter *F*.

When I reach *E* I stop, knowing that my profile is coming soon. I turn the pages more slowly, steeling myself for what I'll find.

Here goes.

My breath catches in my throat. My parents look back up at me from inside the file. This is the first time I have ever seen their faces.

I run my finger over my mother's image. The photo was taken in the lab. It's clear by the white tile walls behind her, the off-camera hunter clutching her arm, the plain gray loose-fitting jumpsuit she wears with a number patch on the chest. She looks just like me. A sob escapes as I take in her red-brown hair so like mine, her pale skin, her green eyes with dark circles beneath them. There's no fight left in them.

When was this taken? What had they done to her?

They'd torn apart her family. My *family.*

"Mom," I whisper, so quietly I can hardly hear myself. The word feels strange on my lips. "I'm sorry . . . I . . . I didn't know you were there."

What would I have done differently if I'd known? If I'd understood this side of our lives as much as I do now? Would I have fought to save her?

Name: *Flora #001462*
Species: *Horse*
Facility: *Roll Point*

"Flora," I say. "Her name was Flora." Am I Flora? Is that what "Flo" is short for? Or am I just "Flo"—similar but not the same? Either way, I'm named after my mother and that means I've carried an extra piece of her along with me all this time without even knowing it.

I look at my father's photo, a little farther down the page. His photo backdrop is the same as my mother's— white tiles. He wears a gray jumpsuit, loose against his lean frame, a number on the chest. His hair is much darker than my mother's; his eyes are, too. His hair is long, tucked behind his ears. It curls outward at the bottom and

I smile at the unruly tufts. When I was nine, Ava cut my hair short for me like I wanted. It'd been just long enough to tuck behind my ears but kept flicking outward at the ends. I pull his photo out of the file.

His name was Warren, a horse. He was at the Roll Point facility, too. There's some comfort in knowing they were together there, though I can never really be sure they saw each other. It notes that Warren died four years ago. Flora's death isn't recorded in this file. If what Ava tells me is true—that both my parents are no longer alive—Dale mustn't have updated it before he died. Or my mother died after he did, which would mean it only happened in the last few weeks.

I swallow hard and look at the information on my sister, pasted at the bottom like an afterthought. There's no photo, and she has no name. Her number is listed beside her information.

I decide to call her Wren.

If I share a part of my mother's name, she should share a part of my father's. I treasure their names for a moment, repeating them in my mind. *Flora, Warren, Flo, Wren*—my family.

The file has notes on the night they were taken. It says we were living on an abandoned farm at the time with another shifter family. The other children, if there were any, must have been too old to be taken to the circus, because it was just me that night—I went to the circus alone.

I'm clutching the photos of my parents when Quinn comes over. He sits beside me, a knot of worry between his eyebrows.

I tuck the photographs under my thigh and wipe at my eyes.

"Why are you a hunter?" I say. "Why do you do this to people?"

"My whole family are hunters—it wasn't something I had much choice in. It was forced on me from an early age. I've only recently started seeing it for what it is."

"And that is?" I ask, imagining a younger Quinn learning to hunt, to kill.

"Complicated," he says. He looks up at the sky and sighs. "You don't understand just how ingrained the hunter drive is from the moment we're old enough to grasp it. This was always going to be my life—I didn't have a decision in that. Just like you were always going to be a shifter, living in hiding."

I shake my head. "Don't make comparisons between us."

He runs a hand through his curls. "The first time I saw a shifter die, it hit me just how real it all was. Before I started training properly with the EOS, going out and facing shifters in the wild, it all seemed like storybook tales to me. Monsters and demons and we were the ones who saved the world by hunting them and destroying them."

I snort. Hunters have always been the villains in our stories, and apparently this is true of us in theirs.

"But I realized it wasn't like that," Quinn continues. "Dale showed me that it wasn't like that, but neither of us ever had a choice to walk away from it all."

"Why?" I ask. "Why can't you expose them? Tell the world about us."

Quinn laughs shortly. "There isn't a happy ending to that scenario. You don't get to opt out—once you know, once you're in, you're in forever. So Dale showed Ivy and me how to change things from the inside, bit by bit. I know it doesn't seem much to you, but Dale was unfortunate in that he got placed in Ethan's unit. Ethan was everything a hunter is supposed to be—textbook. He was always going to do something like what he did to you and your group, and Dale had to go along with it." He pauses, looks at me. "Did Dale ever try to help you?"

I swallow. "Sometimes. But not enough. He seemed scared of Ethan. And he didn't back down when we came back to the cabin for our friends."

Quinn seems almost disappointed by that. Like he expected his uncle to do more to help us. "When they split up Ivy and Maxx," he says. "And dealt with Maxx the way they did, that was a real turning point for me. I know it doesn't seem like it, but I am trying to make changes in the way I do things. It's just not always easy without drawing suspicion. We're analyzed a lot, because of what we do and the lives we take. It's hard to hide."

"Ivy got away," I tell him.

He raises his eyebrows. "Ivy is running. She can never come back. Ava, Hari, and Nora are all on the run, too. I can't do that—not yet."

"So if you're going to help us, what's in it for you really? Why should we put our trust in you?"

"I'm not just helping Ava with all this because she held Rain in the bargain, though that's how she convinced me. I'm helping because I can and because I should. I don't think it's as simple as you're good and I'm bad, or vice versa. It's the choices we make that decide that."

Jett approaches us then and Quinn gets to his feet. "Come find me if you need me," he says.

Jett watches him walk away. "What was that about?" he asks.

I shrug. "I think Ava sent him over. To talk to me about the file."

Jett's gaze lingers on the open pages in front of me. He sits beside me in the space Quinn occupied a moment ago. "He's young for a hunter," he comments.

I nod. "Nineteen, I think."

Jett runs a hand through his hair, making it all stick up at the front. He looks tired. "I'm worried about you," he says. "I was following you over here but Ava told us to give you some space. I didn't know what to do."

"For once she was right," I say with a small smile. I should let him have the file now that I have what I need from it. I've been with it long enough.

"Here," I say, closing the file and handing it over.

"Ava already told me," he confesses. "Not the others, just me."

"How much?" I ask quietly.

"Everything," he says. "She knows how much you mean to me and wanted me to be able to be there for you when you were done. I'm sorry, Flo. About your parents—all of it."

I don't respond. I'm not sure I'm ready to talk about it yet, even with Jett.

"But—a sister, Flo," he whispers.

I put the photos in my coat pocket and wipe the tears from my cheeks. I get to my feet and gesture toward the closed file on his lap. "I haven't . . . I haven't looked at your file, only my own. I don't know what's in there."

Jett places his hand on top of the file. "Okay," he says quietly.

"Share it with the brothers when you're done," I tell him.

"Wait, Flo," he says. He's clutching the file in both hands now. "Do you want to talk first? I can wait—"

"No," I say quickly. "Not yet." My chest feels tight and I don't know what to do with myself. I could walk, I could run, I could scream, and it wouldn't make a difference—it wouldn't make this ache in my heart go away.

Jett casts his eyes down. "We'll figure it out, Flo," he says without looking at me.

I want to say that I know we will, but I don't have the confidence right now. Jett runs his hand along the cover and I know it's time to leave. I turn again, without a word, and get lost between the trees.

THE FALL

Now Ro knew what to expect.

She knew what her days and weeks consisted of. She'd spent two weeks alone in her cell, seeing no one else but the hunters and the doctor. Eating her meals, sitting with her back against the wall, watching the silver sink into her wrist.

Then she started leaving the cell more, and in a group this time rather than alone. She was always with the same eight shifters. The same faces day after day, in the waiting room, in the exercise hall. She still ate her meals alone in her cell, but she saw other shifters almost every day now.

The waiting room was the worst part. It was standard testing, like she'd been experiencing already. She'd be hooked up to machines, injected with serums. They'd draw her blood, hook her up to monitors, test her healing properties and their limits. She'd run, she'd shift, she'd do everything they asked. And they'd write on their clipboards and tap away on their computer keyboards, recording everything.

Then when it was done, the silver was returned to her wrist and she was returned to her cell.

The other seven members of the group weren't her friends, weren't her allies or her pack. They didn't speak to her, or to one another. There was a system, a way of doing things, and Ro was still trying to work it out.

She kept trying to communicate with the girl, without luck.

Today Ro's group was in the exercise room—a large, empty hall. Equipment was stored inside a cupboard. Cameras lined the walls. Hunters guarded every door.

A hunter with a whistle stood in the center of the hall, instructing them to run laps around the hall until she says to stop.

Sometimes they didn't say stop for ages.

Sometimes Ro could hardly keep putting one foot in front of the other.

She knew today would be one of those days, because the hunter with the whistle was the toughest one she'd come across. Whenever she ran the exercise hall, she ran it hard.

The hunters put groups in the exercise hall so that the shifters kept up their fitness and strength, so that they wouldn't die in testing. But Ro thought she might die in here. With the silver on her wrists and all the time she spent in testing or sat in her cell, running laps wasn't as easy as it should have been for her. Ro felt the burn in her calves by lap six, when usually she'd be able to run and run and no one could tell her to stop.

The girl was running in front of Ro. They'd just started their seventh lap and Ro was really feeling it now.

The girl stumbled, tripped over her own feet. She put her hands out in front of her to take the force of her fall.

Ro lunged forward and gripped the fabric of the girl's jumpsuit in her fist, pulling her toward her. Once she had good hold, she threw out her other arm, wrapping it around the girl's waist and pulling her upright.

Both of them turned to look at the trainer. Ro sighed, relieved, when she saw her back was to them. They started running again immediately before she turned and saw.

This time Ro and the girl ran side by side. They still didn't speak, though Ro held her hand to the girl's back when she saw she was struggling. She helped keep her going.

By the time their exercise session ended, Ro was dripping with sweat. Her hair had come loose from her tie and was sticking to the back of her neck.

The girl walked beside Ro as the group was ushered out the door and into the corridors to return to their cells. Two hunters led the way and two walked at the back.

"Thank you," the girl said quietly as they followed the hunters back up to the third floor.

"You're welcome," Ro replied gently. "Can you tell me your name now?"

The girl shook her head. "I don't have one."

Ro glanced ahead and took a deep breath. Looking back to the girl, she said, "What was it before you came here, then?"

"I don't say it," the girl replied.

Ro frowned. "Are your parents here, too? Friends? Where are you from?"

The girl sniffed and wiped at her eyes with the back of her hand. Then she sped up her walk, putting shifters between them, leaving Ro's questions hanging in the air.

23
SLIPPING AWAY

I go from walking to running.

Farther and farther. In any direction. The smoke from the campfire will lead me back when I'm ready, but right now I don't care how far I get, how lost I get. I just want to *go*.

It feels like when I ran away from the circus on my first show night.

It feels like when the hunters attacked and the tent went up in flames.

It feels like when I saw the tiger girls dead in the woods.

It feels like when I chased Ethan into the darkness.

It all weighs heavily on my chest. Every bad thing I remember comes rushing to the front of my mind. I have no memory of the farm—I wish I did, but I don't. I can't picture my sister. I have to keep looking at the photographs of my parents because I feel like the images may slip away if I don't. But the bad I remember, the fire, the deaths of my friends, the hunters, the fear—I remember.

I remember finally thinking we might have found our way at the mountain camp. And then that got snatched away from us just like everything else. Now here I am, back with Ava, back at the beginning.

I stop running and take off my clothes, carelessly throwing them to the cold ground. The sweat on my back, my chest, my neck, turns icy cold when the wind hits my skin. I shiver, but it seems right to be able to feel more than the pain in my heart and the pounding in my head. I *want* to feel more.

I take off my necklace and place it on top of my clothes. Then I close my eyes and call on my shape, eager to be free. As soon as I'm in my horse form, I run.

Wind rushes past my ears as I push harder, gaining speed.

"*We'll figure it out, Flo,*" Jett had told me. And I hope we can. Together. We need each other now. We all need each other. I'm not the only one looking inside that file today.

———

I stop running after a while.

My head feels clearer, and I know I have to go back and face this. Figure out what to do, with my friends and not on my own.

I find my way back to camp, following the thin plume of smoke, and then the sound of voices as I get nearer. I see the brothers on the blanket beneath the tree, looking at the file. I walk quietly past them and over to my tent. I don't see Jett.

174

I sit inside my yellow tent with the flap open. Kanna is sleeping in the one next door. The others sit around the campfire. The flap on Jett's tent is closed, and I wonder if he's inside or out in the woods. I don't know what he found in his file—I didn't look at anyone's information but my own.

———

It's dark before Jett comes back.

He emerges from the trees, walks straight over to my tent. The brothers are long finished looking at the file, having returned to the campfire without a word.

Jett sits beside me. We don't talk, not right away.

Just being together is enough.

He speaks first, his voice quiet. "My parents aren't alive," he tells me. "They never even made it to the labs."

"I'm sorry," I say, my eyes cast down. I'm not sure I can look at him yet, not sure I can bear to add his pain to my own, to carry it with mine. "Did they . . . were there photos?"

"No," Jett says. "The page didn't have much detail. They were clearly insignificant. It was more a record of me and where I came from than about them."

"I'm sorry," I say again.

"Don't be," he says. "I haven't lost anything. Things are the same as they've always been, as I've always believed them to be. It's just hard to think about it all again, to have it dragged up like this. My memories of that day . . ."

I don't have real memories of the day my parents were taken, but I know Jett remembers a lot. I know it's hard for him, and that the file will have brought it all rushing back. The day hunters wrapped his parents in chains, how he fought to get to them, so the hunters wrapped him in silver, too. I reach for the scar on his side, slipping my hand beneath his clothing. He inhales sharply and looks at me. I keep my palm pressed against his skin.

Jett takes my face in his hands, brushing his thumb over my cheek. My eyes meet his, pushing my pain back as his gaze burns into mine. We're both hurting, searching for something that will take some of that away. We can. We're stronger than all of that when we're together.

I give him a long look, and his lips find mine with an urgency we haven't shared before. He swallows my pain, shares his own, we're wrapped up in it, wrapped up in each other. Jett pulls me against him and I take my hand out from beneath his coat. He stops to close us inside the tent, to shut us off from the world for a little while.

Our path has been uncertain since the moment we were born. We have no ties; we're encouraged not to trust, to be cautious. But since I was brought to the circus thirteen years ago, Jett has been the one person I could rely on, confide in, trust, and love.

I sink back onto my blankets and let his touch take everything away, leaving just the two of us here, now, together, knowing that no one else and nothing else can break this one thing that's ours.

24
IMPOSSIBLE HOPE

The light inside the tent is golden.

I sit up to find the space beside me cold. Jett isn't here.

I hurry to get dressed. As I'm pulling on my socks, the zipper opens and Jett climbs inside. "Where were you?" I ask.

The smell of bacon follows him and I realize before he says it. "Bringing you breakfast. Are you hungry?"

I smile. "Yes," I say, taking the plate meant for me. "Thank you."

He leaves the tent flap open and we move to sit in the doorway facing the camp. Hugo is serving breakfast. Jett and I sit close, our sides touching. I take a bite of toast.

"You okay?" Jett asks.

I nod, my mouth full. When I finish chewing, I ask, "Are you?"

He nods too.

As the camp wakes up around us, I look at Jett out of the corner of my eye. "What are you thinking?" I say.

He keeps his gaze on the camp, watches as Ava exits her trailer and makes her way over toward the fire with a mug in her hand. "That you have family out there," he says. "I'm wondering what we can do about it."

I shake my head. "She's so far away from me," I tell him. "A shifter in the labs is more or less untouchable. She probably has no idea I exist, since she was born there. She doesn't even have a name, Jett! She doesn't even know who she is."

"You can be the one to tell her," he says simply. But it's not simple.

I shake my head. "She's in the lab and I'm out here."

"Then we need to get her out."

I look away. The idea seems too impossible. I want to believe him because I want her back. I want her back more than anything. She should be with me. She should be Wren, someone's sister, someone's friend. Not a number.

"How?" I say quietly.

"We've got a hunter in camp. We'll talk it over with Ava and Quinn. There must be a way. Ava wouldn't have given you this information if she didn't want you to do something with it."

I take another bite of toast. Watch the camp while I chew. Jett stays silent beside me.

"Wren," I say when I finish my slice. "Her name's Wren."

"Ava said she—"

"Doesn't have a name, I know," I finish for him. "I named her that, after Warren—my father. My mother was Flora, so . . ."

Jett nods. "It's perfect," he says, linking his fingers through mine. "I can't wait to meet Wren."

I swallow the lump in my throat. "Jett—"

"Don't say it, Flo. Don't lose all hope before we even try this."

My lip quirks up at one side. "Didn't you once tell me not to fill my head with impossible hopes?"

Jett tilts his head. "That does sound like something I'd say."

"You said it hurt you to see me dreaming of better things because it only leads to disappointment," I remind him.

Jett lowers his gaze. "That was then. Before I knew the world was so full of possibility and chance. Our life with the circus was so sheltered. My eyes are open now, Flo, and I believe in this. I believe in you."

I blink, and tears fall. Jett brushes them from my cheeks. "We can go speak to Ava now," he suggests. "She's sitting at the campfire."

I let him pull me to my feet. "Maybe the brothers found something, too," I say, wondering what the file held for them.

"Maybe," Jett says. And we head over to the campfire to find out.

25
THERE'S BAD EVERYWHERE

Lance and Lucas are sitting around the campfire with the rest of the group, including Ava.

Quinn joins us, informing us that Ivy and Rain are staying inside.

I look down at Jett's hand in mine, his thumb tracing circles on my skin.

It was heartbreaking to see Rain yesterday with the knowledge that my sister was in the labs at that age. I know I have to get Wren out. But I also know I can't do it without help. With Quinn still here, I hope he and Ava can give some ideas as to how I might achieve that. And Jett had a point—why would Ava tell me if there was no chance of freeing her?

Jett and I sit beside the brothers. "You two okay?" Jett asks.

Lucas nods. "There was nothing in the file for us."

"Me neither," Jett says.

The brothers look to me then. "My parents are dead," I tell them, my voice shaking. "I have a little sister, though. And she's still there."

Lucas gasps under his breath. Lance hangs his head, his chin almost touching his chest. "So what do we do?" Lucas says.

Lance looks up. "Yeah—we can't just leave her there."

I smile weakly at my friends. "No," I say. "I can't. But it isn't something that needs to involve everyone. Keeping all of you safe is just as important as getting her back."

"Flo," Lucas says, placing his hand lightly on my shoulder. "Whatever it takes, we're helping you. Since the moment we ran from the circus, since the moment we *met,* we've been in this together."

Lance nods. "He's right, Flo. The two of us will always be there for you and Jett."

I fight the urge to cry, blinking hard.

"Thanks, guys," Jett says quietly. "Same goes for us."

Lucas clears his throat, and I notice everyone else in camp is watching us, listening. Lola's eyes shine with tears.

"Flo," Ava says. "We should talk soon. Do you want to do it here or in private?"

I can feel everyone's eyes on me, but I trust my friends and I don't want to keep things from them. I need them. "Here," I say.

Ava nods. "Okay. Well, we know Lucas and Lance's parents are now deceased, as are Jett's, and there's no easy way of knowing if anyone else has anyone related to them in any of the numerous facilities owned by the EOS." She takes a breath. "For that, I am sorry. I would have liked to have delivered more good news. But the reason I sent Quinn and Ivy in search of Flo is that I did have news for her. It is true that Flo has a sister in the labs."

"Do you know how I can get her back?" I ask.

"*We*," Kanna corrects.

"No, I can't—" I begin, but Kanna cuts me off.

"This is nonnegotiable, Flo. We've been through too much not to band together when one of us needs help— whatever the cost. You came for me when the hunters took me. You helped Lola find her sister. We'll help you find yours."

"It's nice to see such loyalty among a pack, and I've no doubt you've earned it with everything you have all been through," Ava says. "It is no doubt a risk to try to rescue Flo's sister—are you all prepared to do whatever it takes?"

"Her name is Wren," I say. "And I am."

"Me, too," Jett adds.

"We all want to help," Lola says. "In any way we can."

"That's good to hear," Ava says. "It is what I had hoped to hear. And Quinn and I are willing to work alongside all of you to free Wren."

I turn to look back at Ava and narrow my eyes. "Why?" I ask.

I figured she wouldn't have shown me the file if there was nothing I could do. I figured the two of them might be able to share some information to help us. But I didn't expect her to offer it up without wanting something in return.

"Because she's—" Ava begins.

"Why?" I repeat, cutting her off.

Ava laughs nervously. "Flo, I—"

"What do you want in return?"

Ava glances at Quinn. "Well . . . the circus," she says.

182

I frown. I don't understand. That's not what I was expecting her to say. I'm actually not sure what I was expecting her to say, but the circus—what does that mean?

The circus is gone.

"I don't understand," I say. I look to the others, but they all seem as confused as I am.

"I want to start over," Ava confesses. "But I want to do it *right* this time."

"You've got to be joking!" Lucas says.

Ava raises a hand. "Now, hear me out. . . . It wouldn't be like it used to be. Hari and Nora are both gone—neither of them will have anything to do with it, ever. We'll go somewhere else, somewhere far from here that the old circus has never touched. It'd be a fresh start, where nobody knows us. We'll start off small, we'll grow and recruit—shifters who *want* to join. And we'll leave all the bad behind."

"There's bad everywhere," Jett says, his tone flat.

"Then we'll beat it back," Ava retorts. "Flo, what do you think? I'll help you if you help me."

I shake my head slowly. "You're unbelievable," I say. "You offer me the one thing I can't turn my back on, then ask me the one thing I could never say yes to. Of course I'm not going to join your circus! None of us are."

"Think about it," Ava says quickly. "It wouldn't be anything like before, I swear to you it wouldn't. Just think about it. Take all the time you need."

"It's not like I have a lot of time *to* think about it." I shake my head again. "Every second I spend deciding what to do is another second Wren is stuck at Roll Point. You've put me in the most impossible situation."

"Is it so impossible, though?" Ava asks, tilting her head to one side. "Was the circus really that bad?"

"You killed shifters and took their orphaned children for your show! *Yes*, it was that bad," I snap.

Ava grimaces. "Flo, it's not going to be like that. It will never be like that. Just, please, give it some thought."

I gesture toward Quinn, ignoring Ava's pleas. "What does he get out of all this?"

"Rain," Ava says simply.

"Ivy already has Rain," I state. "What's keeping him here now?"

The rest of the group watch our exchange in silence. I want to look over at them, see what they're thinking, how they're reacting, but I don't want to take my eyes away from Quinn and Ava.

"I have their weapons and their word. Quinn and Ivy agreed to help if I came through with Rain," Ava says. "And I did."

I pull my hand from Jett's and lean forward. "So there's *nothing* holding him to it?"

"We have an agreement," Quinn cuts in.

"That doesn't mean very much," Kanna says.

She's right—how can we trust either of them? And how can we make promises to people we don't fully trust?

"Ivy and Rain are still on site. They aren't leaving until things are in motion," Ava reassures.

I wish I knew exactly what everyone else was thinking right now. Rescuing Wren could mean we all have to join Ava's new circus—can I really ask that of them? Can I actually do that myself? We escaped that life once.

Are we really all about to welcome it back? It was *my* performance that went wrong—my act that set all of this in motion. How can I go back with that hanging over me? I don't know if I'd be able to perform again—ever.

We'd be captive again. For how long? A few years? Forever? We might never get to leave and lead our own lives. But none of us truly know what we want other than safety, security, the chance to hide away together and live. This could still give us that, in some way.

It's not like I can rescue Wren alone, either. Getting in and out of the labs without Quinn's help would be impossible.

"Dale was family," Quinn adds flatly, like he's trying to keep emotion out of his voice. "I cared about him a lot. I've known Ava for years, and I care about her, too. If I say I'm going to help, I mean it."

I suppose Quinn and Ivy could have taken Rain at any moment. But they surrendered their weapons to Ava and helped her with this in exchange for Rain being returned for them. It feels like they're on her side, on our side. Mostly.

Ava stands. She gestures for Quinn to do the same. "We'll give you all some time to talk things over. Think carefully about this, Flo—it might be your best and only chance to save your sister."

My jaw twitches and I look away, because I know she's right.

26
DISGUISE

I stand up, too, and head in the opposite direction of Ava and Quinn.

"I need a minute," I tell the others. "Just to clear my head. I won't be long."

Jett hurries after me. "Flo," he says. When I don't respond, he reaches for my hand. "Flo, wait." I stop walking and turn to look at him. We're only a little way from the campfire; everyone can most likely still hear us. "We need to make this choice together."

"We will—" I begin.

"No, you're going to make it on your own. You'll come back to the campfire with your mind made up—I know you, Flo!"

"I can't talk about it right now! It's too much to take in. I don't want to make the wrong choice."

"There's only two ways this can go," he tells me. "We make it on our own in a world we're not experienced in navigating, or we put our trust in someone who's betrayed us once before."

"See how hard it is!"

"It's not hard for me," he says. "I already know exactly which option I'd choose—the one with your sister in it. Here, with us. With you."

"I couldn't put all my trust in Ava," I say, shaking my head. "I don't want to transfer my sister from one bad situation to another and drag the rest of the pack down with us."

"Could you live with Ava? Could you live at the circus?" Jett asks me. The question feels impossible to answer.

"I don't know," I say, throwing up my hands. "I could never trust her, not fully. Maybe I could learn to live with her. Maybe I could learn to live that way again, if she sticks to her word that it will be different. She'd have to involve us in everything."

Jett takes my other hand. "Seems like whichever option we choose, we'll be looking over our shoulders all the time. If we couldn't put our guard down in camp with Ava, then should we take a chance and go out on our own? Lola, Kanna, Jax, and Hugo have experience in the wild—they'll help us adjust. But that means it's just us. And it means leaving Wren at the lab, at least until we think of another way to get her out."

I squeeze my eyes shut, hating to admit this. "What hope would we have of getting in and out of the lab without Ava and Quinn?"

"Not much, it seems," Jett confirms. "Probably not any."

I look over his shoulder at the pack around the campfire. They're not talking among themselves, so I know they're listening to us.

"Can I really ask everyone to do this just so I can have my sister back?" I whisper.

"You know they would."

I take my hands from Jett and run them through my hair. "What do you think?" I ask him.

"That it's your choice," he says. "And I'm by your side no matter what. We all are."

"Would you want to be in the circus again?"

"No," he admits, and I'm glad he's being honest. "But maybe I can deal with it if it's different. If we can have some control over the way things are run. If it means we're together. And with your sister, too."

I look past him, past the camp, over at Ava and Quinn sitting on the steps outside her trailer. "Ava still has hunter connections," I comment. "It's likely some of them will still know who we are, where we are. We aren't disappearing into the wild, we're back to hiding in plain sight, under the disguise of the circus. It'll be hard to adjust to that now that we realize how real the danger is."

Jett nods. "It will," he says. "But we've learned a lot, too. We can make things safer for ourselves."

"We could die at the circus," I say.

"We could die in the wild," Jett counters.

I smile weakly. "It sounds like you want to do this."

"I don't feel strongly about either option. Our choices kind of suck. It's just choosing which will keep us safest, and which will get your sister back. That's the only thing driving me toward one more than the other."

"So the circus?" I say.

Jett nods. "I think so."

27
THE DEAL

"If we do this," I say to the group, "everyone has to agree to join Ava's show."

Lola starts to nod. "We already said we'd do what it takes to help you."

"There'll be a bird show for you and Kanna," I say. "Back to balancing on podiums for the elephants. The tiny bicycle for Jett." I leave Jax and Hugo out, still not sure where they stand in all of this.

"Sparkly waistcoats and hats," Jett says. "Bright lights and loud music."

"Can I really ask that of all of you, after everything we've been through to break away?" I say.

"Flo," Hugo says, speaking up for the first time. The breakfast dishes are piled up on the bench beside him, soapsuds drying on his forearms. "Things haven't exactly been easy for any of us—ever. We go from one thing to the next, whatever benefits us most at the time, whatever keeps us alive. Ava's idea for the circus will take some getting used to, but I'm there for you. I'm with you on this. With all of you. As long as we're together . . ."

"Agreed," Jax says. "As long as we're together. Like Kanna said before: you helped Lola find her when the hunters took her. You helped me find Hugo. We've been a team for a while now."

Lola and Kanna nod their agreement. "And a good one," Lola says.

"We tried to join the circus once," Kanna adds with a shrug. "So why not? All else we'd be doing is trying to find somewhere to settle. Maybe we can settle with the circus for a while."

My heart fills with their words and I look to the brothers. This'll be the most painful for them—going back to their act with one member missing. Lucas notices the shift in attention. "If we change the act," Lucas says. "Only if we change the act. We can't . . ."

"We can't do the same as we used to do—the same performance we gave with Logan," Lance finishes for his brother. "So if we change that, we'll join again if it means you get your sister back."

I nod. "We'll make sure that act is changed," I say quietly.

"And be clear with Ava," Lola says. "The only way we will join is if Wren makes it back to us. If anything happens along the way or has already happened to her, if you fail to get her, the deal is off. We only do this if Wren is with us."

"I will," I whisper. "Thank you."

I think about Ursula, Star, Owen, Ruby, and Itch. They didn't want to join the pack in the mountains, but another circus? Would they have stayed if they'd known about this? Owen *loved* being a lion tamer. Could Ruby go back to working the door as the bearded lady once again? And Star—would she be allowed to perform in this new circus, even before she turned sixteen? I know she'd want to. Owen and Ursula would make an amazing double act in their zebra shapes, but they never got the chance before because Owen's still fifteen. Their practices were always impressive, but they never did make it out into the ring together.

I wonder if we'd ever be able to find them and ask. I wonder if I'll ever see any one of them again.

I banish the thought, knowing there's too much else to focus on. And it's too sad to think about when I know the answer to my question is *probably not*. We probably won't see them again. I knew that when they left, but it's still hard to think about.

"So what now?" Jett says.

"We should spend the day thinking on it," I reason. "Just to be sure. We'll tell Ava our decision tonight."

WHERE WE STARTED

Lola and Kanna go out flying.

Jax takes a nap in his tent, and Hugo gathers a towel and soap and finishes washing up. Quinn and Ava haven't come back over to the camp, staying in and around their trailers until we're ready to talk to them.

I can see Ava keeps looking over at us impatiently.

I'm pretty certain we're going to agree once the day is up. How could I not? And Ava probably knows that.

Jett and the brothers sit around the campfire with a pack of cards. I retire to my own tent to lie down and think about what's ahead of us. I just keep seeing a blurred image of my sister beside me, running from the labs and straight into the circus ring.

I turn onto my side, but I can't get comfortable.

I sit up and shuffle toward the tent flap, dragging a blanket along with me to take back outside. I'm restless and don't know what to do with myself.

As I start unzipping the tent, I hear my name mentioned. I stop and stay still, peering through the gap in the zipper.

"Yeah," Jett says. "I trust Flo and will stand by her—always. But now that we're involving sneaking into the labs . . . I'm trying, but it's hard for me to step back with something like that."

"It's her sister," Lucas says. "I'd go into the lab for Lance—I'd do whatever it took."

I see Jett nod. "You're right," he says. "I know Flo can take care of herself and that there's a lot of support here for her. I just hate walking headfirst into danger beside her. I want to keep her safe—to keep all of us safe."

"She's got to do this," Lance says.

"I know," Jett says. "And I know what it's like to be targeted by hunters at a young age. Knowing Wren has been in those labs since she was born, knowing that is all she has ever known, makes me want to help her even more."

"What about the hunter?" Lucas says. "Can we trust him? And Ava too?"

There's a stretch of silence. "I don't know," Jett finally replies, almost too quiet for me to make out. "Probably not. But at the same time, it feels like everyone is getting something out of it: Quinn and Ivy get to leave with Rain, Ava gets her circus, and Flo gets her sister. Everyone wants to see this succeed."

The brothers nod. "Then it's decided. We trust Flo to make the right choices. We do what she wants on this."

Jett sighs. "I'd love to gather up our stuff and run. But this is Flo's sister we're talking about—she'd never leave and I'd never want her to. You're right—we have to see this through."

"Just be on our guard," Lucas suggests.

"Always," Jett says. "Besides, look where running got us—right here, back where we started."

29
ALONE

Night falls.

We're sitting around the campfire, finishing dinner.

I sit beside Jett, replaying his earlier conversation with the brothers in my head. Knowing that they all put their trust in me the way they do is encouraging and also added weight. I don't want to let them down. I don't want to make the wrong choices for the group.

"So what now?" Kanna asks as we stack our dinner plates to wash.

"I guess we should call Ava and the hunter back," Lucas says.

They're both outside the trailers, so I wave over to them.

Ava catches the movement immediately and rushes over. "Well?" she asks. "Have you reached a decision?"

I take a breath. "We will *only* join if we get Wren back. If whatever plan we come up with fails, we'll—"

"Try again," Ava says hopefully. "We'll keep trying until we get her and we won't start the circus without her."

I frown. "Right. But no Wren, no circus. We're clear?" Ava nods. "And there will be changes," I add. "Starting with Lucas and Lance's act. They won't be performing the same way they used to as three."

"Absolutely," Ava says enthusiastically. "Of course, we can do that. I've already had some new ideas."

"Okay, then. Well that's it for now. I'm sure we'll have a lot more to talk about once we get Wren back," I finish.

Ava clasps her hands together. "So you're all agreed?" she asks.

"Yes," I say. I rub my hand over my face, suppressing a groan. I hate that I just agreed to the circus, but the next move is to plan a way to get my sister back where she belongs. I focus on that thought and forget about what comes after. "So what would be the plan—do you have one?"

Quinn steps forward. "We do," he says. "I will take you in—officially. To Roll Point."

"No," Jett and Lola say right away, at the same time. "Absolutely no way," Jett adds. Lucas shoots him a look, a reminder of their earlier conversation I assume, but Jett ignores him. "We thought you'd sneak us in, not walk Flo through the front door."

"That's too dangerous," Lola says.

"Wait," I say, holding up my hand. "Let's just hear all of what he has to say first." I turn to Quinn. "You take me inside—then what?"

"They'll register you," Quinn says. "You'll be wearing fake silver cuffs. Everyone arrives in cuffs so they can't shift. Once we're inside the doctor's room—where all new SuperNats go right away, you can slip your hands out of the cuffs and my pass will get us through the lab and to your sister. You'll have to do that bit alone, though. I can't be involved in the actual rescue part, which is why I can't save Wren alone, or sneak you all in. I need Flo. I need to go in with a purpose and make it look like I've captured her. They have cameras everywhere."

So I have to go into the lab. Alone.

Jett isn't so convinced, now that we know it's just me and not the whole group. And I get it—I'd hate to stay out here while he went inside an EOS lab. But I kind of prefer it this way. It means I'm not putting anyone else in danger when I go in for Wren. It means I can focus on her and not have to worry about the others.

"This needs more thought," Jett says. "It's too vague. Flo needs to know how the passes work, how many doors she'll have to go through before she gets to Wren, how many staff members she might come across, and the quickest way out from Wren's cell."

I smile at him. "You thought of everything."

"Yes," Quinn says sarcastically. "It's lucky we have him here—I'd never have thought of those things otherwise." He pauses. "Of *course* it needs more. I've got it figured out but thought I'd share the details once I told you the basic idea."

Jett folds his arms. "Well write me into it because I'm coming, too."

"No you're not!" Quinn says. "You aren't invited."

"Who's going to stop me?" Jett retorts.

"I am!" Quinn fires back. "I can't take you along. For starters, they won't keep a bear in the labs—got too many already. You would be allowed in the main building but, obviously, they wouldn't allow you to leave. You'd be eliminated."

I shake my head and place my hand on his arm. "You can't come, Jett—he's right."

Jett scowls at Quinn. "How do we know they won't eliminate Flo?"

"Horses aren't as common as bears—nowhere near," Quinn says simply. "And they want this one. Sent a whole team after her."

"Wait!" I say. "I heard Dale say that Head Office wanted me dead. What changed?"

"Your parents died," Quinn says. "Your mother only recently. Your sister is the only horse left at Roll Point. You've caused them problems, but they no longer hunt to kill you—they want you in captivity, Flo."

I take a deep breath. *Your parents died. Your mother only recently.* I picture her face, slip my hand into my pocket to brush against the photograph of her there.

"Quinn," Ava says quietly. "Think about what you're saying."

Your sister is the only horse left. She's only ever known the lab. If she's the only horse, I wonder how much extra testing she has to endure because there are no more of her species to spread it among. I don't know how it works, and I don't want to know. All I know is that my sister is suffering and has known nothing else for thirteen years.

I clear my throat. I need to concentrate on getting Wren outside, not on what she's endured inside. "So what else?" I say, speaking loudly to cover my sadness.

"I need to take you in soon or my team will get suspicious," Quinn says. "I've been gone a while—since the attack on the mountain pack. I'm only taking Flo inside and it needs to be soon. That's the deal."

The use of the word *deal* brings so many bad memories crashing down that I wonder what I'm getting myself into. Should I really be agreeing to this? Should I really be handing so much over? But what I'll get in return if I succeed is my *sister*. I have to do this for her, for both of us.

Ava looks to Quinn. "We'll start getting the plans in order. Right away," she says, and then looks back to us. "Like Quinn says, he's been gone a while—we need to head for Roll Point as soon as possible. Preferably tomorrow."

Tomorrow?

I open my mouth to protest, but think of my sister and close it again. If Quinn and Ava have already spent time sorting through this and planning the rescue, and can bring me up to speed in time, then why not tomorrow? I'd go *now* if I could.

Quinn nods. "I have a few things in the trailer. We should take this conversation inside. Besides," he says, looking up at the sky. "It's going to rain."

30
BEHIND THE CURTAIN

"This is all happening too quickly," Jett says as we follow Quinn to Ava's trailer.

"It has to," I tell him. "I know it's rushed, but we don't have time."

Jett slows his pace and takes my arm. "Flo, I hate this."

I squeeze my eyes shut. "I know," I breathe. "I do, too. But I can't think about anything but Wren. I can't go a minute without thinking what it must be like for her there, what her life must have been like. Nothing can stop me from getting her back."

"Hunters could," Jett says. "High-security could. Silver could. Think about it. Just promise me you won't rush into this if the plan isn't solid."

"You heard what Quinn said!" I say, my voice rising. "I have to go soon. I've done all the thinking I need to. I know you don't like it—neither do I—but I'm going when Quinn says the word. If it means facing all those things again, then fine. It's worth it."

I walk away, picking up my pace to keep up with Quinn. Jett is close behind.

When we reach the trailer, Quinn turns around before letting us in. He looks over my shoulder. "Oh good," he says to Jett. "You're here."

I look between the two of them. "Are you staying?" I ask Jett.

He nods. Quinn scowls and goes inside. The door swings shut behind him.

I turn back to Jett. "I thought you were all for me getting Wren back?"

"I was," Jett says. "I *am*! I was just more enthusiastic about the idea when I thought we'd be going in as a team. Before I knew only you could go and that it's going to happen tomorrow!"

"I understand," I tell him, resting my palm on his forearm. "So what do you suggest?"

Jett sighs. "That we go inside and make sure this plan is tight so you'll come back to me when this is all over."

I lean forward and touch my lips to his, running my hand up his arm and around to the back of his neck. He puts his arms around my waist and pulls me to him. It feels like our first kiss; it feels like our last kiss. Jett's fingers press lightly into my back, like there's not enough time. There's never enough time.

When we part, I'm breathless. Jett smiles softly and takes my hand. He raises it to his lips and kisses my knuckles, his eyes on mine. "Promise you'll come back," he says.

"I promise," I breathe. The words are almost inaudible, but I mean them. I believe in them. I say them again. "I promise."

Jett takes a step back and opens the trailer door for me. Ava's sitting inside on the cushioned bench. Quinn has an array of papers on the main table.

"Come, sit," Ava says. "We're just looking at the Roll Point blueprints. I had Quinn get the floor plan for me when I first found out about your sister."

I can't help but frown. She's been planning this out, even before I agreed to it. Even before she found me. Ava obviously wants this circus as much as I want my sister.

I straighten my face and take a seat across from her. Jett slides onto the bench beside me. Quinn sits next to Ava. "Your sister's on the third floor," he says. "I'll be escorting you to the second. So you'll have to go up one when I cut you free."

I examine the large blue sheet rolled out on the table between us. I watch Quinn's hand as he points to each floor. A mug sits at each corner of the blueprint, holding it in place. The layout is made of thin white lines on a blue gridded background, different areas and rooms coded. I look at Level 2 and my eyes trace the journey up to 3.

"Are the doors to the stairways locked?" I ask. I see several sets of stairs. I place my finger on what looks to be the main staircase to all floors. "This one?"

Quinn shakes his head. "You'll almost definitely be seen if you go up there. You don't need a key card for the main staircase or the fire escape stairwells, but you do to access the floor facilities on each level. You'll take mine when you escape from me."

"What about getting back out?" Jett asks.

"There's a set of stairs here," Quinn says, pointing to the plans. The stairwell is on the opposite side of the building to the one I'll go up from second level to third. "Wren's room is along here," he says. "The emergency exit stairway will lead you right down to the ground floor and you can get out the door you'll see there."

I rub my forehead. "Okay," I say.

"Don't worry—we'll go over all of this again and again until we're completely clear on each step. The emergency exits are signposted. Once you're in the stairwell, it's just a straight run down and out."

"What's the security like on that exit?" I ask. "Alarms?"

"There's no key code or swipe system to leave the floor, in case of emergency evacuation. But there are alarms and guards outside it, and they will be armed."

"Then how—?"

"I'll have sympathizers stationed there. I'll inform them and they won't stop you. You can outrun the backup the alarms will bring. The facility will rely on the guards already stationed there to stop you escaping—no one will know they let you go. This is why it's so important that you leave on *this* stairwell," he says, pointing to it again. "You must *not* go back the way you go in."

I nod. "How much authority do you have?"

"Enough to help you through this," he says. "I run ops, lead my own team, have some say in how they're positioned around the labs when we're not on field duty."

"And where will non-sympathizers be while all this is happening? You know, the ones who won't hesitate to kill Flo and her sister," Jett says. I flinch at his words and he angles himself slightly toward me, taking my hand in his under the table.

"It's unlikely that anyone would straight up kill her inside the labs," Quinn says, irritation clear in his voice. "We use tranquilizers first. The mission would be to recapture."

"And if they couldn't catch me?" I ask quietly.

"Flo," Quinn says. "You know the answer. We all know the risks here."

A muscle moves in Jett's jaw, but he doesn't say anything. Quinn turns to address Ava, their heads bent together over the unrolled blueprint. Jett watches them silently. I look out of the window beside me as it begins to rain.

The murmur of Quinn and Ava's conversation fills the small trailer. I catch snippets as they discuss the hunters who'll be stationed outside my emergency exit. Ava gives her approval.

The rain picks up, marking the window and distorting the view of the forest. There's something relaxing about it. Like I'm somewhere it can't touch me. Where nothing can touch me. Hidden behind the curtain at the circus where no one could see me. I close my eyes and listen to it for a moment. I wonder if Wren has ever seen rain. I wonder if she's ever been outside.

"Flo?" Quinn says. "Are you still with us?"

I open my eyes. "Yes, of course." I sit up straighter.

"Okay," Ava says. "Let's run things through again now that we're clear on the exit plans. Unless you have any questions?"

"Some," I say. "Maybe. Let's run through and I'll ask as they come up."

Ava nods. "Quinn," she says.

Quinn clears his throat. "We'll pull up at the gate—you'll be cuffed."

"Who's at the gate?" I ask. I notice Jett shift in his seat beside me, sitting up and paying close attention to all the little details we're going over now.

"There will be two guards controlling the gate," Quinn answers. "They won't be on our side. They'll ask for some information about you, then should send us through."

"To the doctor?" I ask.

"Yes," Quinn confirms. "On the second floor. I'll take you to her and she'll take a blood sample and some other things—I can't remember."

"Try," Jett cuts in, his voice harsh.

I nod my agreement. "I need to know what she'll do."

Quinn raises his eyebrows, holding his hands up in front of him. "I don't know. Truly. I usually stand outside the room for the majority. Or sit in the corner while she works—I don't pay attention to her procedures."

I glance at Ava and she shrugs one shoulder. "It can't be helped, Flo," she says. "Quinn's tried to remember, but he's no expert on that side of things."

"Is it always the same person?" I ask. "Do you know her well?"

"We all have a doctor to report to," Quinn says. "She's part of my team now. So there are more, but I always go to her."

"She's not a sympathizer?"

"Definitely not."

"If we don't know what the doctor is going to do to Flo, how do we know she won't give her something like the tranquilizer serum?" Jett says. "She can't be unconscious at any point—I don't think I need to explain *why*."

"I'd wake up in a cell," I breathe. "And it'd all be over."

Quinn extends his arms. "Now, wait a minute. No one is getting knocked out.

Ava puts both hands on the table in front of her, her fingertips touching the blueprint. "It's going to work. Quinn and I have been planning this before we even picked you up," she says. "I wouldn't let Flo go if I didn't think she'd be able to get back out."

"And what's the backup plan?" Jett asks. Our fingers are laced together, our hands resting on his thigh. "If something does go wrong—what do we do then? I could never leave her there, you know that."

Ava smiles calmly. "We wouldn't leave her, Jett. We'd come up with a way to get her and Wren out again." She turns her gaze to me. "Flo, get a couple hours of rest and we'll wake you when it's time to leave. We can go over the plan again on the journey to the facility and make sure we're all clear on route and strategies. Yes?"

"All right," I say, even though I know I'm letting her control me again. It feels just like it did back at the circus the night we figured out hunters were watching us. She told me what to do then, and it all worked out for the worst. What's she doing now? Is she genuine this time? I have to believe she is, because she wants the new circus and this is her way of getting it.

31
DARKNESS

I lie inside my tent, wrapped in Jett's arms.

He leaves soft kisses on the back of my head, my neck. His body, pressed against mine, is warm. Safe. My back is against his chest, my head resting on his arm, my mind somewhere else entirely.

Wren. The lab. It's all I can think about.

The lines of the blueprint are etched to the backs of my eyelids. Every time I close my eyes, I see them, see the layout, see the obstacles between my sister and me. There's no way I can sleep.

Jett's breathing slows as he drifts off, getting some much-needed rest. His arms loosen slightly as he relaxes into slumber. I try to follow him there, hoping to escape my thoughts and to get some rest before I leave for Roll Point, but I can't. My mind is too active, running over everything that I'll do tomorrow.

I slip outside, craving some fresh air around the campfire, some time alone before this all starts. I'm careful not to wake Jett.

The campfire is low and I carry a few extra logs over. "Thanks," Ava says as I approach. I startle in the dark, then throw the logs on, poking them with a stick until they catch.

"I didn't realize you were out here," I say. She is sitting mostly in the shadow cast by the low flames.

"Couldn't sleep," she says. "You too?"

I sit down beside the fire.

Rubbing her hands together, she says, "Do you feel like you can trust me with this?"

"Not totally," I admit. "I know you want the circus, but I don't know why you want us. I'm having trouble fully understanding what you're doing."

"I'm being open with you, Flo," she says. "I know it's hard to take my word for it, after everything. But I want the circus, and all of you in it. There's nothing more."

A moment of silence passes between us. The logs crackle as they catch fire.

"I never wanted the circus at first," Ava says with a small smile. "It was all Hari's idea. But once we'd set up, I kind of felt like it was what I was supposed to do. Sometimes I even forgot the threat of the hunters and enjoyed having this pack, this family to call my own and work alongside in making something successful."

I rest my elbows on my knees and hold my head in my hands. I don't know what to say.

"There was some time where we were really popular, you know. But there was always that dark side to it. My memories are tainted, and I want it all back without that darkness. I want to help rebuild the good parts of it, the parts where the shifters in our care felt safe. Make it a home—a place shifters can come and find shelter and family, and perform to earn it. It's the only way I know how to live."

"It's the only way we've ever known, as well," I tell her. "But we wanted something new, something of our own. And now we've traded that to go right back to the beginning with you."

Ava wipes her eyes. "I don't have anything anymore. My brother and sister are gone. Dale's gone. I'm sorry if you didn't want to be found, but the circus children are still important to me—still family to me, even after everything." She looks at me. "Do you remember when you first arrived at the circus?"

I shake my head.

"Hari brought you and introduced you to Nora and me. You squirmed in his arms, wanting to be put down. You were always going somewhere."

I turn away, hiding the tears that spring to my eyes.

"As soon as Hari lowered you to the ground, you took off and ran face-first into the elephant triplets, who'd come over to see what was happening. Those three were as curious as they were mischievous, even then. You and Lucas bumped heads and both fell on your backsides. Lucas started to cry and his brothers helped him up, leaving you there on the ground. Jett rushed over to help Lucas, but then he saw you. He pulled you to your feet and the two of you have been inseparable since."

"I don't remember all the details," I tell her.

"You were so young," she says. "I looked after you a lot when you first got to the circus, but as you grew a little, so did your confidence and your friendship with Jett. Then you were off on your own, fitting right into day-to-day life there. You were happy."

"I didn't know I'd been taken from my parents, or that they'd been sent to the labs with my sister."

Ava lowers her head. "And that's what I want to take away from the new circus. I want the happiness, the growing and learning and sense of community. It's my chance to do something right by myself."

She gets to her feet. "You should try and get a little sleep before we go. I'll come wake you in a few hours."

32
NO SAFER PLACE

"Flo?"

I returned to my tent after Ava left the campfire, but I don't remember falling asleep.

It's still dark out. Ava taps at the side of the tent. "Flo?" she whispers. "Are you ready?"

No, I think. *I'm not ready. But I have to be.*

I groan quietly and roll onto my side, Jett's arm still draped over me. I gently lift it off me and sit up. It's time for me to go to the EOS lab and for Jett to stay here in Ava's camp. The thought brings a fresh wave of panic, which I hurriedly shove back down.

"I'll be out in a minute," I say quietly, my voice hoarse from sleep.

I softly shake Jett awake. He blinks, forcing his tired eyes to open. I put my hand on his face. "Go back to sleep," I whisper. "I just wanted to say bye to you. You don't need to get up."

He pushes up onto his elbows. "I do," he says. "Is it time?"

I nod, then realize it's too dark for him to see me. "Yes," I reply. "It's time."

212

He pulls me close and buries his face in my neck. He kisses me there, like he did last night and the night before. I tip my head back. "I have to go."

"I know," he says sadly.

"I'll be okay," I reply, kissing him lightly. "You know I will. Here—" I unclasp my necklace and drop it into his hand— "Look after this for me. Give it to me again when I get back."

"Flo—"

I close his hand around the chain. "I don't want to lose it."

He runs his free hand down my arm. "All right. I'll keep it safe for you. Come on."

I'm already dressed—I went to sleep in my clothes—so I pull on my boots and coat and climb out of the tent. I look up at the clear sky and wonder what time it is and what time we'll arrive at the lab.

I see a flashlight beam and two figures over by the van. I make my way over to it with Jett beside me.

"Flo," Quinn says. "Pick up the pace—we have to get moving."

"It's still dark out. Are the doctors even there in the middle of the night?"

"It's six-thirty in the morning," Ava says.

"Dark mornings are the worst," Quinn mumbles. I wonder how he became a leader at such a young age. Sometimes he seems ruthless, like a natural leader. Other times he seems childish, caught up in something he doesn't fully understand. But speaking to him, I've come to learn that he does understand. He's sure of what he's doing and what he wants.

"We've got an hour's journey," Ava says. "The doctors arrive on site around eight thirty. We want to get in early so there's less staff in the building. That should minimize our chances of things going wrong."

I nod. "Okay. Thank you—for thinking of everything."

Ava tries to hold back her smile. She bows her head. "You're welcome. You'll have to ride in the back once we're close," she says apologetically. "But sit up front with us until then—okay? We can go over things together and make sure we're one hundred percent ready."

Quinn climbs into the van and starts it up. He turns the headlights on.

"Have you got the floor plans?" I ask.

Ava holds up the roll.

I turn to Jett and place my hand on his cheek. He leans into it. "It'll be fine."

Jett's expression is pained and I drop my hand.

"It's okay," Ava says, touching my arm. "I know this is happening fast and it's stressful and scary—for both of you. But I'm here and Quinn will help us, and I believe that this will work. That you'll get Wren back, and then . . ."

Ava trails off, but I finish her sentence for her. "And then we all join your circus."

"It's not going to be like last time," Ava says quietly. A moment passes in silence, and then she hugs me, surprising me. I keep my hands by my side. She lets go and takes a step back. "I promise."

I don't reply. She seems genuine, like she's trying to do the right thing. I can't believe she'd want to put me in danger, and I do believe that she wants the circus as much as I want my sister. Especially after what she told me last night.

"I think it's a beautiful name you chose for your sister, by the way," she says. "I see what you did—it's very clever and sweet."

I hear voices and turn to see the others making their way over. Lola waves. "We came to see you off."

"Yeah," Kanna says. "Good luck. We're looking forward to meeting Wren."

I smile at look at Ava. She's smiling, too. She glances back at the van before saying, "I've instructed the others to pack up and move my trailer to another site close by. Wait there until we get back." She looks to the group, her voice low. "Keep watch at all times. Be aware that Ivy is still here—she could alert Quinn of your movement. We'll leave as soon as we return."

"What's going on?" I say. "Has something happened?"

The driver door swings open and Quinn leans out. "Time to move," he says.

He shuts the door again and Ava's startled expression relaxes a little. "What's going on?" I whisper.

She shakes her head. "Precautions," she says. "I don't want anyone to know where we're going other than us. Too many people—too many hunters—know where we're camped right now. Quinn has been a good friend, but once this is over, I want to separate myself from hunters entirely, no matter who they are."

Ava rounds the van and climbs into the passenger seat, leaving me to say good-bye to Jett and my friends. I remind myself that it's not good-bye, not really.

"What are you thinking?" Jett asks.

I offer a small smile. "About getting back here with Wren. Introducing her to everyone and telling her about our lives. Learning about her, letting her discover what she likes, who she is. I want her to be happy with me, Jett. I want her to be safe. Do you think she'll have all of that?"

"I can't think of a single place safer for her than with her big sister," he says. "Can you?"

I shake my head, with tears in my eyes. "No," I reply, my voice catching.

He steps forward and kisses my forehead. "Go get her," he whispers.

I take a step away from my friends, reluctantly turning my back on them. I wave as I climb into the van, then shuffle in beside Ava. She moves to make room for me. "See you soon," I say to the others.

"You will," Lola replies as I close the door.

THE AFTER

Ro sat beside the girl in the waiting room again.

She dipped her head and whispered, "Hello."

The first number was called. The girl took the movement as opportunity to reply. It was the first time she had since the gym. She glanced up and said, "Hello."

A small smile tugged at Ro's lips. She looked at the girl, at her unwavering gaze, like she wasn't afraid of anything.

But she was. She had to be.

They all were.

"Why did you run away last week?" Ro asked.

The girl shrugged. "I don't like to talk."

"About your life before the labs?" Ro prompted.

The girl shook her head but kept her eyes down. Ro glanced up to find one of the hunters watching them. She quickly looked away and didn't speak again until the next number was called. As others moved around the small room, Ro said, "I don't have any family. Not that I know of anyway."

"I do," the girl offered. "A big sister. My . . . my mother told me about her."

"Is she here?" Ro asked.

"No," the girl said. "I don't know where she is. The hunters . . ." She looked up and bit her lip. Lowering her voice, she continued. "The hunters took my parents and me and left Flo behind."

"Flo," Ro says. "It's a pretty name."

The girl nodded.

The door opened again and the guard called the girl's number. Ro had it memorized, like her own.

The girl stood and glanced at the guards. She turned back to Ro and lowered her voice. "I was called Hope," she whispered. "Before."

"That's still your name," Ro said.

The hunter called the girl's number again. "No, no," she said quickly. "Not now that they're gone."

33
THE PLAN

I study the floor plan, running the route with my fingertip.

Ava watches me.

"What if she's not there?" I ask. "Inside her cell."

"What?" Quinn says. "Why wouldn't she be? Where are these questions coming from? We've been over everything."

Ava puts her hand on Quinn's arm. His hands grip the steering wheel. "Quinn," she says softly. "We're nervous—you must understand that."

He shakes his head. "I do understand. I'm nervous, too. I don't want anything to go wrong, either—so trust me. She'll be there. Everything is done to a schedule. For the time we're there, Wren will be in her cell. Okay?"

I stay quiet. I don't like his tone. He might be nervous, but this is way bigger for me.

Ava clears her throat and answers for me. "Yes," she says. "Flo is just being cautious. It's important she feels confident."

"And do you?" Quinn asks me.

"Not entirely," I tell him, folding my arms over my stomach.

"Would it help to run over things again? The whole thing?"

"Yes," Ava and I say at the same time. She gives me a sideways glance and smiles. I still don't feel like I can return it, so I look away.

Quinn starts from the beginning—when we'll stop to cuff me, where we'll park, the gate. "Then I'll take you into the doctor's room," he continues. "I'll get her to leave—"

"How will you do that again?" I ask. "Is she likely to leave us in her room?"

"Quinn has organized for someone to call her away during your examination."

"What if she doesn't go?" I say.

"She'll go," Quinn says confidently.

I lean back on my chair. "This whole thing is . . . " I sigh. "It's insane."

Ava remains silent.

"Then why are you doing it?" Quinn asks.

"Because I want my sister back," I say simply. "This is my best chance, and I know if something goes wrong that my friends won't leave me, that they'll know what happened to me."

"I won't leave you," Ava adds.

I look at her and she nods. "So we're doing it," I finish. "No turning back."

"Then let *me* worry about the doctor," Quinn says. "You just worry about what comes next."

"Go over it," Ava prompts. "Focus on Flo's role now."

"When the doc leaves, hit me—not too hard." He shakes his head. "Then you'll take my card, like we said." He wrestles it out of his pocket and shows it to me. "This one."

"She should probably hit you hard," Ava says. "To make it seem more realistic."

Quinn glares at her and I turn my head toward the window, a smile tugging at my lips. "Then," Quinn says stiffly, "I'll need to raise the alarm, almost immediately. Too long and they'll get suspicious."

"Too soon and I'll get caught," I retort, whipping my head back around to face him.

"Right," he says. "So run fast. Up the stairs, to Wren's room, out the fire escape."

"I'll be in the van waiting," Ava says. "It's simple when we break it down like this, don't you think?"

I furrow my eyebrows. "Yes, but I doubt the rescue will happen exactly in line with our step-by-step plan. Do you?"

Ava hesitates for a moment. "It might."

Quinn says, "It will. Stop doubting it. If you keeping waiting for something to go wrong, it will go wrong."

I turn to look out of the window, the floor plan still unrolled across my lap, and pay attention to the direction we travel. I run things over in my mind without interruption from Quinn or Ava. I go over and over each step: through the gates, to the doctor, take Quinn's badge, go up a flight, Level 3, along the corridor, free Wren, out the fire escape, to the ground floor, and out the doors. The sympathizers will let us pass and I'll return to the van.

Ava will take Wren and me back to the others.

Then the whole group will leave to join the circus once more.

34
RIGHT AND WRONG

"We're close," Quinn says after a while.

It's still not light outside, but it's getting there.

"You're going to have to move to the back," Quinn tells me as he pulls over on the side of the road. I climb out, followed by Ava.

We go around to the back of the van and Quinn unlocks the two doors. I see a shape in the distance, floodlights bouncing off its white exterior. The lab.

Quinn climbs into the vehicle, pulling a duffel bag along the floor of the van.

Ava turns to me while Quinn is occupied. She grabs my hand and whispers, "Trust your instincts today, Flo. Take the cuffs off first chance you get. Don't let them strap you to anything or inject you with anything."

Quinn jumps down, cuffs in hand. His feet scuff the tarmac. He dangles the fake silver in front of him, looking at Ava. "Who wants to do the honors?"

Ava swats his arm. "This isn't a joke, Quinn."

"All right," he says, lowering the cuffs. "I know, I'm sorry. Just trying to lighten the mood."

Ava looks over at the building in the distance. "Let's all concentrate now."

I hold my hands out and Quinn steps forward. "Keep your wrists out of sight when we walk in there. It's unlikely, but I wouldn't want anyone to realize your skin wasn't burning."

I grit my teeth at his casual tone. He has no idea how much silver hurts us. None.

Quinn secures the cuffs around one of my wrists. "Try to get used to them because they'll be on you until you reach the doctor's office."

I nod. They're a little clunky but they're lightweight and fastened loosely.

"Take them off," Ava says.

I think of it like a circus trick and slip one hand out easily, then the other. The cuffs drop to the floor. "Done," I say with a smile.

"That was quick, Flo!" Ava praises. "Well done."

"It was quick," Quinn says and I see the "but" coming before it does. "But don't drop them in the lab. Hand them back to me. If anyone finds fake silver handcuffs, there will be questions."

I frown but nod. "I won't."

Quinn bends to pick the cuffs up from by my feet. He places them on my wrists again. He checks his watch. "We should go. Practice more on the way if you need to." He ushers me toward the back of the van. "But make sure they're secure before we stop," he adds.

I take my heavy construction coat and scarf off and throw it into the back, not wanting the extra layers to slow me down or affect my movements once I'm in the lab. I shiver a little in only my sweater, jeans, and boots. I try to keep my hands steady as I hold them out again so Quinn can put the cuffs there for the final time.

Hands bound, I climb back into the van. Quinn closes one door, then the other. I crouch in solid darkness, shuffling toward the back to find a place to sit for the rest of our journey.

The van starts up again, and now all I can do is wait.

35
THE DOCTOR

Only a short time passes until we stop.

The driver's door opens then slams shut. One set of footsteps comes around the side of the vehicle. The back doors open. The weak morning light slices through the darkness and I blink. I lift my bound hands to cover my face, my eyes stinging.

"Ready?" Quinn says. I nod in response. "Let's go."

I shuffle forward. "Where's Ava?"

"She's got to stay in the van. It's dangerous for her to be here, too."

I climb out of the van, into the morning. I stumble a little, my steps clumsier with my hands cuffed. Quinn links his arm through mine. "Sorry," he says. "Got to play the part now."

I nod. "I know. That's fine."

As we near the gate, Quinn tightens his hold on my arm, digging his fingers in. I suck in a breath. It doesn't hurt, just startles me. "Too hard?" he whispers.

"No," I whisper back, keeping my eyes trained forward.

As we get closer to the facility, I don't have to fake my fear.

We stop at the gate, but I don't see anyone around. I look up and see the cameras: two of them, pointing right at us. I look away.

"Q-two-seven-six," Quinn says. I look to his right and see a speaker on the wall. "With one SuperNat."

The speaker crackles. "Species?" a voice says.

Quinn pauses for a moment. This is it. "Horse," he says with confidence. "Female."

The voice on the other side of the speaker whistles. It comes through all static and high-pitched. Quinn scrunches his face up at the horrid sound. "Someone's going to be the favorite around here," the voice says.

Quinn smiles now, only briefly, but I catch it before he catches himself and wipes it from his face. I don't know why he smiles—the owner of the voice can't see him. Unless . . . I look up at the cameras again.

"She the one you've all been tracking?" the voice asks.

"She is," Quinn says, his manner returning to professional. "Let us in."

There's a beep and the gate starts sliding open, rattling as it does. Quinn and I move through it—Quinn first, then me roughly tugged forward to meet his pace. I pretend to struggle, in case anyone's watching.

"Quit it," Quinn snaps.

We're playing the part now.

He drags me through the courtyard and I look back at the tall barrier topped with barbed wire. More cameras are above us—on poles, on the walls—pointed in every direction, seeing *everything*.

There are cars parked in a small lot, but only a few. The parking lot outside the gate was quite empty, too.

A small strip of grass on either side of the entrance is the only area not white, gray, or black. We head for the glass doors, passing a guard stationed outside them.

"This place is well protected," I comment, noticing the guard's weapons belt. I recognize a tranquilizer, a silver gun, a pair of silver cuffs, a clearance badge, and a small radio. "Not easy to get in or out, is it?"

Quinn jostles me a little too hard. "Shut up."

I startle at his aggression. I'm about to respond when I realize we're close to the guard. The guard nods toward us and gestures we go through. The guard scans his pass on the door and Quinn thanks him.

Quinn and I walk through the foyer to a set of elevators, me following with my bound hands hidden behind him. There's not a lot to see, the room empty but for a man sitting behind a single desk. Two corners of the room are fitted with cameras, both pointing toward Quinn and me. I wonder who's watching us right now.

"Quinn," the man at the desk says. "Good to see you—your team has been worried."

Quinn nods. "Could you put out a message to them and schedule a meeting for later this afternoon?"

"Certainly," the man says. He picks up a phone and dials right away.

"Can you also put in a request for weapon replacements?" he asks as we walk past. "Lost mine in the field."

The man looks from me to Quinn. "Yes," he says. "Sure. I will do."

"Thanks, man."

Quinn calls the elevator. I make note of a set of stairs to my right, remembering them from the blueprints. I call up the plans in my mind, placing things according to the layout I pored over on the way here.

The elevator dings and the doors open soundlessly. Quinn and I step inside, then the doors close. Quinn still doesn't relax inside the elevator. I look around for a camera, but I don't see one. I turn toward Quinn, open my mouth, but he says, "Don't speak."

I scowl and turn away from him. Maybe there's a camera in here.

The elevator doors *ping* a second time and open to Level 2, and Quinn grabs my arm again and pulls me along with him out into the corridor. He roughly escorts me down several corridors that all look the same. I remember the layout from the floor plan and feel calmer knowing I can recall it all in my head. If I ran away now, I'd know exactly how to get out of here. But I'm not going anywhere without Wren.

We stop outside a door that reads: DR. J. FINCH. Quinn doesn't ask if I'm ready before he knocks and enters. He opens the door without waiting for a reply and looks inside.

"Quinn!" Dr. Finch says. "They called and said you were on your way up." She looks at me. "The horse. I'm so glad it was you who found her. Sit over there, will you?"

She's younger than I imagined her to be, with brown hair tied back in a neat bun and dark plum-painted lips.

She wears a white coat like Greg did, with a blouse that matches her lip color and black wide-legged pants beneath. Turning her back to us, she prepares a syringe.

I look wide-eyed toward Quinn. He doesn't echo my concern as he walks me over to a chair. I notice there are straps on the arms and legs.

Don't let them strap you to anything or inject you with anything.

I turn in Quinn's grip. His eyes are fierce. His expression tells me to play along, but I don't want to anymore. I shake my head no. He nods sharply: *yes.*

"Get her to leave," I hiss. "Your friend—where is he?"

Quinn looks toward the doctor. "What a lot of trouble you've caused," she says over her shoulder, her comment aimed at me.

She's lining up equipment, making notes on a clipboard beside her.

I slip out of cuffs on my wrists—I don't care if it's too soon. They clatter to the floor before I can catch them and the noise alerts Quinn. I kick them under the chair with the straps on the arms.

Quinn shoves me the rest of the distance to the chair. I crash into it and the doctor turns around as Quinn bends the retrieve the cuffs. I stumble a bit, but hurry to right myself. Quinn stands and tucks the cuffs into his pocket.

The doctor returns to preparing her equipment. I catch a glimpse of silver on the countertop in front of her. "I have to say, Quinn, this is all very exciting. To finally be working on this horse after all we've heard about her and her group. What did you do with the rest of them?"

"We captured and destroyed the ones that didn't get away," he says. I flinch, even though I know it's not true.

"Shame," Dr. Finch says. "No more for me?"

Quinn shakes his head even though she has her back to us. "Nothing else worth bringing in."

The doctor turns around and smiles. "Your team will get a lot of praise for this mountaintop mission of yours, Quinn. From what I've heard, it's been a great success."

Quinn smiles back at her. "It has."

The doctor turns back around and picks up the syringe and what looks like a silver cuff—just like the one Ivy placed on my wrist before we were forced into their van and taken to Ava. "We can start testing as soon as tomorrow." She nods toward the chair.

"Sit in the chair," Quinn says.

I shake my head at him. "Quinn, no," I whisper.

He pushes me back and pulls one of my arms toward the restraint. I push off from the seat, forcing him away.

"Hold her still, Quinn!" Dr. Finch says. Quinn grabs my arms, trying to pin me in place. This doesn't feel right. The doctor shouldn't still be here.

Trust your instincts.

I turn quickly and shove Quinn into the wall. It's surprise more than strength that knocks him back.

"What are you doing!" Dr. Finch shrieks. Her wide eyes look from Quinn to me. She reaches for a phone on the wall. "Do we need backup?"

No.

"No," Quinn says, standing. "I can handle it."

Dr. Finch looks between us again and, ignoring Quinn, pulls the receiver from the wall. I hurry toward her and swat it from her hand. It swings on its cord, hitting against the tiles. Dr. Finch tries to go around me, but I draw on my strength, on my other side, and knock her back, too.

I block her way, and I'm not really sure what I'm doing now. Quinn has failed on his part so I think I'm on my own now. Maybe I always was.

"Do something!" Dr. Finch yells at Quinn. An idea then seems to spark in her mind—her expression suddenly switching from panicked to determined. She turns rapidly and dashes for the syringe on the countertop she'd prepared for me moments ago. She snatches it up with one hand, reaching for the silver cuff with the other.

Quinn tries to grab my leg, but I move too quickly. His fingertips only graze my boots. I reach Dr. Finch and slam my hip against her, pinning her against the counter. The silver cuff drops to the floor and I wrestle the needle from her hand. She scratches my arm with it, drawing blood, but I get it free from her grip. "What is this?" I say. "What's in it?"

Quinn gets to his feet and advances. I hold the needle to Dr. Finch's skin. She puts her hand up to Quinn: *stop.*

"It's just something to calm you down," Dr. Finch says, her voice trembling. This can't be the first time she's been attacked by a desperate shifter in here.

I press the needle into her flesh and she releases a quiet scream. Maybe she didn't think I'd really do it—I didn't even know if I would. But here I am, pushing the end down and depositing the serum into her system.

"Flo!" Quinn yells.

Dr. Finch loses consciousness alarmingly fast, slumping in my arms. I let go and she drops to the floor. Quinn stands still at the other side of the room. "That was meant for you," Quinn says. "It's too large a dose for a human."

I look down at Dr. Finch. "She's still breathing," I tell him.

Quinn scowls. "That's not the point. I need to call someone—now."

"No!" I say. I pull the cord on the phone until it snaps.

"Flo! What is all this? This isn't our plan," Quinn says, his voice getting higher with shock, panic, or something else, I don't know.

"You weren't sticking to the plan!" I argue. "I didn't like where it was going."

"Well you've just made everything a hundred times worse."

"Then I need to move fast." I'm so close to my sister, I can't let this spoil anything. "Give me your access card. Shall I hit your face or . . . ?"

"No, Flo," he says. "Josephine needs medical attention."

I shake my head. "Give me a head start—just a couple seconds."

I look down at Dr. Finch—Josephine—then at the cut on my arm where she scratched me with the needle. Flesh wounds heal. Shifters' bodies fight against infection and poison. Shifters aren't invincible—silver can stop us, can kill us—but we are strong.

Humans, though. Humans are fragile. The hunters have to use something strong to take us down, to fight our healing strength and sink into our veins so we slip into unconsciousness. And now I've put that inside Josephine. Her system won't fight it like mine would. It can't.

A twinge of regret tugs at me, but there was no time to think. It was Quinn's fault as much as mine—he pushed me to act. I look back up at him and he lowers his eyebrows. I suddenly don't recognize him.

"Did you really think I was going to let you leave the lab?" he says. I hold my breath, afraid to move. "That I would risk so much for someone who killed my uncle? Ava might have forgiven you for Dale's death, but I haven't. Not for his, not for Willa's."

I stare back at him. I exhale and it comes out sharp and fast. This can't be happening. "You're betraying us? After everything? You led me here with no intention of helping? But you're a sympathizer! Or did you lie about that, too?"

"I am a sympathizer," he agrees. "To *innocent* shifters. You've killed people, Flo. You deserve to be locked up. In the human world, you would be—why should the rules be different because of what you are?"

I laugh harshly. "*Everything* is different because of what I am. I've lived my life fearing hunters, wondering when they'd come for my friends and me. Kill us or capture us—I don't know which is worse."

Quinn shakes his head. "You have this coming, Flo. You deserve this."

"No," I say. "I don't. You're not doing this. We're sticking to the plan. I'll get my sister and you can call medics in here for Dr. Finch a few minutes after I leave with your pass. You never have to see me—any of us—again."

"I'm not letting you go," he says flatly. "Do you know how many shifters beg for release when I bring them into this room?"

I shudder and squeeze my eyes shut for a moment. Blink once, twice. How scared they must be. My sister has only known this. She has only known fear.

"The others will come for me," I say.

Quinn shrugs. "I've already sent a team to bring them in. You're all killers."

"And what are you?" I ask sharply. "How many shifters have *you* killed?"

"None," he says. "I have seen death, but I have killed none. I bring them all to the lab."

"And the lab kills them for you," I say. Quinn snarls at me and I take a step forward. "And Ava? What about her? Did you trick her into coming here, too? You know they will kill her, no question."

"No!" Quinn retorts. "Ava's fine. I wouldn't do that to her. I'll tell her something went wrong and that you were captured. She'll go back to the others for backup to break you out, but my team will get there way before she does. I told Ivy to leave with Rain the moment Ava and I left with you. There will be no one left, and Ava will have no choice but to back off. You can't win this, Flo."

I hide my relief at the flaw in his plan: the others are already gone. Ava saw to it that they were out of harm in case anyone came for them, and she was right. I feel a strong sense of gratitude toward her that is both unwelcome and deserved. At least she's safe from Quinn. If I could just get to her . . .

"I'm leaving with my sister," I tell Quinn. Then I close my eyes and hurriedly call on my shape. The transformation is fast, as I willed it to be. I barely have time to register the change before it's on me, responding to my urgency. I feel everything all at once: the intensified senses, the strength, the rapid beating of my heart.

Quinn doesn't look surprised.

I charge at him, ramming him against the wall. He doubles over and I lift up onto my back legs, kicking him full force with the front. The blow knocks him to the ground. He looks up at me dazedly, a large cut on his forehead. *Now* he looks surprised.

The metallic stench of his blood mixed with the sterile scent of the room is nauseating. I need to leave—I've spent way too much time in here. I kick Quinn again and he goes still.

I hurry to shift back and check that he's still breathing. He is. I take his pass then hunt for clothes. Mine are ruined, so I take Dr. Finch's long lab coat, doing up all the buttons, and slip my boots back on. I take Dr. Finch's key card, too. Then I head out of the room, clipboard in hand, trying to blend in. I try to stay out of sight as much as possible and take the back stairs, like Quinn advised, even though I'm beginning to question everything he told me.

I enter the stairwell that'll take me up to the next level. When I reach Level 3, I find a door that needs a swipe card. I insert Quinn's with shaking hands and swipe down. The yellow blinking light turns green and the door unlocks.

I glance at Quinn's photo on the ID before shoving the door open. He was setting me up to fail, and I let him.

Because it was the best chance you had, I tell myself.

I think about Ava then. Of her hushed words and secret plans. Suddenly grateful to her for saving the others from Quinn. Now I just need to save myself and my sister.

The door closes behind me with a soft *whoosh*, knocking against my back and forcing me farther into the Level 3 corridor. I quickly scan my surroundings, taking in as much as I can. This is Wren's corridor—I remember from the plans. I know I'm in the right place.

A few others are up here—doctors in white coats, escorted by hunters. There aren't many people around, and the ones who are check door charts, make notes, look through small hatches on the doors, and discuss the shifters inside.

I start walking and grip Quinn's key card tightly as I approach the first door I come to. I decide that I'll give the shifters a chance to get free and leave this place. Help as many as I can, while I can.

I swipe the first door, the first shifter to set free. I doubt there are sympathizers at the exit as Quinn promised, so I form a new plan: chaos.

36
ONE OF THEM

I realize that I should have planned to do this anyway.

I was so caught up in getting Wren out that I forgot about everyone else who's trapped in here—those who've known the outside world and those who haven't.

I push the door to the first room open. The boy inside is sitting on the floor in the middle of the room. He doesn't even look up at me until I speak. "What are you?" I ask.

He lifts his head. "What?"

"What shape are you? Can you shift?"

He holds up his arm and I notice a silver bracelet on his wrist. "No," he says. "Is this a test? You take this off during testing hours." I step farther inside the room, noticing how horribly scarred his wrist is beneath the bracelet.

"How do they take it off?"

"They?" He frowns. He tilts his wrist up. "You're not one of them?" There's a thin space for the card on the side. I press it in and the bracelet opens. "You're not one of them," he says again, not a question this time.

I shake my head and help him to his feet. "I'm like you. I'm going to try and get you out of here. Everyone."

His smile lights up. "How did you escape?"

"I didn't," I tell him. "I came in. For my sister."

His eyes spark with hope. "And you're helping everyone?"

I nod and the boy shifts to a cheetah.

He follows me out of his cell.

I swipe the next door.

The cheetah charges down the corridor, scratching and biting at the hunters and doctors already on this floor. Most of the doctors flee toward the exits, but the hunters hold their ground, trained for this kind of thing.

As I make my way to door number six, I still haven't reached Wren, but have released two monkeys, a warthog, and an elephant. The five of them join the cheetah. They charge through the facility, clearing the path as more hunters come.

I swipe door number seven. I wonder if I'll know Wren when I see her. If I'll recognize my parents in her, or if I'll recognize myself in her hair, her eyes, her voice.

A young blond woman sits in room seven, wearing a gray jumpsuit that's frayed at the edges. It's the same as the other shifters were wearing; the same as my parents wore in the photographs in Dale's file. She sits with her back to the wall, hugging her legs to her chest. "Hey," I say, like I did to the others. "What shape are you? Can you shift?"

She blinks, dazed. "What?" Looking around me, she seems to notice that something isn't right. That something is happening outside her cell. "Who are you?"

"I'm Flo," I say. "A horse. I'm freeing the shifters on this row—do you want to help? They'll soon be outnumbered out there."

She gets to her feet. "Flo? You came here to save us?"

"Yes," I tell her. "My sister is here."

The woman smiles and walks toward me. She pulls me into a hug. "Flo! I know your sister."

My eyes widen. "Is she okay?"

The woman nods. "I think so." I take her hand, removing the bracelet with the swipe card. She sucks in a breath and holds her wrist to her chest. "That's better. Thank you, Flo."

"What's your shape? Can you help?" I ask, eager to keep moving. To make sure backup doesn't arrive before I can free more shifters. That this doesn't end before it starts.

The woman nods and I smile at her. "Yes," she says. "I'll help you. I'm Ro. A lion."

37
FIGHT

My smile breaks.

"Rowena? Tia's Ro?" I say quickly.

"You know Tia? Is she with you?"

Do I tell her?

"She's not here," I say first. "But we helped her look for you, after the warehouse."

"Is she—?"

"A lot has happened," I say.

Ro lifts her hands to her face. "She's not okay, is she?" she says through her hands. "I can tell by your face."

I look away, not that I can hide it now. Not that I want to. She deserves to know, but now isn't a good time to tell her. *When is a good time?*

"Ro, I'm sorry—the hunters, they took more of the group. They attacked us. We went up against them and Tia didn't make it."

Ro clutches her stomach and sits down on the edge of the bed. Her head dips and she lifts her hands to her hair, balling it into her fists, her freedom forgotten. Her forehead rests against her knees. She's so still, while outside the cell shifters and hunters fight against each other. I don't know what to do. I can't stand here when Wren is still waiting to be set free.

Animals and hunters rush past the open door.

"Then what's the point?" she finally says. A growl startles me and I almost miss what Ro is saying.

I take a shaky breath. I know this feeling. I remember the emptiness when I thought Jett was gone, that a hunter had taken him from me. I got him back, but Ro won't get Tia back. It breaks me to know that feeling isn't going to go away for her.

"There's always a point," I tell her. "Even if you can't see it yet."

Ro shakes her head. I'm losing her.

"But," I add. "You do have a choice to make. I'm sorry, but you have to decide how to act now. Come with me or stay in the labs."

"I don't know what to do," Ro sobs.

"What would Tia tell you to do?" I say quietly.

"Fight," Ro answers. "But she'd want to be here with me, fighting by my side."

"And if she couldn't be with you?" I say. "Would she still want you to go out there?"

Ro lifts her head and looks at me. Her eyes shine with tears and her mouth is set in a thin line, her lips trembling. "Yes," she says with certainty. "She would."

"She fought for you, Ro," I tell her, reaching out my hand. "Are you coming?"

Ro draws a breath and takes my hand.

38
A TRAP

I have to set more shifters free before the hunters overwhelm us.

I have to find my sister.

Ro stays close. "Is Chase here, too?" I ask her as I swipe the next door. Rowena shakes her head. *Oh.*

I turn away from her and focus on releasing shifters from their cells. A door at the end of the corridor swings open. Shouts and the sound of weapons firing draw my attention. I throw myself into the cell and release the shifters silver band without any explanation. There isn't any time now. "Go!" I yell. "Shift and go!"

The boy transforms into an eagle and flies out of the cell. Backup is here, and there are now more hunters than animals on Level 3. I rush on to the next door, Ro just behind me.

I'm getting closer to the fight with each door. I knew it was only a matter of time before someone tried to stop me when a hunter seizes my wrist. I shake free and she reaches out for me again. But the hunter doesn't touch me this time as Ro, in her lion form, throws herself at the hunter and the two of them fight it out.

I work my way along the doors, and Ro protects me from the fight while I work. One after the other, shifter after shifter.

I reach Wren's door. This is it.

I swipe the card and pull it open, charge inside, and—

She's not here.

The cell is empty. "Where is she?" I scream.

Ro shifts back to human and grabs my wrist, backing us out of the room. "Come on," she shouts over the noise. "We have to keep going."

"She should be here," I say, looking around the small room. "She should be here." They must have moved her. Quinn led me into a trap. He got me to walk into Roll Point willingly and my sister isn't here.

I turn to Ro. "A hunter took her away this morning. I thought he'd have brought her back to her cell but—"

"But what?" I interrupt. "Where would they take her?"

As if sensing my desperation, Ro runs, pulling me along with her. She takes Quinn's key card from my hand, using it to open the main door. She wedges it open so the shifters can escape any way they can.

I take the doctor's card out of my pocket and hand it to the cheetah boy, instructing him to release the other levels.

Shifters charge to join the fight on Level 3 and it seems like there could be more shifters than hunters now, but in the chaos I can't be sure.

I note blood on the walls and floors, the scent of silver in the air. I hurry toward the emergency exit right behind Ro, her grip on my arm is strong.

"They came for her this morning during exercise hall," Ro shouts. "Nothing ever changes in our routine, but then a hunter showed up and called her out."

"And you know where she is?"

An eagle flies over us, a piece of skin stuck to its talons. It stops by the fire exit door and shifts back into a girl. She shakes her hand, flinging the piece of skin away.

"I have some ideas," Ro shouts back.

We reach the emergency exit stairwell. I don't want to use the stairs Quinn indicated to me in his plan—I don't want to follow any part of the original plan, which was most likely designed to get me caught anyway—but for the main staircases, we'd have to pass through more fighting and more hunters. The chance we'd be captured or injured is far greater.

As Ro and I run down the stairs, our feet echo and clang on the metal steps. Our breaths mingle, loud in the open, empty space. I hear another set of footsteps from a few flights above and hope it's not a hunter. Alarms blare to life overhead and as suddenly as they started up, the lights go out.

As the alarm continues, a buzzing sounds from the backup generator and fills the stairwell with a dim blue light. Quinn explained this compound procedure to me. Told me it might happen if the hunters are alerted to my break-in. The lights flicker a bit, but it's enough to see.

We hurry down the last small flight of stairs, leading to a fire door that should take us outside. The sign beside it reads G for ground level.

I hesitate in front of the door—this is where Quinn told me to go. I wonder what's on the other side. *Who* is on the other side.

Ro pushes on the bar to open the door. "Don't!" I yell over the noise, but the door doesn't open anyway. Another way for Quinn to stop me leaving. Ro slams her shoulder into it. When nothing happens, she steps back with her head in her hands. "What are you doing?"

"I was hoping the others would be able to get out this way," she says. "Us, too, when we find your sister."

I back away from the door. "Which way?" The alarms cut out and I scream the words into the silence.

Ro jumps. "Come on."

We exit the stairwell and start along the ground floor corridors. My ears are ringing from the alarm. The sudden silence feels deafening, weighing heavily on my senses.

The ground floor corridors are lit with the same dull blue as the stairwell. But instead of cells, the rooms look like offices and meeting rooms.

Ro and I are alone now. It doesn't feel like there's any activity at all on this floor. Still, my heart races with each turn and the two of us stay quiet. There are faint noises— the distant sound of the shifters and hunters fighting against each other, our footsteps on the tiled floor, each breath we take.

Then I hear something else. Something familiar, but something I didn't think I would ever hear again. I hear it in my dreams, my memories, and now here is it for real. My heart feels like it stops altogether when the musical sound of laughter reaches us.

39
GAMES

I press my back against the wall, pulling Ro beside me.

I listen carefully for the direction the laughter is coming from, but echoes throw me off, and it sounds like it's coming from all around us. It closes in. Too close, too far, I can't determine the distance. Quinn told me he'd captured the Laughing Sisters in the woods—who let them out?

"What's down here?" I whisper.

"The main testing rooms," Ro replies. "That's probably where they're holding your sister if she's not in a cell."

The cackling, biting, hooting reaches us again, echoing through the corridor. There's no way to avoid it. No escaping it unless we go back. And that isn't an option.

"What *is* that?" Ro hisses.

The sounds stops, cut off abruptly. I put a finger to my lips.

The silence that follows is almost as bad as the noises the sisters were making moments ago. It's too still now. I feel too vulnerable, out in the open, standing in the corridor, not knowing where they are. *Do they know where we are?*

"It's the bear from the woods," one of the hyenas sings. My breath catches in my throat. *They know we're here.* They're listening, just as we are. I still can't tell where the trio are, which direction the voices are coming from.

"*You?*" Ro mouths. She's asking if I am the bear from the woods.

I nod, remembering the way they surrounded me on the mountain, sniffing at Jett's shirt. Then they chased us. And I still can't bring myself to think about what they'd have done if they'd caught us. Now they hunt me again, only this time I'm cornered. There's nowhere to go.

The three sisters laugh again.

"Hyenas," I whisper to Ro. "Three of them."

I continue along the dimly lit corridor, only the soft blue light to guide us. I don't know if we're walking away from or toward the three sisters. They could sneak up from behind or pounce from in front.

I move away from the wall.

"What's happening?" Ro whispers, keeping close to my side.

"Funny running into her again," I hear from a little way down the corridor, closer now. "Here of all places."

Laughter drifts down the corridor. They're almost here—I can hear their feet slapping on the tile floor as they run toward us.

"Tell me what to do," Ro says.

"Be ready to fight," I tell her.

"Tut, tut." A single silhouette at the far end, black against blue. "Not a bear, though, is she? The little pony lied to us."

"Viv," I call out. I try to keep my voice steady as two more figures step into view. "Zoe, Eve, this isn't the time for games!"

Laughter rises, echoing all around me. "There's always time for a game," Viv replies, rushing up to me. "Boo!"

I push her backward. Taken off guard, she stumbles. I turn to run but Eve grabs my arm. "Naughty," she says. She pins my arms behind my back. *They're so fast.*

I struggle. "Get *off!*" Elbowing Eve in the stomach, I break away and start to run away. Ro follows.

And then they're gone again.

"Where did they go?" I breathe. "How are they doing that?" I look around, full circle. It's too dark, too unfamiliar.

Ro searches the darkness, too. "I don't know," she breathes. "I don't like them. They weren't wearing cuffs— someone took them off already."

I swallow hard. "Come on." We take off down the corridor. I urge Ro in front of me to lead the way to the testing rooms.

"A chase!" I hear from behind. "Let's go!"

I'm drawn back to the last time this happened, the memory so fresh in my mind. This time, I'm trying to protect my sister, though. And I'm not letting them make her a part of their game.

I hear a high-pitched scream. Viv's call to stop. The laughter cuts off and the footsteps fall away. The building is suddenly silent again, expect for the rushing in my ears. *Where'd they go? What happened?*

I slow my pace, eventually stopping. Ro does the same. "What's going on?" she whispers. "We should go!"

I hold up my palm. "Just a minute."

I walk back slowly, breathing as lightly as I can as not to make any sound. Then I hear a crash.

I peer around the corner and see the three of them standing outside one of the doors that line the corridor. Eve crashes into it, snarling. Viv tells her to try again, pushing Zoe forward to join her sister in breaking down the door.

"Come on!" Ro hisses, gesturing for me to follow.

"Wait," I whisper, then nod my head for Ro to look. To see what I'm seeing. Ro shakes her head. She won't look. "They stopped," I tell her. "There must be a reason."

"Unless it's a trick," Ro says. She reaches out for me. "Let's go."

I hear a series of bangs then as the sisters knock into the door, trying to get inside. Laughter bubbles up again from around the corner. "They've found something," I whisper.

I peer around the corner. "A prize inside," Viv says. "Someone was trying to hide."

"A new pony," Zoe says. "Her scent is just like—" her head whips around to face me. She smiles, a wicked grin.

"Sisters," Eve finishes, the word like a hiss. She looks at me, too. "Just like us."

Wren is behind that door.

"Not like you," I say, stepping out. "We're nothing like you."

That's where Quinn hid her, locked her away.

I strip off the lab coat and step out of my boots.

40
FIRST BITE

I close my eyes and shift.

Eve charges at me before the change has fully taken place. She whacks me into the wall with her whole body and my shape slips from my hold, knocking the air from my lungs. My naked form crumples to the ground.

I struggle back up to my feet. Zoe laughs, but Viv looks annoyed. She steps forward and grabs Eve by her jumpsuit, pulling her backward. "What was that?" she scolds. "Did I say to do that?"

Eve starts to giggle, and Viv puts her hand over her sister's mouth. She snaps her teeth at Eve and the laughter dies down, but the sound of it still echoes through my mind. They look beaten down from their time in the labs. Smaller. Dark circles beneath their eyes. But their energy pushes through. Their love of the chase and the game overrides whatever else they must be feeling.

Viv shoves Eve over to Zoe, who quietly scolds her. Then Viv looks at me. "I don't want Eve having all the fun, especially not before I have a turn." She tilts her head. "I always get first bite."

FIRST BITE

She swings back around to Eve, and Eve recoils. "I didn't bite her," she says nervously. "The first is yours."

"You still touched her," Viv says. "You shouldn't play with other people's food. Not until it's your turn."

"Food," I breathe. I shake my head. "No. No way." I move, putting myself in front of Wren's door. "Wren," I call to her. "Wren, are you okay?"

She doesn't answer. She doesn't know that name. I hear movement inside—a crashing sound. Something thumps against the door.

I watch the hyenas, their slow, teasing advance. Viv looks so pleased with herself.

"Just hold on a bit longer," I call back to Wren. "I'm going to get you out."

A lump forms in my throat as I realize that Wren doesn't know what leaving with me will mean for her. My chest hurts with the enormity of it. With what it will mean to both of us to be outside of Roll Point together. I've imagined what she will think of sitting around a campfire beneath the moon and the stars, of being deep in the forest or watching the sunset turn the ocean violet, of my friends and their shapes. Of the circus.

The three hyenas circle me, Viv calling Eve and Zoe forward with one simple rule: don't touch. They form a moving wall around me, forcing me away from the door, nipping, snapping, laughing.

I have to beat them back. I *have* to.

I shake my head. The hyenas are closer still. Viv scratches my bare stomach, drawing a thin line of blood.

253

I hiss and move back, crashing into Zoe. She pushes me away like I burned her and checks for Viv's reaction.

"She's not doing anything," Eve whines. "It's no fun if she isn't doing anything."

"She will," Viv says with a cruel smile.

Movement catches my eyes, momentarily drawing my attention away from the circling hyenas. I think I see Ro at the end of the corridor, a shadow. The sisters don't seem to notice her, being so caught up with me.

Viv scratches me again, and I cry out but don't lose my balance this time. A second line of red joins the other.

Ro roars and charges into view. She doesn't stop when the Laughing Sisters block her path to me. Viv shifts and throws herself at Ro. Her torn clothes scatter, and Eve picks up the pieces and throws them in the air, squealing with delight before she joins her sister in the fight.

I back up against the door and close my eyes, finding my shape as Zoe does the same. Zoe springs at me, and I lift up my front legs and knock her back. She whimpers, and Eve makes a horrible high-pitched sound that makes me feel cold all over.

Ro counters the cry with a roar of her own, and I join the chorus as I keep Eve and Zoe busy while Ro tackles Viv. It's clear that Viv doesn't stand much chance up against Ro's claws, teeth, and size.

Zoe stalks around my side, coming up behind me while Eve occupies the space between Ro, Viv, and me. Zoe jumps up on my back, scratching. I release a shrill scream and rear back, knocking her off.

More people suddenly join us in the corridor. I'm so caught up in the fight that I hardly register them. But when I notice flashes of black and a group of hunters filling the space around us, I stop and shift back, raising my hands for what good it'll do to block their silver bullets. The hunters only aim at the hyenas, though, taking them out all at once.

I lower my hands and take in the group of hunters in front of me, ignore the Laughing Sisters on the ground around me. Am I next?

Ava pushes through the hunters. "Flo!"

I stumble back against the wall, the tension leaving my body as the hunters lower their weapons.

My leg is bleeding, my stomach scratched, and there's a chunk of flesh missing from my shoulder. I can see a bruise forming on my hip bone, too. I put my hand against the wall to steady myself. Ava grabs my lab coat from the floor and hurries over to help me into it. She buttons me up. Blood stains the white fabric.

"The gates are wide open, staff are fleeing, animals are *everywhere*, and one side of the building caught fire. Did you do this? Where's Quinn?"

I look over her shoulder at Ro. She's still in her lion form, teeth bared at Ava's back. The hunters train their weapons on her.

"Don't!" I shout. I don't even know whose side they're on, not after everything, but if they're with Ava, I have to believe they're helping her. "She's with us, she's helping me."

Ava turns around, but Ro doesn't change her threatening stance or her form.

"Ro!" I say. "Shift back. Come on!"

Ro does as I ask, but I realize it's only so that she can speak. "You," she says to Ava the moment her transformation is complete. "The woman in the woods."

"Ro, what are you *doing*? Ava's helping us."

"She's a liar," Ro spits. "She's the reason I'm in here! She's the reason Chase is dead."

My eyes widen. Ava captured Ro and Chase in an attempt to exchange the two of them for two of us, and Ro remembers her. Ava doesn't speak, doesn't blink. Does she care about what she's done?

"She's the reason a lot of people are dead," I admit, tearing my gaze away from Ava. "But we don't have time for this. We can't stay in the building!"

"We don't have time for a lot of things, do we Flo?" Ro snaps. "No time to mourn Tia, no time to get revenge on our enemies, only time to find your sister and leave."

"That's why I came here," I tell her, trying to act as if her words don't sting. "You didn't have to stay with me but you did. You helped me. You said you were her friend. Ava has been helping me. Your friends are waiting for us, Ro. Please. We have to go."

"I'm not going anywhere with *her*."

"We are," I say. "We have no choice. Our friends are there. Lola and Kanna, Hugo and Jax. They're waiting for us. Please come with us."

"If you're not with us, you're against us," one of the hunters says. She's short with freckles and looks a similar age to Ava. Behind her are three other hunters—two women and a man—all waiting for instructions. *Sympathizers?*

I look to Ava. "They're helping get us out," she says. "I assumed things didn't go quite to plan when I saw the building burning."

I look between them. "Quinn betrayed us," I say carefully. "And my sister is behind that door. Quinn hid her there."

A knot forms between Ava's eyebrows. "Bastard," she growls.

"He did it because we killed Dale."

I move around Ava and take Ro's arm. "We can sort all of this out," I whisper. "Let's just get out of here first."

Ro glances at the door Wren is locked behind and nods. "Okay. Just until we get out."

"Guard the corridor," Ava calls to the hunters. "Let's get this door open."

41

LITTLE SISTER

Inside the room is a girl.

She sits in the corner, her hands covering her ears, her face buried in her lap.

She doesn't even know I'm in here.

Her chestnut-brown hair is long, falling in curtains around her face. The tips touch the floor.

There's a blank screen at the front of the room. Clear plastic chairs tucked under long metal tables face the screen. The walls are mostly bare but for a few large prints, displaying graphs and numbers I can't make out and probably wouldn't understand.

"Hello?" I say, moving slowly toward her. She's half hidden behind a chair. "I'm here to help you."

The girl doesn't look up, but she must sense me because as I move closer, she shrinks away, though there's nowhere for her to go.

I crouch down in front of the girl and take her hand. She resists, but not much. I used Quinn's key card to get inside, and now I use it to take her silver bracelet off.

Ro approaches. "Hey, Hope," she says gently. "Look—it's your sister."

"What's your name?" I ask.

She shakes her head but looks up at me, tears in her eyes.

"She was called Hope," Ro tells me. "But she doesn't like to use it anymore, since—" She hesitates. "Since your parents died."

I lick my dry lips. "Hope? That's what they called you?"
She nods.

I take a shaky breath. "I'm your sister—Flo."

She lifts her chin a little more. Tears fall freely and I reach out for her. I've run out of air. I can't feel the tears on my cheeks or my hand on her arm. I'm numb to all of it.

"Flo," Ava says from out in the corridor.

Ro rounds on her. "Give her a minute."

"It's not safe to wait around like this," I hear Ava hiss back.

Wren regards me for a long moment. "I know," she starts, her voice scratchy and quiet like she hardly uses it. "I know about you."

I let out a sob and reach for her. She doesn't move away.

Ava and Ro continue to argue. The hunters join in, taking Ava's side in hurrying us up. There are distant sounds—thumps and shouting, gunshots and shattering—that remind me there's a fight happening in this building, remind me we should leave. As much as I don't want to rush Wren, I have to.

"I only just found out about you," I tell her quickly. "I was only three when they took our parents—you weren't even born yet. I didn't know I had a sister until yesterday." I put my other hand on my chest. "I'm named after our mother, Flora—I think. I've been calling you Wren, after our father. I didn't know your name was Hope."

She shakes her head. "It's not," she says. "Not anymore."

I wipe at my eyes. "What can I call you, then?"

Her eyes light up. She pulls herself to her feet. "I like Wren."

I laugh pathetically, tears running off the end of my chin. "Wren."

"You look like her," she says, touching the ends of my hair. "Like our mother." She looks at me. "You've given me a new name."

I nod. "But I want to give you more than that."

42
TRUST ME

I keep hold of Wren's hand as we follow Ava and the sympathizers out of the compound.

Wren is slightly smaller than I am but not by much. She trails along beside me, keeping close, holding tight.

The shifters ahead stop, holding their hands up for us to stop, too. "The fighting has reached this level," one of the sympathizers say. "We can't go any farther with you, Ava. You'll have to get yourself out."

Ava turns back and must read the panic on my face. "It's okay," she says quickly. "We're nearly there."

"We'll try and clear the way for you," the sympathizer says. She hugs Ava quickly and the hunters leave through the door, leaving it ajar for us.

I wonder if other shifters have broken out yet. If they've passed the gate and gained their freedom.

"Stay close," Ava says. "Stick to the edge of the room and follow me. Call out if something happens."

I look back at Ro to see if she's following Ava's instructions. She scowls, her eyes trained on nothing in particular. "Ro, did you get that?"

"Yes," she says, her teeth gritted. This isn't going to be easy. And I know nothing I say can make it better. I can't convince Ro to forgive Ava for what she did. *I* can't forgive Ava for all she's done.

Wren and I stay put between Ava and Ro, keeping them as far from each other as possible, and go out into the foyer. The desk I saw earlier is broken and dented. The guy who sat behind it is gone. The elevator doors are stuck open, a body dressed in black stopping them from closing. The white and gray walls are disturbed by blood-stains and burn marks. Shifters and hunters fight in here and it spreads outside. As promised, the sympathizers try to clear a path for us.

Wren trips over her own feet. Her grip on my hand strengthens.

"It's okay," I say. "Wren? It's all right. I'll get us out of here, don't worry." I have to speak up over the noise of the building—sirens, shouting, rumbling.

"I don't like blood," she says. "It's everywhere and it smells so strong."

"It's silver you can smell," I say. "Just silver." Though I know it's both.

She presses herself against my side, pinching my arm in her effort to hold on tighter.

When we get outside, Wren relaxes her hold and the four of us run full pelt for the gate. I squint against the sun as we dash across the stone courtyard and parking lot. The gate ahead is open, only a small gap, but still open. Shots ring out and I duck my head, leaning toward Wren, protecting her with my body. We don't slow and no additional shots follow. I don't even know if they were aimed at us.

We run through the gap, slowing slightly to pass through in single file. Ava goes first, then I push Wren through, following close behind.

Ava only slows when we get out into the large parking lot. It's pretty full now, and Ava positions us between cars for cover as we make our way back to the van.

"I don't like this," Ro whispers behind me. "We can't trust her. We should go now—leave her here."

"I've known her my whole life," I tell Ro. "I know what she did to you. If you can't trust Ava, then trust me? Please."

Rowena scowls. "I don't know . . ."

"She's the reason a lot of my friends lost their lives, too," I remind Ro. "I'll explain everything when we reach the camp. But Ava's the only way we can get back to the others."

Ava turns back. "Flo?" I hurry to catch up with her, pulling Wren along with me. "What really happened with Quinn? Is he alive?"

"Yes," I say. "But he blamed us for Dale's death. Willa's too. So he tricked us into getting me here, then sent a team for the others."

"The others aren't there," she says. "The hunters won't find anything."

"I know," I reply. "Still, I can't help but worry . . . Quinn had a pretty solid plan of his own."

"Well so did I," Ava says. "Everyone's safe. You're here now too and worrying won't get us anywhere. Running will. Keep up."

Quinn's van isn't far and Ava reaches it first.

"Quickly," she says, swinging open the driver's door. I run around to the passenger side with Wren. When I round the vehicle, Quinn leaps up from his crouched hiding place. I don't have time to react before he opens the van door, taking me off guard, and slams it into my face. I stagger back, my hand wrenched from Wren's, my vision faltering. Blood runs into my mouth and I reach up to cup my nose.

"Flo!" Wren calls out, startling me.

Ro grabs Wren and pulls her back so she's behind me. I hold my nose, blood on my hands. I don't want Wren to see.

Ava hurries around the side of the van. She gasps. "Quinn! What are you *doing*?"

"This is my van," he growls.

"You loaned it to us, for this mission. Which Flo tells me you screwed up. I thought we had a deal?"

Quinn cocks his head to one side. "Stay out of this, Ava."

"I won't!" she replies quickly. She moves forward, pushing me behind her. Blood coats my teeth and I recoil from the taste. Wren puts her hand on my cheek. I shake my head. "It's fine," I tell her. "It'll heal soon."

"I can't believe what you tried to do!" Ava yells at Quinn. "We're not doing this. It's over. You lose. Now move out of the way."

"No," Quinn says, standing a little taller. "You don't get to tell me what to do."

"You're forgetting that I'm a lion," she tells him. "And these girls are horses. Would you be saying the same if we were in our alternate forms? Because that can be arranged."

"She's right," Wren says fiercely, surprising me. I nod, too.

Quinn reaches for his belt. I stagger back, pushing Wren with me, but his hands come up empty. Ava smiles. "Unprepared?" she says. "Your weapon is in the van. Now get out of my way." She pushes him hard and ushers us inside. Wren and I get in and lock the passenger door while Ava and Ro run around to the driver's side. Ava locks her door too and wastes no time starting the engine.

I look out of the window, watching Quinn. And I realize he's laughing.

43

THE HUNT

"You're very quiet," I say to Wren.

She watches out the window, and I keep expecting questions from her that don't come. I thought she'd be bursting with them, and I kind of looked forward to answering them. Wren continues to stare out of the window, her hands pressed to the glass. "I'm looking," she replies. "For now."

I lean back and give her space to take things in at her own pace, figuring she'll ask when she's ready.

Squashed between Ava and me, Ro says, "Pull over first chance you get. I'm not riding like this the whole way." She sits as far away from Ava as she can, which isn't far at all, pushing me into Wren and Wren against the door.

Ava stops right away. A car behind us presses on its horn as it passes the van. "There are clothes in the back for all of you," Ava tells us, then jumps out. Ro moves to do the same. "You coming?" she asks.

"Where?" I say.

"To change and sit in the back. I have questions for you, too."

I'm wearing the doctor's lab coat and Wren is in her jumpsuit from the lab—we don't need to change. Besides, I know what Ro's questions are and I'm not ready to answer them.

I shake my head. I want to stay here with Wren. I want her to be able to see outside, not be shut inside the windowless back of the van.

"Flo. My girlfriend is dead—you owe me some answers now that we're outside. You promised."

"I'll keep my promise," I tell her, noticing the shine in her eyes. "When we get back to camp. Lola and Kanna are there. Jax and Hugo, too. They will know more than I do about what happened after you left the warehouse."

"We argued," she says.

I look out the front window. Ava has walked a little ahead, stretching her legs, waiting for us to finish. Ro stands out in the road. She'll have to move if another car comes by, but at the moment the road is quiet.

"I'm sorry," I reply. I'm not sure what else to say.

"Me too." Ro dips her head. "I never got the chance to make it right."

"Tia was worried about you," I say. "She really wanted to find you. She didn't hold any bad feeling from what I could tell."

Ro's tears fall now. I lift up my pack from by my feet, where I'd left it before going into the lab, and empty it out. "Here," I say, tossing it to her. "It was Tia's. I've been using it. Your name is sewn into the bottom."

Ro wipes her eyes and turns the backpack over, running her finger across the sewn heart with her name inside.

"There was also this," I say, bending down to retrieve the threaded string bracelet from among the belongings strewn out at my feet.

I pass it to Ro, and she secures it on her wrist. "This is mine," she says. "I was wearing it when the hunters took Chase and me. She found it?"

I nod. "She went out looking for you and came back with it. That's when we knew for sure the hunters had you."

Ro closes her eyes.

"There's more," I tell her. "A few things, back at camp. I emptied some of it out." Ava had given us new packs as well as clothes and tents, so Jett and I had distributed everything between us. But I'd wanted to keep Tia's bag, because it meant something, because it wasn't something to be thrown away and replaced.

Ro nods. "Thank you."

She walks around the van and opens the back doors. I feel a shake as she climbs into the back and shuts herself in. Ava makes her way back over and sits beside me. I move over a little, giving Wren some more room.

"Ready to carry on?" Ava asks.

I nod and she buckles herself in.

She starts the engine and checks her mirrors. I watch her squint and hesitate. Then she yells, "Shit!" and presses down on the gas so hard that Wren and me fly forward. The seat belt digs into my collarbone.

"What's happening? What is it?" I yell as I move over to Wren's side to look in the side mirror. My breath catches as I see two black vans chasing ours. They're close.

"Quinn?" I gasp. "Is it him?"

Ava doesn't answer. She focuses on the road ahead, the dial on the speedometer creeping up and up.

I clutch the dashboard and check that Wren is okay. She looks pale and there's a red bump on her head, but otherwise she seems unharmed. She watches the mirror, too. Watches the vans coming closer, closer.

"What do we do, Ava?" I say. "We can't lead them back to the others."

"We have to. If they catch us as we are, we won't stand a chance against them."

"No!"

"We *have* to, Flo," she snaps and leans forward, willing the van to go faster.

I look back in the mirror, my breath coming fast. If we can go fast enough to shake them off, maybe we can give the others some warning before they catch up with us. Maybe I'll have time to get Wren to safety and out of the fight. Maybe we'll stand a chance.

But with them this close, they'll arrive seconds after us. No one will have time to get ready to fight. The hunters will know what's coming and the pack back at the camp won't.

I shake my head. "Your plan, Ava—"

"Is all we've got." She glances at me. "We can't take them alone."

"We could outrun them," I suggest.

"Not likely. I'm going as fast as I can."

"Not with the van," I say.

44
BLINK

The van screeches as it stops, throwing us forward again.

We dip into a low ditch, tires skidding in the soft mud as Ava brakes.

As lions and horses, we can outrun the hunters in the woods and go back to the new camp on foot. They don't have us cornered this time. We aren't forced to fight our way out. We can run—we can escape them and leave all of this behind. I've got Wren. My friends are safe. We're so close.

"They were probably tracking the van," Ava says, breathless as she unbuckles her safety belt. Wren and I do the same. We push the doors open and spill out onto the side of the road.

One van flew past us as we braked. It's turning around now to come back for us. The other is close behind.

The back doors swing open and Ro stumbles out. She's dressed in jeans, brown boots, and a cream jumper now, with Tia's backpack slung over one shoulder.

"We have to shift and run—we're being chased," I tell her quickly. I put my hands on Wren's shoulders. "Are you ready for this?"

270

She nods fiercely. She's not going back there.

Wren closes her eyes and becomes a horse within one blink and the next. Her coat is chestnut-brown like mine. It shimmers in the late morning sun.

I follow her lead, leaving our clothes shredded by our feet.

Ro shifts into her lion and scoops up Tia's backpack in her jaw.

"Run!" Ava shouts as the hunters' vans both reach us. Then she's a lion, too, and the four of us are running and gunshots ring out between the trees.

I keep Wren in front of me. Ro runs by my side.

The wind rushes by as I dodge tree trunks and jump over roots and gnarled vines.

Ava is right behind, keeping close. We're faster than the hunters are.

Once we're far enough away, Ava overtakes and shifts back, halting us.

The rest of us stay as animals while she speaks. "I'll lead us back to camp," she says. "Well done, Flo. Let's keep a good pace."

—

After a while she stops us again, and tells us all to shift back to human.

It's getting later in the day, but I can't tell how much time has passed. I'm hungry and tired, but when Ava tells us we're close, I'm hit with a dose of energy. I want to get back more than I want anything else.

Ro empties out Tia's backpack, which she'd filled with some of the clothes from the back of the van earlier. "Those were for everyone," Ava remarks.

"I'm giving them to everyone now," Ro replies.

There are two pairs of leggings, which Wren and I claim. Ro hands Wren a black T-shirt me a blue one.

She pulls a loose, short-sleeved dress over her head and hands a pair of jeans and a blouse to Ava. I recognize the dress—it used to be Ursula's. Ava must have collected up whatever wasn't destroyed after the circus fire and kept it all.

"That's all I've got," Ro says. "No shoes. Nothing warmer."

Without another word, Ava leads the way back to camp. Ro and I walk on either side of Wren.

"Did you know our parents?" I ask Wren. "Did you ever see them?"

"Sometimes," she says quietly. "But not very often."

"You said I looked like her," I say. "Like our mom."

Wren nods and looks at me now, squinting against the sun. "You do. Sometimes we were together for training or testing, but not much. I saw her a few times a year at most."

"What about Dad?"

Wren shakes her head. "No," she says. "When he died, I found out because the doctors were talking about it—right in front of me. The next time I saw our mother, she hugged me close. She couldn't stop crying. They separated us and I saw her even less after that."

I wipe at my own eyes. "And what about. . . . What about when she—?"

"They told me," she says. "Because they took me for extra testing to fill her loss. They're interested in the different species and comparing our results, so I had to make up for that. I saved my tears for my cell. I missed her and I knew I was never going to see her again. But you never even got to meet her, or Dad."

"I don't remember anything about them," I say. "I don't even know if the few memories I do conjure up are real."

"They remembered you, always," she tells me. "There weren't many things Mom got chance to tell me, but she told me about you."

"When did it happen?" I ask.

"In the last few weeks," Wren tells me. "I don't know how long exactly—it's hard to keep track of time in there."

"I'm sorry," I tell her.

She looks away, tears in her eyes. "Me too," she says.

I follow Wren's gaze, up at the trees around us, and reach for her hand.

45
LOST TIME

Ahead of us, Ava starts to run.

"Look!" She yells back, pointing ahead to a plume of smoke. It could just be the campfire, but it seems too big.

I hurry after her, pulling Wren along with me and calling for Ro to follow.

Ava's trailer is backed up against the tree line, and its door is swinging open in the breeze, bullet holes in its side. The other is engulfed in flames.

My hand flies to my chest as I stop and take in the scene ahead. *What happened here?*

Wren stops beside me. "Stay close, okay?" I tell her.

"What is it?" she asks, eyes wide.

"Something's not right," I say. "I don't know what. We have to go check that our friends are okay. Stay by my side, and we'll keep each other safe like back at the lab and out in the woods. We can do it again, can't we?"

Wren nods determinedly.

Ava emerges from the abandoned trailer. She turns to Wren and me as we catch up with her. Ro has moved into the trees, but I can still see her, Tia's backpack strapped to her shoulders.

"They should have moved in time," Ava says. "I don't know what happened." Her voice shakes with uncertainty. Could Quinn have found out where we were heading and beat us here? Did the hunters find them anyway?

"Over here!" Ro shouts from inside the woods.

With a sudden jolt, the three of us are running for the trees, following Ro's call. I turn in a circle when I reach her. "Where?" I pant. "Where are they?"

"Look," Ro says, pointing to a bloodstained leaf. She runs her finger through the air, following a path of trampled foliage. "This way?"

I nod and she leads off.

First we find a trail of discarded supplies, and then we find our friends. I see Jett first and rush ahead. "Jett! *What happened?*" Wren yelps as I tug her along so suddenly. Ava hurries to follow.

Blood runs from Jett's eyebrow, down the side of his face, which is covered in healing bruises. Hugo is on the ground beside him, a wooden spear through his leg. I raise my hand to my mouth then quickly turn Wren away.

Hugo is pale, clutching at his leg. Jax is on his knees beside him, trying to help him. Jax has cuts on his face, his tears mixing with the blood. Ava rushes over to them, lending a hand. She's dealt with injuries at the circus, and probably while she was a wild shifter, too. Hugo should heal quickly if the wound is cleaned up and cared for, but seeing him like this isn't easy.

Kanna's unconscious but breathing—Lola confirms it. "Ro?" she says in disbelief. "Ro, is that you?"

Ro cries out and launches herself toward the sisters, falling to her knees beside Kanna and hugging Lola. They both cry and press against each other harder, clutching at lost time.

Lance and Lucas are crouched by a tiny unlit campfire, the side of Lance's face badly burnt. I don't know who to help first. "What can I do?" I say to Jett.

Instead of responding, he gathers me into his arms. I'm still holding Wren's hand, so he pulls her in, too, and holds us both close. He kisses my hair then leans back to look at Wren.

"I'm Jett," he says quietly.

She steps back. "You're bleeding."

He lifts a hand to his head and winces when his fingers find the cut. Jett smiles at Wren, despite the blood running down his face, despite whatever it is the camp has just been through—I came back with Wren. *Wren is here.*

"Are we in danger?" I ask him.

"Not now," he confirms.

"Quinn betrayed us," I say.

Jett nods. "I know. I was so worried about you, Flo. He had a group of hunters spying on us, so when we moved, they followed and attacked us. I couldn't stop thinking about you in the lab with someone who'd turned against us."

"I kicked him," I say with a small smile. "And released the shifters."

276

Jett grins and shakes his head. I leave Wren and Jett to get to know each other and make my way around the camp.

I move to crouch down beside Jax first and put an arm around his shoulders. "I'm sorry," I whisper. "He'll be okay, won't he?"

Jax nods his head. He squeezes his eyes shut. His face screws up while he cries, and I rub his back. Jett takes Wren over to the unlit campfire. He sits beside Lance, gesturing that Wren take a seat on his other side.

Jax sniffs, wiping his hand over his face. "Did you get your sister?" he asks.

My heart swells. His cousin is badly hurt, but he still asks about Wren. "Yes," I whisper.

"You should," he sniffles. "You should go to your sister. Make sure she's okay."

I look at Hugo. He's pale, unconscious, only the soft rise and fall of his chest indicating that he's alive. His pant leg is coated dark with blood. Ava's ripped the fabric away and is working at the wound.

"Are you, though?" I say. "I don't want to leave—"

"Go to her," he insists. "Really. I'm . . . I just want to make sure I'm here when he wakes up again. He's lost a lot of blood and I know we have to leave soon."

I nod and get to my feet. "Call me over if you need anything," I say.

He looks up at me. He reaches for my hand and squeezes it, the way Hugo would. I swallow hard and Jax lets go.

I return to where the others are gathered. Kanna's awake now, and Wren's sitting between her and Jett. She shuffles over when she sees me coming, making a space for me.

"Is everyone else okay?" I ask the group.

"We are," Lola says. "It's just Lance's face . . ."

"It'll heal fine," Lance says. "Right, Flo? Your stomach was way worse than this and that's okay now, isn't it?"

The side of his face looks sore and scabby, but seems like it's already begun to heal. The skin is growing pink and fresh. All I can do is nod, remembering what the touch of fire and singed flesh felt like.

"So it's just—" Lola takes a breath. "Just Hugo."

"Where are they now?" Wren asks. "The people who hurt you."

"The hunters are gone," I say quickly.

Kanna makes eye contact with me. "Definitely gone," she says. "Don't worry."

I remember Quinn laughing as we drove away in his van. He knew what we'd find on our return. We should move again, before he sends more hunters or comes here himself.

"Yes, don't worry," Lola adds. "Hello, by the way— I'm Lola."

"That's a pretty name," Wren says, smiling shyly.

"I like yours, too," Lola replies.

Wren leans against me, her hand finding mine.

"Where are the hunters?" Ava asks, coming to join the group.

"A little farther that way," Lola whispers, pointing toward where the trees are the thickest. Ava nods and makes her way over there. I can't find it in me to think of the bodies through the trees, only relief that everyone's okay. I look behind her, see Jax patting Hugo's shoulder. Hugo blinks, looking up at him. He's coming to. He's going to be all right.

Ava notices too. "I'm going to go and look. You should all get ready to move on. We'll take the remaining trailer—as soon as possible. If the hunters followed you all here, they could have informed others of the location of this camp. More could be coming."

We pack up and move quickly through the trees, carrying what we can. We pile ourselves and our belongings into the trailer with bullet holes in the door.

Ava catches up. She claps her hands together as she approaches the trailer. "Quickly! Let's go!"

As soon as we're all inside, Ava climbs into the driver's seat and starts the engine. I take a breath and think about what's ahead.

Moving on means starting the circus. This part of the journey is over—I have my sister—and the next part is about to begin whether I'm ready for it or not.

As the trailer bumps over the clearing and toward the road, my attention returns to Wren, then to the whole group squashed in around us. We're all going to be all right. We always were going to be, because I realize now that the home I wished for was right in front of me the whole time. Jett is my home. Wherever he is—that's home. And the others now, too—including Wren. We've been through so much together. I might have known Jett and the brothers the longest, but Lola, Kanna, Hugo, Jax, and even Ro are just as important to me now. And I have my sister to think about and care for.

But not Ava. Never Ava.

Ava wants to put us back in the circus. Pull us back to that life. Drag Wren down with us. Now that I have her, now that we're here and the danger is gone, it's only a matter of time before it starts again. Ava is the danger. The circus is the danger. I can't let it happen. I can't wait for Quinn to come back for us.

He knows to look for a circus. And the way he laughed when we drove away from him, the attacks that followed both here and on the road, tells me he won't stop looking for us. It's not Ava he's after. She can stay and she'll be safe from him—from his team of hunters—but the rest of us won't be.

I'm going to have to break my promise. I'm going to have to betray Ava as she betrayed us. I'm going to have to become just like her to protect my family.

46
OUR OWN SHOW

I don't remember the names of the places we've traveled to.

I don't remember what the jump I've been practicing is called.

Everything is unfamiliar. Everything but the feeling of being trapped inside a cage, with rules and limits and boundaries I want to get away from. It's temporary, but it feels the same way it did before.

We're not joining Ava's circus. We're all agreed on that.

I meet with Lola and Ro to plan our route. Each night, when the camp is dark, we find each other, and we plan. We've been planning for months behind Ava's back, practicing for months when she's watching us. I don't know if she suspects anything.

This is all unfamiliar to the rest of them, too. Progress is slow because of that. The wild shifters in our group don't know what to do around here, how to fit in. They spend the day longing for the night when they can be themselves again, be true, stop acting. I'm used to playing

281

this part, but that doesn't mean it's easy when I thought I'd left it all behind me.

We followed Ava to the first location. We explored while she set up. We found different routes, different places, potential homes. Worked out our direction. Planned. And soon we'll leave.

We're putting on our own show now.

Ava has recruited nonanimal acts to her new circus. She has acrobats, a strongman, a bearded lady to replace Ruby, a lion tamer, a ringmaster. Humans. All of them.

We have to hide away even more now. We're living with people who can't know what we are. Opening night is only a few weeks away. Ava's got it planned—she had it all planned before we even said yes to joining her.

We've got our own plan, but it is moving slowly.

I watch Wren jump a hurdle in a clearing beside the circus. Ava promised no fire.

The show is creeping up on us. Will we have to perform again? I don't want that. We have to be gone before then.

We take turns traveling a little farther each day to see what's around us. We have to be careful that Ava doesn't notice us coming and going. She seems to notice the wild in our group less than she notices ex-circus members. So Lola, Kanna, Hugo, Jax, and Ro go, and they report back, and with each couple days that pass, we have more of an idea of where we're heading and what we'll find when we get there.

Sometimes they're gone longer than a day. I don't like it when they're gone longer. I don't like staying here, wondering what's happening while they're out there. But I can't take my sister into the unknown and have everything unfold like it has in the past.

"When are we going?" Jett asks, approaching my side. His shoulder touches mine. He keeps his eyes on Wren as she jumps and jumps again. A row of hurdles, a ring to leap through, a course set up that's better than the one I had before. Not that any of it matters. Or at least it won't soon.

Kanna and Lola are flying the route now. They left two days ago. "Maybe tonight. Maybe tomorrow," I say. "We've got to be sure of where we're heading—no more trouble."

"And they definitely think the place Ro found is empty?" Jett asks.

I nod. "It's far from here. I was worried Ava would notice her missing for all the time she was gone. She hasn't spoken to me much."

"She hasn't spoken to anyone much, only Lola," Jett reassures.

"Lola thinks we're ready."

Jett nods. "I do, too."

"I wish I could have seen it myself," I say, even though I know I couldn't have. It's too far—Ava would notice me gone. It'll take a little more than a week for us to reach it, but the parrots can fly it quicker. Ro found it originally— she comes and goes and no one questions it. She isn't part of the circus, but she became part of the deal and Ava has to let her stay. It was the least Ava could do after what she did to Ro—something I reminded her of.

"It's too far," Jett says.

"Is it far enough?" I ask him. "Ava could come looking."

"Ava's busy," Jett says. "Unless she abandons everything. Are we that important to her now that she has her acrobats, tightrope walkers, and magicians?"

"Yes," I say with certainty. "We are. She'll look."

"She won't find us," Ro says. I didn't notice her come by. "She is the last person I'd want to find us. I never want to see her again."

As the months have passed, I've become increasingly worried about Ro. She disappeared for a while, so long that I didn't think she'd come back. But she did, and she brought the news of a place she'd found for us with her. She doesn't eat with us, sleep when we do, talk to us. She only plans with us. She only wants to get away.

—

Once evening rolls in, the parrots return to camp.

"The mountains in the north," Lola whispers beside the campfire. "They're perfect."

Kanna nods along beside her. "It'll take a while to reach them by foot, but we can make it there. I mean, really make it."

My eyes widen, my heart beats fast with excitement. "What's it like?"

"Pine trees and sunshine and caves," Lola says. "Humans aren't allowed to camp up there. They can't climb without permission."

Kanna waves a hand. "But we can avoid them if we pick the right place. Where the trees are thick, where the path doesn't reach. We can disappear."

"No shifters?" I whisper.

Lola shakes her head. "It's steep and secluded where we're looking. But if we follow our planning, set up resources, camp near freshwater, I think we can make it work."

"And if not?" I ask, leaning in.

"We move house," Kanna says with a smile. "The road is our home, Flo. We can go anywhere. We just need somewhere Ava can't find us for a while—this is it."

"There's snow," Lola says, to no one in particular. "On the peaks of the mountains, there's snow."

"I've never seen snow," Wren says, stirring beside me.

"I thought you were sleeping," I say softly.

"Ish," Wren replies with a mischievous grin. Her personality has come out in the past few months, and I don't know where she gets the mischief from—definitely not me. I think the brothers have been influencing her.

"I'll show you the snow, Wren," I say, brushing my sister's hair back. I think about what it might be like when we get there, what I'm hoping we'll find. I've traveled up mountains, lived in the woods, in the circus, an abandoned warehouse. I've been in the labs. I've seen a lot. And this feels right. This is what we were looking for— somewhere we could hide and feel safe. We used to think we had that with the circus, and we thought we'd find that with the mountain camp. But this time it's just us— we're making our own decisions, we're not relying on anyone but each other, and no one is getting in our way.

When we found the mountain camp, I thought it would give us time to think about what to do next, where to go, what we really wanted. But I realize now that this whole time we've just been trying to survive. Trying to get through the next thing that was thrown at us. Trying to find somewhere safe to rest and think. And now— somewhere safe to *live.*

I turn to Lola and Kanna. "Okay, it's late now. We need time to gather our things, get everyone together. Spread the word—we're leaving tomorrow."

"Tomorrow's show night," Lola says.

"Ava's got the rest of the crew and her new performers."

"You don't owe her anything, Flo. None of us do," Kanna says.

I nod. "I know. So we're leaving on show night. Ava will be so busy—she shouldn't notice until it's too late for her to do anything about it."

Kanna grins wickedly. "It'll be an opening night to remember."

47
SHOW NIGHT

I part the red–and–white striped curtain and look into the ring beyond.

The audience is bigger than I expected.

Ava's performers will have to be enough; her animals are leaving.

It's time we stopped letting others make decisions for us and carve out our own path. We almost got there before, and I believe we can make it work for us this time.

I've seen too much, lost too much. Gained too much. Ava can't take that away. So we had to trick her, like she's tricked us time and time again. Kanna's right—we don't owe her anything, not really. She saved us from the hunters, but she was the reason we were mixed up with them in the first place.

The music starts, loud and grand. The stage lights point toward Ava, fixing her in the spotlight. It's where she wants to be—where she belongs.

"Are you ready, Flo?" Jett says behind me. I release the curtain and turn around to face him, a weird sense of déjà vu taking over for a moment.

I reach out for him. He's there. He's always there. My sister is beside him, and they're waiting for me to go with them.

"I'm ready," I tell him. Wren leaves the big top first. She's wearing a backpack that's half the size of her. The straps dig into her shoulders. "Are you all right with that?" I ask her.

She turns around and nods, excitement twinkling in her eyes. "Your pack is outside."

"Both of them," Jett says with a smile. "Get it? Your pack is with your pack."

I laugh. "I get it. Let's go!"

The audience is cheering as we exit the circus tent. The night is cool. "Hurry," Wren whispers, urging Jett and me on. Knowing Ava is no longer in the ring, having stepped out of the spotlight for the first act to take the stage, fills me with panic even though I know she won't take her eyes off the show tonight.

In the darkness, the others wait. Backpacks and camping equipment are on the floor around them. Ro stands a little away from the rest of the group, Lola beside her.

"Finally," Kanna says as the three of us join them. I pick up my backpack, looping my arms through the straps. There are pans hanging from it that clang in the wind. A rolled up sleeping bag pushes my head forward.

It's time to go.

Time to follow our own path.

Time to leave all of this behind.

We don't need the help of a large group, the elders, the circus. We don't need anything but each other. We've been through enough, and we know how to take care of ourselves. We'll adapt, we'll defeat everything that moves against us, and we'll do it together.

EPILOGUE
THE FOUND

This is home.

It's been just over a year since we ran from Ava's circus. Longer still since we ran from everything we'd ever known. There were times when I didn't know what I wanted, and times when I thought I knew. But this is it. *This is home.*

I step out of the cave and breathe in the crisp air. Spring is coming and the sun warms my face as I look up at the sky. Kanna and Lola are flying.

There are others in the air: two eagles and a hawk. Just three of the new shifters we added to our pack.

The longer we spend here, the more shifters we find in the mountains or farther out. Usually in small groups or alone in the wild. There isn't a day where I don't think of Ursula, Star, Ruby, Owen, and Itch. Kanna and Lola fly out to search for them sometimes, but we've never found them or heard anything about them.

We've built our own community now, and I still hope they will join us someday. That we will find our way back to each other.

THE FOUND

Lola is in charge. We don't make anyone fight to join or make anyone stay against their will. Everyone checks in and out with whoever is on watch when they come and go—just to make sure we cover ourselves and keep as hidden and safe as possible.

I don't know how they found this place. The cave entrance doesn't give away the size of the space inside. There's a small pool tucked away at the back, but the water is really cold.

Ro said she'd squeezed through every gap up here to find the perfect spot and when she found it, she just knew.

Wren comes running up the steep path, Jett right behind her. Her face is tanned and freckled. She smiles, gap-toothed and carefree. "Hey, Flo."

I smile back at her. "Hey. What have you found?"

There's a pinecone in her hand. She collects them. She holds it up for me to see. "That's a big one," I say.

"I'm going to go add it to my box," Wren says, taking off again toward the cave.

We sleep inside and outside of the cave. Wren chose to stay inside—it's what she's used to and she couldn't sleep out in the open. So Jett and I set up close to her.

Jett wraps his arms around me and I breathe in this new Jett, who smells like forest and mist. He stands beside me and watches the camp start the day. The smoke from the campfire, the smell of breakfast cooking, the clang of cups and pans, the sound of voices.

We have made our home into something like the mountain camp that was taken from us so quickly—the sanctuary we'd been looking for ever since leaving the cabin. This place has that, plus a bit of the circus and a bit of the wild in it.

It's perfect.

How long will it last? I don't think about that anymore. We could be here for another week, another year, or ten years from now. All that matters is that we are here, we are together, we are careful, we are building our numbers and keeping one another safe, and we will continue to do so until that day comes. If it comes.